A Denazen Novel

TREMBLE

Book Three

A DENAZEN NOVEL

TREMBLE

BOOK THREE

JUS ACCARDO

Entangled Publishing, LLC
2614 South Timberline Road
Suite 109
Fort Collins, CO 80525
Visit our website at www.entangledpublishing.com.

Edited by Erica M. Chapman and Liz Pelletier
Cover design by Danielle Barclay

Print ISBN   978-1-62061-018-3
Ebook ISBN   978-1-62061-019-0

Manufactured in the United States of America

First Edition May 2013

The author acknowledges the copyrighted or trademarked status and trademark owners of the following wordmarks mentioned in this work of fiction: Jell-O, *Annie*, Technicolor, *The Twilight Zone*, Coke, Chippendales, Reese's, Nike, Band-Aids, Bruce Wayne, Nerf, Chevy, Volkswagen, Gmail, Energizer Bunny, Sunoco, Barbie, *Sleeping Beauty*, Advil, Leatherman, Starbucks, Showtime, Netflix, *The Walking Dead*, *Dexter*, Frisbee, Batcave, *Rain Man*, *Sopranos*, Disney, Taser, "Old MacDonald Had a Farm," *West Side Story*, Snoopy, Six Flags Great Adventure, Sponge Bob, Powerman 500, Cheshire Cat.

Welcome to the
Edmonton Public Library

Date due: 11/4/2014,23:59
Item ID: 31221109005517
Title: The perfect mistress

Date due: 11/4/2014,23:59
Item ID: 31221101937352
Title: The bride wore black leather

Date due: 11/4/2014,23:59
Item ID: 31221109055785
Title: Tremble

Thank you!
www.epl.ca

September 26-28, 2014

Discover • Experience • Celebrate

Thousands of FREE family-friendly events!

From concerts, dance demonstrations and backstage tours; to historic exhibits, film screenings, culinary workshops and so much more - there's something for everyone!

Visit AlbertaCultureDays.ca to find out what's happening in your community.

SEARCH FOR EVENTS ON THE GO:

Alberta Culture

For James...
I've always got your back

1

There were too many people and I had nowhere to run. My heart pounded, and I swallowed back the thick lump of worry caught in my throat. I didn't need this. Not now. Not tonight.

He moved across the room slowly but with determination. I'd tried to duck out of sight when he came through the door, stepping into the middle of a larger crowd and stooping low to avoid detection, but it'd been pointless. Like radar, he locked onto me immediately.

I took a deep breath and braced myself, convinced this could only end one way—in disaster. I'd had a feeling about coming here tonight. You'd think after all the crazy crap I'd seen over the last few months, I'd pay more attention to stuff like that.

Apparently not.

For a brief moment, I thought about mimicking. Using my Six ability to become someone else and slink away unnoticed. He couldn't possibly follow if he didn't know who I was, right? Unfortunately, there were a few problems with that scenario. First off, there were too many people here. It would be impossible to mimic without being seen. Maybe if it were later in the night and people were a little drunker... You'd be surprised the things you could explain away when Jell-O shots and schnapps were involved.

Next, I wasn't willing to mimic a dude. I'd done it twice and it wasn't something I wanted to do again. *Ever.* Extra body parts and things dangling in places they shouldn't? No way. And mimicking another girl would be useless.

This guy?

He'd follow *anything* with boobs.

"Dez, baby!"

I stepped out from behind a large guy with a beer in each hand and forced a smile. "Curd. 'Sup?"

"Cookies, babe. Just cookies."

Curd was intent on creating his own language. The sick part was, a week from now everyone would be saying it. I had no idea how he did it, but the guy was like a verbal infectious disease. I scanned the room for help. The bastards who'd dragged me here against my will were, of course, nowhere in sight. "Here alone?"

Curd winked. "I won't be as soon as I find my Love Goddess. She's with you tonight, right?"

"Of course," I mumbled. He was talking about Jade, my epic-rival-turned-reluctant-guard-dog. He'd seen her at a Halloween party in October and had been obsessed ever since. She'd gone as Venus, the goddess of love—Curd had gone as the devil. Unfortunately for him, the attraction only went one way. She preferred her guys a little taller with a side of ninja. I knew because she'd tried to snag Kale from me. Tried—and failed. "But I'm pretty sure she'd disagree with the *your Love*

Goddess part."

"All in time, baby. All in time. So what about you? You stag tonight?"

"She's here with me," Alex said from behind. Sure. *Now* he showed up. I made a mental note to kick him in the balls as soon as we got outside. You don't drag a girl to a party, then slink off and leave her to drown. There were social rules to follow, dammit.

Curd looked from Alex to me, right eyebrow rising slightly. "That's the third time in two weeks I've seen you two partying together. What's the deal? Be honest—you back together? 'Cause I was starting to like the weird dude. Plus, I think he owes me a pair of shoes…"

At the mention of Kale, it felt like someone dropped a house on my chest. If I were being honest—something I didn't do often these days—I would have admitted I had no desire to be here. This was just a lame, half-assed attempt at going through the motions in hopes of finding something real. A spark of the old me. The one who used to exist on shallow, pointless things like parties and cheap thrills.

And what had I gotten out of it? A big fat nothing. All I felt was the same empty blackness that had settled in my soul the moment Kale walked away with Marshal Cross—AKA my dad. The kind that comes complete with an über helping of pain and an unhealthy dose of irrational guilt.

The kind you know will crush you someday.

"We're just hanging," Alex said. He turned, eyes affixed to mine. "Kale had to go out of town for a while, but *he'll be back.*"

He'll be back.

I turned away, trying hard not to laugh. It'd been months and we hadn't found any sign of him, Dad, or Denazen. It was like they'd left planet Earth entirely—which was weird. Denazen, a company looking to control the Six population, wasn't usually known for duck and cover. Ginger, Kale's biological grandmother and head of the Underground, had assured me she had people working on it around the clock. The Underground, a small group dedicated to seeing Denazen dismantled and in ruin, had their ear to the door. So far, the bad guys hadn't made a sound. The more time that passed, the less hopeful I became that we'd ever find them.

In the weeks following Kale's return to Denazen, I'd gone back to the town where we'd found my half sister, Kiernan, and torn apart her house. Of course, I hadn't uncovered anything worthwhile. The place was in exactly the same shape we'd left it the day we'd gone to get her. She'd never been back. I spent the entire day there, going through her drawers and papers, sifting through closets and tearing apart boxes in the garage. I hoped for an address or picture. Something—anything—I could use to find out where they might be. I would have even settled for something on Supremacy—the Denazen science project I was an unwilling part of.

Denazen had taken a group of regular Sixes and given them a drug to enhance their abilities. It'd been a failure. All they'd gotten, instead of the powerful army they wanted, was a handful of crazy and death spanning across several decades. Word on the street was that there was a cure, but we'd yet to dig anything up. Finding something at Kiernan's place would have made sense, since she was, after all, the only one who'd been given it.

All I found was jack crap.

Alex and Jade—with her stupid promise to Kale to *watch out for me*—had made it their mission to shove me back into my old life whether I liked it or not. This was the third Nix—

people without a Six ability—rave they'd dragged me to in a month, and I *wasn't* feeling the love.

"Jade was over by the bar last time I saw her." Alex's lips lifted with a truly evil smile. *His* mission in life had become making hers miserable. The two were like oil and water. "She was actually looking for you," he added.

Curd's eyes grew wide and he swaggered off, chest puffed, without another word.

"That's not gonna earn you a good-night kiss," I said, leaning back against the wall. While I had no desire to be out and about, the one thing that made it even remotely bearable was watching Jade and Alex take verbal swings at each other. I had a bet going with Mom's boyfriend, Dax, on who would take down who first. My money—surprisingly enough—was on Jade. She was kind of ruthless. If I didn't hate her so much, I could have totally seen us hanging. "Are you pretty much ready to go? This whole scene is lame."

Alex frowned. "Already? We just got here."

I shrugged but didn't answer. Technically we'd gotten here more than two hours ago, but there was no point arguing with him. He'd dubbed himself the designated driver and conveniently had the car keys stashed out of reach.

Resigned to my fate, I skimmed the crowd for something to focus on. It was nothing but the same scene I'd lived a thousand times before. It felt almost shallow to be here. Knowing there was something like Denazen out there made everything about my old life seem really small. It made the things I used to love feel insignificant and pointless.

I angled myself toward the door, about to tell Alex I needed some air with the intention of sneaking back to the cabin—I'd start walking if I had to—but a girl across the room caught my eye. She reminded me of the way I'd looked at the beginning of summer. Tight low-riders, a red bustier, and killer black boots. Her hair was even similar to mine—blond with the ends dyed black. She moved to the music, grinding suggestively against the guy she danced with. At least I thought he was a guy. There were too many people in the way. One of her arms was slung across his shoulder, the other wrapped possessively around his waist.

A few months ago that had been me—only I was a better dancer.

As the ending beats of one song seamlessly melded into the opening of the next, her date disengaged himself to head toward the bar, and the girl turned in the direction of the stairs. I couldn't see her face at first, but something about her kept me riveted, overshadowing my escape plans. There was something vaguely familiar about the way she moved... Her determined stride and the almost stiff set of her shoulders.

She waded through the crowd, swallowed by the sea of people for several moments before emerging on the other end of the room. Yeah. Definitely something familiar, but I couldn't put my finger on it, and it was driving me nuts. She obviously knew people, laughing and chatting as she went, but I couldn't place her. Then, just before she rounded the corner of the stairs, her head tilted sideways and I saw her face. "Sonofa—"

Even over the loud music, I heard Alex's surprised cry when I shoved him aside and bolted across the room without warning. A couple drifted into my path. They were focused so intently on each other and never saw me coming. I elbowed them apart and cut through the middle without apology, determined to keep up.

There was a flash of blond as I rounded the corner. Someone behind me called out, but I ignored it and kept going because losing her *wasn't* an option.

Casually, she ducked into a room at the end of the hall as I made it to the top of the steps. The door was just about to click shut when I reached it, wedging the toe of my shoe between it and the frame. Kicking out, I sent it flying into a bathroom. It bounced twice before hitting the tile wall with a noise that reverberated, sending an annoying rattle echoing through the small room.

The girl whirled around, surprised, and stumbled sideways as I burst in. "What the—"

Fist balled tight, my hand shot out and cracked her in the side of the head before she could finish. There was only one thing I wanted to hear coming from her mouth. Answers. "Where is he?"

She let out a howl and clutched her head. Tripping backward, she caught the edge of the sink and toppled over, yanking the role of paper towels and a small container of hand soap down with her. They clattered to the floor, the plastic top on the soap cracking in half and spilling soft pink liquid across the tacky blue tile.

Brown eyes rose defiantly to meet mine and, knowing what I knew now, I couldn't figure out how I'd missed it before. They were the same color as the ones I saw in the mirror each day. The same shape. They even held that same mischievous spark. She had a slightly narrower, heart-shaped face, with a chin that came to more of a dramatic point like Dad's. I remembered her once joking that she could cut glass with it. The resemblance was there, though. We even had a similar personality. Overly confident, sarcastic, and just a little bit crazy.

"Where is he, Kiernan?"

Eyes narrow, she pulled herself upright using the edge of the tub and folded both arms in defiance. With an attitude I'd grown to love—*before* she went dark side—she said, "Screw me sideways, bitch."

I knew it wouldn't be that easy, and that was fine. Better than fine, in fact. It meant I got to hit her again. And I did. I'd had dreams that started like this. Me getting the opportunity to kick the crap out of the girl who'd been the catalyst for the destruction of my life. The problem was, the dreams never ended well—for me.

As soon as she went down, I grabbed her wrist and dragged her back to her feet. There was a comb on the sink beside me. Picking it up, I concentrated on one of Mom's kitchen knives.

A shudder rippled through my body, along with the tiniest twinge at the base of my temple. A tickle and nothing more. The physical cost of mimicking—which was what I called my Six ability—had, for the most part, become a joke. Bigger things still took a lot out of me. Mimicking an entire person knocked me for a loop, but the days of debilitating pain and gut-wrenching agony had passed and left me with one hell of an advantage.

One I was eager to test out on Kiernan.

The plastic handle of the comb grew cold and smooth as its weight changed. Now, instead of feeling flimsy, it was solid and heavy. The whole process used to fill me with a sense of dread. Now I found it oddly comforting.

Kiernan snickered and shrugged, not the least bit worried. She'd always been the cocky kind. It'd gotten us in trouble on more than one occasion. "You don't have the guts."

I pressed the blade against the back of her forearm and moved it a slip. A thin line of red appeared a moment later. "Wanna put it to the test? I think you might be surprised what I have the guts to do now." I straightened. "You should be proud, actually. You drove me to it."

She laughed. "Me? It's the other way around, *sister*."

A part of me wanted to know what the hell she was talking about—I'd never been anything but friendly to her—but it was a small part. The rest only wanted to know one thing.

"Tell me where he is." A small voice inside my head goaded me to make another cut—this time deeper. Kiernan had provoked me by lying and, worst of all, helping Dad recapture Kale. She'd posed as my friend, infiltrated the Underground, then not only fed Dad important information but gave him an all-access pass to the Sanctuary hotel that ended with its destruction and the death of Rosie, one of our own. Did I have the guts to hurt her?

She laughed, unfazed by either the knife or my threats. "Oh, Dez. Dez, Dez, Dez. You sure you really want him back? He's not the guy you thought he was, trust me." She leaned closer and blew me an exaggerated kiss. "He's a screamer, did you know?"

Did I have the guts?

Oh, hell yes. Yes I did.

I jerked the knife away, dragging it hard against her skin. This time, she let out a hiss and tried to yank away from my grip, but I held tight. For a moment, neither of us said anything. A stare-down of epic proportions.

I'd been working with Mom to learn how to fight, but I had a long way to go. Maybe force wasn't the right tact. Maybe appealing to something deeper would get me the information I was so desperate for. Kiernan was Dad's lapdog, but she was also my sister, and that had to mean something.

"How could you let him do this?" I released her arm and took a step back to give her some room. "You know what he's doing to these people—to us! He's using you just like he is the rest of them. If we stick together, we can — "

"*Stick together?*" She pushed away from the sink and advanced. "How could I possibly trust you? You turned on your own father!"

I blinked. "Turned on my own father? Have you met the guy? He's a monster."

"What he and Denazen are doing is best for all of us." She shook her head and leaned closer. "Besides, I know you knew about me. You begged him to leave me."

"Weren't you there the day we met? Did I look like I had any clue you were my sister?"

"All an act."

An act? She'd never seen me in the school production of *Annie*. I had a bit part as an orphan and blew it when I caught sight of Uncle Mark and Brandt in the audience halfway through. I broke character and started waving like an idiot. I'd never lived it down.

"What's going on?" someone asked from behind.

I froze. The tiny hairs along my arms and on the back of my neck jumped to attention. That voice played on repeat each time I closed my eyes. It was the soundtrack to my dreams and the thing that kept me from slipping over the edge of crazy. I almost didn't want to turn for fear that I'd finally lost it, and the whole thing was in my head.

When I got the nerve, I turned and found myself face-to-face with the most amazing crystalline blue eyes I'd ever seen.

Kale's eyes.

2

It was like I'd landed hard after a wipe, air knocked from my lungs and blobs dancing like a Technicolor kaleidoscope behind each eye. He stood in the doorway dressed in worn blue jeans and a long-sleeved black button-down shirt. His hair was longer than the last time I'd seen him. Shaggier in the front and reaching down just below his ears.

Our eyes met and every inch of me filled with a happiness I never expected to get back. Kale. Here. In one piece.

He stepped across the threshold, blue eyes on mine for a moment before moving to Kiernan. "Are—are you okay?"

I started to reach for him, the smile on my face going from ear to ear and probably making me look goofier than the Cheshire Cat. "I—"

"I'm fine," Kiernan said, knocking my hand away. She shoved me aside, stepped around, and as I watched in shock, pulled him close.

With a wink, she twisted and covered his mouth with

hers, and my entire world grew dark. It was like Jade all over again—only worse because of the way he responded. Fingers knotting into the back of her shirt, he dragged her tightly against him like he couldn't bear the thought of space between them.

I wanted to move—needed to move—but it was like my feet were superglued to the tile. The feeling that built in the pit of my chest was like acid. Chipping and chewing away at the bones until it reached my heart. And it did. The burning sensation, followed by a total lack of oxygen in the room, made me dizzy. I couldn't look away and I couldn't breathe. This was a nightmare. That was the only explanation. At the moment, I was warm and safe in my bed, snoring softly while this horrific scene played out in my head. It couldn't be real. I knew that for several reasons.

First, *my* Kale would never be sucking face with Kiernan. She'd betrayed us all. He might want to touch her, but there sure as hell wouldn't be kissing involved. Second—and more importantly—*my* Kale *couldn't* suck face with Kiernan. He'd vaporize her on contact.

"What the hell, Dez? You take off like someone lit your ass on fire—" Alex rounded the corner and stopped short when he got to the doorway. "Huh. Someone slipped something into my drink. I've obviously entered the *Twilight Zone*…" He leaned to the side, peering around Kiernan and Kale to me. "You okay?"

"Popular question tonight," I mumbled, still staring at them. Good. My voice. I found my voice. Maybe that meant air wasn't far behind.

Kiernan pulled away, grinning like a cat that ate an entire flock of canaries, and hooked a finger possessively through one of the front loops of Kale's jeans. "She's fine and dandy as candy."

"I was on my way back from the bar when I saw this girl run after you. Do you know her?" Kale's gaze shifted between Alex and me, then fell back to Kiernan. "She looked angry."

Alex let out a sharp whistle. "You've gotta be kidding me, brother man."

Kale's expression darkened. "I'm not. Who did you say you were?"

"I *didn't*," Alex answered, taking a step closer.

"Was there something you needed, then?" Kale growled, drawing himself up. "If not, you can leave now."

With the boys distracted—their dislike of each other apparently transcended memory issues—I grabbed Kiernan's arm and spun her around. She still hadn't lost the shit-eating grin and, more than anything, I wanted to wipe it from her face.

Possibly using an electric sander—or a cheese grater. Pavement would have worked, too.

"Told you he wasn't the same." She knocked my hand away and pushed back, catching me off guard. I lost my grip on the knife and it bounced across the floor, clattering loudly against the tile before landing at her feet.

It happened fast. We dove for the comb-turned-blade at the same time, but she was just a hair closer and reached it first. There was a *whoosh* of air as she swung, accompanied by a glint of silver. I dodged the attack and knocked her back against the wall, still determined to get an answer. "What did you do to—"

The rest of the sentence caught in my throat. So did the airflow. Kale had me flipped and pinned against the wall in Kiernan's place, fingers tight around my neck as she stepped to the side, smiling. Something bubbled in my stomach. *Déjà vu.* The night we'd met. Only this time the look in his eyes was different. Unapologetic and cruel.

Alex made a move to come forward, but I held up a hand to stop him. Something was wrong—obviously—but Kale was still Kale. And that meant he could flatten Alex without batting an eye, not to mention we had no idea what was going on with his ability.

"I'm asking again, Roz. Do you know this girl?"

"Kiernan," I said, trying to pry his hands from around my neck.

His fingers relaxed a bit. "What?"

"Her name is Kiernan." I felt his fingers twitch with each word I spoke, the vibration of my voice making their hold just a bit tighter. "Who the hell is Roz?"

The question seemed to confuse him. Good. I could work with that. Confused Kale was better than homicidal Kale any day of the week. His grip loosened, head tilting a hair to the left. The coolness in his eyes cut like a chainsaw through my core. There was absolutely no recognition there, and it was taking every ounce of my control not to break apart. "Listen to me. I don't know what they did to you, but you know who I am. I'm *Dez*. You lo—"

Kiernan sighed and placed a hand on his shoulder, pulling back. I was tempted to hit her, but one look at Kale and I squashed the idea. Something told me that in his current state it wouldn't go over well. "She's right, Kale. You *do* know her… you just don't remember."

For an insane moment, I thought for sure she'd had an attack of conscience and was about to come clean. We might get this whole crazy mess sorted without any bloodshed.

I was an idiot.

"This is Kiernan McGuire, the girl Daddy told you about."

I nearly fell over. "Are you *serious*?"

Kale's eyes darkened and the right corner of his upper lip pulled back. I knew that look. It was the one he frequently wore while thinking about his years at Denazen. While thinking about the people who hurt him. At the moment, that was *apparently* me. "*She*'s the one responsible for my accident?"

There was the smallest twinge of doubt in his voice. I might have been able to pick at the edges and pry something free, but Kiernan jumped right in. "Think hard, Kale. *Kiernan*. You know the name… How does it make you feel?"

"This is crap," I spat. "Don't listen to her. She's so full of shit her eyes are brown!"

"Kiernan." He repeated the name, eyes still on mine. Falling forward, he released my throat and placed both hands against the wall on either side of my head, boxing me in. "It makes me feel angry."

Worry bubbled, but I stuffed it down. "Of course it makes you feel angry. She screwed us all over."

Alex moved farther into the bathroom and inched closer, but he froze when Kale turned. Alex threw up his hands in a show of surrender and nodded in my direction. "You're confused, brother man. This is *Dez*. You don't want to hurt her."

"He's right, Kale," Kiernan said, somber. "Daddy would be pissed if something happened to her. She's part of an earlier trial of his Supremacy project."

Kale's eyes traveled over me with a hint of disgust, and something inside shattered into a million tiny pieces. Seeing him kiss Kiernan had been horrible, but seeing him look at me that way was unbearable. Like I was one of *them*. It was one of the worst moments in my life. "She's Supremacy?"

"I know. Makes no sense, right? But it was the test round.

They weren't picky about subjects. She lives. For now." She waved her cell and pointed toward the door. "We have to go. Stuff to do, remember?"

He held my gaze, and for a second—just a second—I could have sworn I saw something spark in his eyes. Recognition? A feeling? Maybe a flash of something familiar. But it didn't matter. Whatever it was disappeared within a half beat of my heart, leaving his stare cold and empty. He turned and crossed the threshold without a word, Kiernan following close behind.

As she stepped into the hall, just before rounding the corner, she turned back to me, smiling. "Did you know the first *official* stage of the Supremacy decline is loss of the ability to feel pain?"

And then she was gone.

"Dez, your arm." Alex grabbed my hand and twisted. The sleeve of my new green sweater was ripped and oozing red.

"Crap," I hissed, wrapping my hand tight to stop the bleeding.

"You don't feel it?"

"Of course I feel it!" I lied. Did it with a straight face, too. Pretty impressive considering the raging storm of *holy freaking crap* brewing in my chest. "Hurts like hell." I nodded to the door. I could freak later. The Supremacy thing would still be waiting—unfortunately—but Kale wouldn't. "Hurry. We can't lose them."

We charged from the bathroom and into the hall, taking the steps two at a time. It took a minute, but I finally spotted Kiernan's newly blond head bobbing through the crowd, Kale at her side. We needed to move faster. They were already across the room and by the door. Another few seconds and they'd be out of sight.

The party had gotten even more crowded in the time we'd

been gone. An unending sea of bodies stood between us and them, making it impossible to cut fast through the middle of the room. "Shit! We're gonna lose them."

Alex took my hand. He stopped short and tugged me to the side, jaw set in determination. "No we *won't*."

We'd talked about Alex using his abilities in public. More specifically, around our friends. He'd grown a little careless, and in an epically weird turn of events, I found myself being the voice of reason. It was one thing to make a napkin float across the room in a crowd of drunken people. It was another to make said napkin conveniently dive into the cleavage of the hot foreign exchange student.

This was an exception. With the smallest flick of his fingers, he parted the crowd down the middle, allowing for a narrow, straight path between them and us. There was a little confusion, and a few people yelped, but no one seemed to realize what had happened. It was like a handful of people inexplicably tripped backward at the same time.

With a grin, Alex propelled me through the middle of the newly separated crowd and right out the front door. Easy peasy. We made it onto the lawn in time to see Kiernan and Kale reach the sidewalk. They stopped, and Kiernan pointed to a couple standing a few feet away. I didn't recognize either of them, but that didn't mean anything. Parkview had one hell of a reputation. Kids came from neighboring towns just to party.

We ducked behind a tree and I sucked in a deep breath, trying to process everything that had happened. "He had no memory of either of us. He touched me and nothing happened... He *touched* her."

"He did a little more than touch—"

I glared, daring him to finish the sentence.

"Sorry. Old habit. The guy brings out the worst in me."

He leaned forward and cursed. "Oh, wow… The memory and touching? Yeah, that's not the only thing that's different."

I pushed him aside and peered around the large tree trunk to see Kale bent low to the ground just beneath a streetlamp, hand flat against the sidewalk. The concrete in front of him shimmered and twitched as something dark—like a thousand tiny shadows clustered together and churning like chaos—gathered. The mass of black convulsed twice, then sank into the ground.

It moved like a snake, skating not along the ground but *inside* it. Just under the surface, bouncing back and forth between the edge of the lawn and the curb, and then heading straight toward the couple. When it reached them, there was a surge of darkness beneath the guy's feet and, within seconds, he exploded into a million dustlike particles that were carried away on the breeze.

"Holy shit!" Alex stumbled back behind the tree as the girl's hysterical screams cut through the night, drawing people out from inside the house. He tried to drag me with him as a crowd started to gather on the sidewalk but I resisted, too sick to peel my eyes from the sight.

I covered my mouth to keep from screaming.

A small pile of dust remained in front of the girl. She'd fallen to her knees, uncontrollably sobbing while rocking steadily back and forth. Seeing something like that—even when you knew these things existed—could mess you up. I wondered if she'd ever be the same. I wasn't sure *I'd* be.

When I finally managed to tear my gaze away from the girl, I found Kale staring at me. Kiernan noticed, too. She hooked her arm around his shoulder and blew me a kiss before leading him away as sirens split the air.

"She knew we were standing here," I breathed, finally

letting Alex tug me around to the other side of the tree. "She wanted us to see that..."

3

"It was freaky, Dax. He was actually kind of a dick." There was a snap, and a flame flickered to life from the tip of Alex's lighter. Lifting a cigarette to his lips, he took a long pull and said, "More so than normal, I mean."

"Alex," Ginger warned. I figured she'd tell him to put out the cigarette because she hated the smell, but instead she waved her empty cup back and forth. "I'm not getting any younger here."

He rolled his eyes and disappeared with the cup—cigarette still between his lips—to refill her drink.

After Kale and Kiernan left, we'd gone back into the party to find Jade. Miraculously, she hadn't heard the screaming or its resulting chaos. I was pretty sure she was the only one and that it had something to do with the fact that she'd been flirting hardcore with Tom Bozeman, Parkview High's basketball captain.

I'd wanted to follow Kale, but Alex wasn't having it. He

threatened to throw me over his shoulder if I tried. I decided that, since he was bigger he'd probably win, and besides the embarrassment factor, it was probably for the best.

Aside from his inexplicable personality adjustment and nifty new use of his ability, Kale was dangerous. Denazen trained him to be an unstoppable killing machine from the time he could walk. The fact that Kiernan seemed to have him wrapped around her sleazy little finger and convinced I was the enemy only made it ten times worse. We needed to approach this situation with caution.

"They did something to him. That wasn't Kale." It was the first thing I said since getting back to home base—AKA the cabin Dax had moved us to. Every eye in the room turned to me. They probably thought I was going into some kind of shock or something. "I mean, obviously it *was* Kale, but they scrambled his brain. Confused things. Kiernan told him *my* name was Kiernan, and he was calling her Roz."

"That makes sense, Dez." Alex reappeared with Ginger's cup. He blew out a puff of smoke and handed her the drink, then turned to me. I didn't like his expression. Pity and something else. Sympathy. It didn't look right on him. Not that Alex was unsympathetic or cold, but he didn't normally sugarcoat things. "As much as I hate to say this, I'm betting nothing anyone could ever do to that freak could erase you completely from his mind. I saw it right away; I don't know how you missed it."

"Missed what?" As Alex sat down, Dax pulled the cigarette from his fingers and took a long drag before handing it back.

"The blond hair. The black tips. The way Kiernan was dressed. Hell, even the name she's using. *Roz*? Come on…"

"Cross swapped them," Ginger said, banging her cane

against the floor. She lifted the cup to her lips and took a sip. "Of course."

"It's an identity theft nightmare," Alex agreed. "He gave Kiernan's name to Dez's face and Dez's name to Kiernan's face."

If that were the case, it'd explain why there was so much hate in his eyes when Kiernan mentioned her own name. Somewhere deep inside, Kale must remember she'd help create this mess. And if that was true, then he was still in there. There was hope. "But *how* did they do it?"

"Another Six, maybe?" Mom chimed in. She was sitting across from me, next to Dax.

"But that doesn't explain the change in his ability," Alex interjected. "It was wicked. I can't see that being the result of another Six's power."

"We need more information." Whatever they did to Kale, it could be undone. It had to be. I just needed to figure out how.

"Need to be careful, though." Alex dropped the butt of his cigarette into an empty Coke can. It gave the tiniest hint of a sizzle. "Judging from the way he was all over—" He frowned and tapped the table. "I mean, *touching* Kiernan shows he's ten times more dangerous than he used to be. He's got control over it now. That allows him to move around more freely. We can't go rushing in until we know what we're up against. This is a game changer."

"Agreed," Mom said. "Plus, we still don't know where they are."

Ginger downed the remaining contents of her cup and turned to Dax. "Call Henley. Tell him I need an update. Have him here first thing in the morning."

"Henley? Who's Henley?"

Ginger heaved herself out of the seat and flashed me an

impish smile. "We have a man on the inside."

• • •

I woke the next morning with a stiff neck and an uneasy stomach. Dreams of Kale had haunted me the entire night. The way he killed that guy. The look in his eyes as he turned to me. It was cold and so incredibly distant. A voice deep in the back of my mind whispered horrible things. A rush of scenarios that came to light in my worst nightmares kicked their way to the surface.

Kale fought so hard against the person Denazen wanted him to be. What if this change meant they'd finally succeeded in creating the monster they'd always wanted? An unstoppable killing machine loyal to their cause. What would happen if he never remembered me? If I'd lost him forever? No. I couldn't think like that. This wasn't the time to be negative. Not when I'd finally found him.

I slid out of bed and stumbled down the hall toward the kitchen. It was early. The clock on the wall above the door read 7:12, but someone was always up around here. It made me think of Rosie, the desk clerk killed in the Sanctuary fire. She'd never slept.

Thinking about Rosie made me think about coffee. We'd always butted heads, but the girl had an appreciation for coffee rivaled only by my own. I rounded the corner of the kitchen, intent on beelining to make a pot, but someone had beaten me to it.

"Deznee." Ginger raised her mug and gave it a little wiggle. It was an old white ceramic thing with Chippendales dancers on the front. Knowing her, it was full of fruit punch, not coffee. "Good morning."

I stopped in the doorway and took in the room. Ginger wasn't alone. Dax was there with Mom, as well as Vince, a Six Kale and I met over the summer while visiting the names on the list my cousin Brandt had given us. A Denazen raid had destroyed Vince's home shortly after we'd lost Kale, but thankfully I'd given him Dax's cell number and we were able to bring him in safely. He'd been with us ever since and had started taking more of an active role in things. In recent weeks, he'd gone out with Alex and several of the others in search of new Sixes. He felt the need to pay forward the favor we'd done to him by warning others.

"Morning, Dez." Vince nodded.

"Come in. Sit down." Ginger pointed to the other end of the table at the one person I didn't know. A tall guy with black hair and linebacker shoulders. Our eyes met and for a second, I was sure I'd seen him somewhere before, but then he spun away. "Deznee, this is Henley."

I circled the table and pulled my Xtream Scream mug down from the cabinet with a nod in his general direction. "Oh, yeah. You're the man on the inside, right?" The smell of the coffee was comforting, and when I sat down across from Mom and took that first heavenly sip, for one brief moment all was right with the world.

Then that Henley guy opened his mouth.

"So anyway, they've decided to terminate them. The order went out early this morning."

I let the cup thunk to the table. Cream-colored liquid sloshed over the edge, collecting in a puddle at the base. "See, that's not the kinda thing I really wanna hear first thing in the morning. Who ordered what terminated? Someone catch me up here."

Dax sighed. "Denazen has been playing in the kitchen

again. They've officially started the third Supremacy trial."

"Officially?" I laid my hand across the table, right at the rim, to keep the spill from going over. Mom, with a roll of her eyes, tossed me a paper towel. "I didn't even know there was an unofficial."

"There is," Henley said with a frown. "And it seems they got it right—for the most part. Incompatibility for the new drug seems to be sitting at fifty percent. And what's worse? They don't need babies anymore. Any age will do."

"Wow." I took another sip and set the mug down. "Way to ruin a morning, dude."

"That's me," he said with a wink. Pulling something from his pocket—a Reese's peanut butter cup—he unwrapped it and popped the small candy into his mouth. "Always happy to bring the sunshine."

Mom frowned. This was a touchy subject for her. She and I were part of the second trial—one that, so far, had proved unsuccessful. While pregnant with me, she'd been given a drug to enhance my Six ability. It worked—but with some hefty side effects: an increase in abilities, followed by insanity, and then eventually death. Sometimes I thought she felt guilty about the whole thing. She was the one given the drug, and yet I was the one with the pendulum swinging over my head. "So they've started using it? The new drug?"

Henley opened his mouth, but I beat him to it when something dawned on me. "Oh my God. That's it. They used it on Kale! That explains the difference in his ability."

Henley finished chewing his candy and swallowed. "I can't say for sure, but from what Ginger told me, yeah—though it shouldn't have messed with his memory. Either way, he's lucky to be alive. Like I said, there's only a fifty percent survival rate." He frowned. "But the new trial isn't the only bad news."

"Aren't you just a ball of happy," I mumbled, downing the entire cup of coffee in four long pulls. "Can't say I'm really thrilled to make your acquaintance at this point…"

Henley flashed an apologetic smile and kept going. "This morning they declared all the old models obsolete. They're not going to wait for the rest to turn eighteen. They've ordered them—"

"Terminated," I finished for him. That's where I'd walked in on the conversation. Perfect. "How many are there?"

Mom leaned back. "Including you? Twelve."

"That's a lot of potential crazies to hunt down," Alex said, leaning back in his chair. "With all the resources Denazen has, we'll never get to them all in time."

Henley nodded and pulled out another piece of candy. I resisted the urge to jump up and snatch it away. The smell of peanut butter was making me sick. "Twelve total—but you have two already, so, really, only ten. And not all of them are still out there. Some have already been terminated."

"Two—me and who else?"

Henley turned, pinning me with a look that sent chills down my spine. "Me."

This kept getting better and better. "Do we know which of the ten are already dead?"

He shook his head. "Unfortunately, not without going to check on each one. We have someone else on the inside. She's good with a computer, but they're keeping the info pretty close to the cuff. They erased all the files. Our guess is they're playing it safe and using paper."

Wonderful. "Do we have names? Addresses?" I glanced back at the coffee machine. Vince had just poured the last of the pot into his cup. Perfect. I was going to need more caffeine to deal with this. Like, *much* more. "Please tell me we have something to go on because otherwise this is going to be an epic needle-in-a-haystack thing."

Henley looked uncomfortable. "We have the names and last-known locations, but that's no guarantee you'll find them there. I'm pretty sure it's an old list."

"And we can't get an updated one because they're not keeping it on the computers anymore. What about you?" I nodded to Henley. "Can't you go in and dig something up? Isn't that what you're there for?"

Ginger shook her head. "Henley's position on the inside is no longer viable. He's here to stay."

Henley stood. "I've got a massive headache. Do you mind if I crash?"

"Of course," Ginger said, standing as well. "Deznee, could you please show Henley to five twelve?"

"No," he said, glancing at me from the corner of his eye. "You can just tell me where it is. I can find my own way."

Ginger narrowed her eyes. "Deznee will take you." Without another word, she turned and exited the kitchen through the door on the opposite end, Dax following close behind. Mom hung back for a moment, then left as well, leaving Vince at the table shoveling away at an enormous bowl of cereal. I'd never seen anyone eat as much as he did. Anytime I saw him, he was chewing on something. The guy's metabolism must operate on triple speed because he was thin as a rail.

"Well, I guess you're showing me to my room." Henley turned and started for the door. As he stepped away from the table, I noticed something bulky in his side pocket. Something round—like a wheel. There was only one person I knew who carried a wheel with them everywhere they went.

Brandt.

I waited until we were down the hall, past the common room, before I stepped in front of him. "So that's it? You're not planning on saying anything?"

He stopped just short of crashing into me, eyes wide. "Huh?"

"Really? You're gonna play dumb? With *me*?"

"I don't understand. What are you—"

"The *skate wheel* is sticking out of your pocket, brain trust." The wheel was from his favorite skateboard. It was the one and only thing he'd taken before leaving Parkview behind.

He patted his hip like he'd forgotten it was there—totally unlikely, since he never went anywhere without the damn thing—and cursed. "I can explain."

"I doubt it," I said, bitter. One foot in front of the other, I started walking again, a confusing mix of anger and elation twisting my gut into a knot. "I haven't seen you since before Kale left. I waited—you obviously knew what was going on. You had to know I needed you."

"Dez—"

"What could you possibly have to say, Brandt?" I was angry, but more than that, I was hurt. Whenever the bad crap went down in my life, Brandt always had my back. He was a Soul Jumper, which meant that when my cousin's body died, his life force jumped into the nearest person. In the event that person was a Six, he inherited their abilities.

Brandt had obtained incriminating information about Denazen, and Dad had him killed. They didn't know it— and hopefully never would—but he was alive and well. After his first death, he'd jumped into Sheltie's body, the Six who'd murdered him. Sheltie could invade your dreams, so even though my cousin had to stay out of sight, he was in my dreams when I really needed him.

Until one day he just wasn't.

He grabbed my arm to stop me, then leaned back against the wall. "Just 'cause I was out of sight doesn't mean I wasn't looking out for you."

"I didn't need anyone looking out for me. I needed my best friend."

Brandt shook his head. "I'm sorry. Nothing I say is going to seem like a good enough reason."

"Try me."

"I did visit your dreams, Dez. I visited, and I got so freaked by what I saw that I made myself stay away."

Not what I'd expected.

He pulled the wheel from his pocket and rolled it between his hands. The Brandt equivalent of a nervous twitch. "You were hurt and terrified. The way it manifested in your dreams really hit me. I—I was afraid if I kept seeing stuff like that, I wouldn't be able to stop myself from running home—and I couldn't do that. Not when there's so much else at stake."

I understood—sort of—but it didn't make me feel any better. Brandt had been my rock. Not having him there, with everything that had happened, was hard. I'd missed him. "So that's it? You're here now?"

He nodded and we started walking again.

It took exactly six steps for it to hit me.

"No—"

"Dez, don't."

I froze, heart nearly seizing. "Ten—you said—you and me…" Forming a coherent sentence was nearly impossible. "You jumped into the body of a *Supremacy victim*?"

Brandt sighed, stuffing the wheel back into his pocket. "I didn't plan it, Dez. It just happened."

"I don't understand," I said. Deep breaths. In through the nose. Out through the mouth. Nice and easy. "What happened to the Sheltie suit?"

"It's a long story." He glanced down the hall, like he was checking to make sure we were alone, then leaned closer. "Cross and Kiernan were wrong. A few months ago they told you they'd found a cure — but they hadn't."

He was wrong. Had to be. "Kiernan is over eighteen. I know that for a fact."

"They gave her something they *thought* was the cure, and it did work — for a while. After a few months, though, it started breaking down. She began showing signs of decline."

She'd seemed perfectly fine at the party. "But you're saying she's okay now?"

"Ginger will fill you in on the bulk of it, but the short

version is yes." He gestured to himself. "But that's where my new body comes in. To make the cure work, they needed something from someone. A man named Wentz. Ginger sent me in to get to him first, but I failed. I died trying to stop them."

"And you ended up in the same boat as me," I said, the knot in my chest getting bigger. "So now not only am I on death row, you're there with me. Your strategy leaves a lot to be desired."

He took my hand and squeezed. "We are *not* on death row."

I pulled away and opened my mouth to argue with him.

He cut me off. "Dez. Look who you're talking to. Soul Jumper, remember? Other than dealing with the current effects, I'm not in any real danger." He thumped me lightly on the shoulder. "Come on, you *know* that."

Wow. Duh. He had a point. Why hadn't I seen that for myself? Because my own brain was starting to scramble, that's why. Easily distracted and unfocused, I found my mind wandering lately. The Supremacy drug—it had to be. But that didn't matter. Not now. For the first time in months, things were starting to look up. Time to suck it up and take back my life. "But what about the cure? If you failed, how—"

"Ginger will kick my ass if she knows I'm telling you about all this. Let her fill in the rest of the blanks." He swayed a little, and I felt bad for badgering, but there was one more thing I had to ask.

"What about Kale? Do you know what they did to him? He—he's so different."

The sympathy in Brandt's eyes bugged me for some reason. Maybe because, for the past few months, I'd seen it in everyone's eyes. Annoying compassion for the poor, lost girl. "The new Supremacy drug would account for the change in Kale's ability, but I've never heard of it messing with someone's memories. I guess it *could* have been the thing that scrambled his eggs, but I doubt it. They've given it to twenty people. Nine or ten survived, and as far as I know, their heads are still in working order. If I had to place bets on the cause, I'd go with a Resident."

Residents were Sixes who willingly lived and worked alongside Denazen. Their own personal superpowered butt monkeys. "Any ideas which one?"

He shrugged. "Wish I knew."

We came to a stop in front of room 512—six doors down from mine. He looked a little pale, and every once in a while I swore I saw him tremble. "I have to ask—and I expect the truth. The headache—is that body declining?"

He brushed the lightest of kisses across my forehead. "Lemme crash for an hour or so. Then we'll plot world domination, 'kay?"

Not the answer I'd hoped for. Hell, not even an answer at all. But for now it would have to do. I had a boyfriend to rescue and ten science project offspring to hunt down before they popped their lids—or Denazen did it for them.

Oh. And a cure to find so Brandt's current body and I didn't die a horrible, insanity-laced death.

Easy. Reeeal easy.

• • •

Showered and dressed, I found everyone clumped in the living room talking quietly. Dax and Mom looked cozy on the couch, while Alex was crammed into his beanbag chair—an essential piece of furniture for every living room, according to him.

Ginger sat in her normal armchair by the door, wooden folding tray upright in front of her. There were a lot of Sixes under our roof, but the people gathered here had formed a sort of leadership chain. We were the enforcers of Ginger's little army.

"So what's the plan?" I asked, flopping down next to Mom. There was a renewed energy humming through my veins. Having seen Kale last night and getting Brandt back this morning had recharged my batteries some. A direction and a goal. We were facing one hell of a mountain, but I had my climbing legs back and wanted to get started. "How are we gonna use the info we have to get Kale back?"

"We're not," Ginger said. She picked a manila envelope off the tray beside her and waved it back and forth, accidentally smacking Vince as he walked in the room.

"Come again?" I'd heard her wrong. Had to have.

"We're not going to do anything about Kale. At the moment, he's not a priority."

The temperature in the room plummeted and everything blurred to a filmy haze. "Not a *priority*? You've gotta be shitting me!" I jumped up and jabbed a finger at Mom, who seemed oddly unbothered by Ginger's words. "Tell me she's kidding."

Mom opened her mouth but Ginger, with a stern look and sharp shake of her head, cut her off.

Wow. So my own flesh and blood wasn't going to side with me? She'd raised Kale inside Denazen as though he were her own for Christ's sake. "He's *my* priority. If he's not a priority for you guys, then he's one for me. The *only* one."

"Deznee—" Ginger tried, but I steamrolled her.

"No way. No excuses. This is crazy. He's your grand—"

"Dez!" Alex roared. He slammed the coffee table, rattling the cereal bowl Vince had just set down. "Sit down, shut up, and let her finish."

I glared, wanting nothing more than to punch him, but sank onto the couch. Lately Alex seemed to have subscribed to the Church of Ginger. He backed her decisions—even when they made no sense. Made excuses for her—even when it was obvious that she was wrong. And now he was ready to let Kale flop in the wind because Ginger *said so*?

Okay. Maybe that one wasn't such a big surprise, given the shared animosity between the boys.

Ginger cleared her throat. "As I was trying to say, there are more pressing matters. We know Kale is unharmed. He's not going anywhere for the time being. Denazen is going to move on the Supremacy subjects swiftly." She shot a glare in my direction. "In case you've forgotten, Deznee, that includes you and Brandt."

I hadn't forgotten. I'd *tried*, but I hadn't forgotten. They wouldn't let me. Mom was constantly bringing it up, working it into conversations at the most random times, and Ginger dropped hints on an almost daily basis.

"We haven't long to find them." She ripped open the envelope and leafed through a file, pulling out a wallet-sized black-and-white picture. Handing it to me, she said, "We *must* get to this woman before they do."

Reluctantly, I took the picture. I was still pissed—but curious. The girl in the photograph was pretty, somewhere in her twenties with big hair and out-of-date clothing. I flipped it over. In small, blocky handwriting, it said, PENNY MILLS, 1974. "Who is she?"

"She is the last remaining survivor of the *first* Supremacy trial."

Alex took the picture from me and let out a wolfish whistle.

I snagged it back and rolled my eyes. "Ew. She's, like, *old* now."

Across the room, next to Dax, Mom cleared her throat.

"Older," I corrected quickly, waving the picture at Alex. "Too old for *you.*"

Dax snickered and threw his arm around Mom's shoulders. "Smooth."

I coughed and turned back to Ginger to avoid Mom's stare. I'd made the mistake of mentioning makeup to her once, and she thought I'd implied she looked old. Didn't take it very well. "Didn't Denazen kill everyone from the first trial? That's what Dad said…"

Ginger took the picture from me and stuffed it back into the envelope. I didn't miss how she snapped the file shut, either, as I leaned in to get a closer look. "This is the one that got away. She is, in part, how Marshal Cross was able to cure Kiernan."

I froze. "Kiernan?" This must be what Brandt was talking about. The *component.* "You mean this chick has the cure for the crazies? She can save us?"

"She *is* the cure. Like Kale's blood renders Sixes pliable, Penny Mills's blood cancels the negative effect of the Supremacy drug. From the information Henley gathered, we believe they combined it with a formula stolen from a scientist named Franklin Wentz to create the third generation."

"If she escaped back when the first trial went live, how did they get her blood?"

"Henley said they didn't know about the blood until June. Each Resident has a vial on file. Mills's was lost in storage, and because they thought her dead, they had no reason to go looking for it. You see, the first trial's symptoms were ten times worse. After it was clear that batch wasn't viable, they simply turned them lose and let them fade away."

"So they didn't monitor them at all?"

"There wasn't any reason to. The trial was conducted in private; none of the volunteers knew the names of the other participants. When nothing happened right away, they were informed the experiment failed, and they were released—Denazen found the fatal flaw in its formula and knew the members would all grow sick and die."

"But Penny Mills didn't."

Ginger shook her head. "No. She didn't. Recently they discovered she was the only one still alive. Of course they went after her, but by some miracle, she evaded them. They assumed Penny's survival was genetic and searched for the blood. What they found was a component that bypassed the side effects as well as bridged a gap in Wentz's research, making a successful trial of Supremacy possible and curing Kiernan."

"So we find Penny Mills and, what? Get her to bleed on me?" If they thought I was drinking some chick's blood, they were in for a surprise. I'd start digging my own grave now.

"The blood alone won't cure you because it stopped working after a while. However, with Franklin Wentz's formula and some of the blood, we can duplicate a cure."

"They had the blood in storage," Mom mused. "That would be why there wasn't much to go around. The vials are only several ounces. They take them from all Residents."

"And since they can't find Penny, they have no way of getting more," Dax said.

I hated to be the naysayer of the group, but someone had to put it out there. "If they've already started producing the new trial—which uses the blood—what are the chances there's any left for the cure?"

"Henley has confirmed that a small amount remains."

It bugged me that she kept calling him Henley. His name was *Brandt*—no matter what his outside looked like. And worse than that, I hated that she'd involved him at all. If Dad were to get his hands on someone like Brandt, with his soul jumping ability, the potential damage could be catastrophic. Denazen could simply kill Brandt off a thousand times, allowing him to gather multiple Six abilities, giving them an all-powerful weapon.

This whole thing was a disaster and I was torn. On one hand, I wanted to try talking some sense into Kale. If anyone could get through to him, I was sure it'd be me. On the other hand, while I'd always been a little careless with my own life, ten others were now on the line. "Okay, so we need to get the blood, like, yesterday. But say we do find this Penny Mills chick—we need the formula Denazen stole from that Wentz guy."

"Technically we don't need the formula. We have something better. We have Wentz," Ginger said with a grin. "He's been here for about a week now."

"He's here? As in, right now? How have I not seen this guy?"

Mom rolled her eyes. "He's a little bit…different. Ginger set him up in a lab on the third floor. He doesn't come out much."

I hadn't known we *had* a third floor.

Ginger tapped her cane against the floor. "We need that blood."

"And Denazen has the blood. Maybe Kale can help with that. He's obviously been on the inside. Maybe if I talk to him—"

Alex snorted. "Are you really that stupid? You saw what he did to that guy last night! What the hell makes you believe he'd

think twice about doing it to you? In case you missed it, you're
nobody to him anymore. Worse than nobody. You're the girl he
blames for all this. The person he *hates*."

I flinched as if each word were a physical blow. Knowing
it was one thing, but hearing it was another—especially from
Alex.

His eyes widened and he shook his head. He'd gone too far
and he knew it. Alex had always acted first and thought later.
Most people got better with age—he'd gotten worse. "Dez…"

Alex could be a dick—hell, he'd perfected it to an art
form—but I knew he was only trying to keep me safe. He was
wrong, though. Kale would never hurt me. Not really. He might
not remember my face, but I'd seen something in his eyes at
the party. Something deep down that could never let me go.
Kiernan was proof of that. She had to dress like me, make him
call her a name that sounded like mine, and had to redirect his
anger by slapping *her* crappy name on *me*. All I needed was a
little time and an opportunity.

I turned away from Alex and focused on Ginger. "If I
could just get him alone… It seems like we'd have a better
chance pursuing Denazen to get the blood rather than a
woman who could be God knows where. The world is a big
place. Kind of the ultimate needle in a haystack, don't ya
think?"

She shook her head. "We find Penny and the others first,
then we'll deal with him. It's late December, Deznee. You'll be
no good to Kale if something happens to you. For the moment,
he appears to be safe."

She was right. My birthday was only a few months away,
and whether I admitted it to them or not, I was beginning to
show signs. I asked Mom once why it happened at eighteen.
She told me that the way she understood it, there was a protein

in the original formula that kept replicating. By the time the subjects reached eighteen, it was too much for their bodies to handle. The sand in my hourglass was almost gone.

I hadn't felt Kiernan hit me with the knife at the party, and I couldn't be sure if it was Supremacy—or stress—but lately I found myself easily distracted, my mind wandering to nonsensical things. Other than the little Mom knew, we had no one to ask about the stages of the Supremacy decline. We just had to wait it out and take things as they came. Finding Penny Mills *was* the logical first step.

Still, doing nothing about Kale, when Kiernan was throwing him right under our noses, would be hard—if not impossible. At least for me.

I stuffed down the lump threatening to crawl up my throat and tried one last time. "He's not safe with Denazen. *No one* is safe with Denazen. What about the damage he does before we get to him? How will he live with himself? He *killed* someone last night."

"Do you really think he'd want you pursuing him if there was a cure to be found? He'd want you to find it first." Mom leaned forward. I didn't miss her hand resting atop Dax's and I felt an irrational pang of envy. My hand was cold. And empty. "He won't be able to live with himself if we don't find it in time because you went after him instead."

Again, I wanted to argue, but they all made sense. Annoying, piss-me-the-hell-off sense, but still. Sense. This was hard for my mother, too, even if she wasn't showing it. She'd raised Kale inside Denazen like her own child. But one of the few things I'd learned about Mom in the short time we'd been together was that she was coldly logical when it came to sizing up dangerous situations. Emotion took a backseat. It made sense. So many years with Denazen taught her to push her feelings aside to get through tough situations.

I sighed and kicked at the edge of the chair. "Fine. Where do we start?"

"Penny Mills will take some time. She's deep underground and Denazen, with all its resources, has been searching unsuccessfully for her since October." Ginger pulled out another picture. Scribbling an address on the back, she handed it to me. "In the meantime, we start tracking down the others."

The girl looked about my age with an infectious smile and bright blue eyes. Her long brown hair was twisted into an artful knot with a pair of wooden sticks to hold it in place, and there was a blue smudge across her right cheek. Paint. She looked happy, and I wondered how long ago the photo had been taken. Where was she now? Did she even know about Supremacy?

Was she even alive?

"Deznee, I'd like you to take Alex and go to Kelpsbergh. That's the address we have for Ashley Conner."

"What's her 411?"

"Looking over the bit of information Henley provided, it would seem she's a remote viewer."

"What's that mean?" Alex asked, taking the picture from me.

"Ashley sees things that are happening in other places. She's living with foster parents who I assume are Denazen agents, but I can't be sure, so proceed with extreme caution."

I stood and took the picture from Alex. "We can save time if I check out Ashley and Alex beats down the door of another. Two birds in half the time."

Ginger narrowed her eyes. "You're not going alone. I'm not asking you to make out with him, for Christ sake." A truly wicked smile slipped across her lips. "I suggest you leave now before I insist you take Jade along as well."

That was all the motivation I needed. As much fun as it was to watch them snipe at each other, I wasn't in the mood. I grabbed Alex's arm and headed for the elevator.

5

It took us almost an hour with traffic, and I laid into Alex in the car for siding with Ginger about Kale. He and I once had an intense relationship—until he cheated. I found out later it had been an act, staged to keep me safe, but there was no going back. He insisted he still loved me and nothing could ever change that, but if we couldn't be *together,* he wanted me in his life as a friend. Friends, though, didn't side against you. They had your back. Apparently, Alex hadn't gotten the memo.

We arrived on Ashley Conner's doorstep a little after ten in the morning. There weren't any cars in the driveway, but I saw someone moving around in one of the rooms upstairs when we pulled in.

Alex raised his hand to knock, but I grabbed it and pulled back. "Wait a sec. Ginger said she thought they might be agents. This chick's foster parents."

"So?"

"*So*? If they're agents, wouldn't they know who we are and

why we're here? They're not exactly gonna want to invite us in for cake and cookies, then spill their secrets."

He stuffed both hands into his pockets and sighed. "You think Denazen has your picture plastered all over a Most Wanted list? You're hot, but come on now—"

"I'm being serious."

He hesitated, then stepped back and took a long look at the house. The downstairs was quiet and dark, but the room in the corner on the second floor had the light on. "Well, either way, they'd be Nix, right? Agents are always Nix. Easy to take out."

"Let's check things out first."

Rubbing his hands together, Alex waggled his eyebrows. "Play Peeping Tom? Twist my arm. The girl in the pic is a hottie. Maybe we'll catch her doing something naughty."

I rolled my eyes and shoved him back down the stairs. "You've been hanging out with Curd a little too much lately."

We crept along the side of the house and around to the kitchen window. The lights were off, and there appeared to be no one around. From there, we peeked in the small, grime-covered window on the side door of the garage. No cars.

The backyard was also deserted. The only things in sight were an old tire swing hanging from a questionable-looking branch, a peeling picnic table missing a leg, and a lawn with small patches of snow from the first storm of the season.

We circled the house, coming back around the other side with the intention of knocking on the door. "Wonder which one is her room. Maybe she's in there undressing?" Alex said. He clasped his hands together and flashed me an impish grin.

"Not likely, since she's standing behind you," a girl's voice snapped.

We whirled around, nearly knocking each other over. The

brunette from Ginger's picture, complete with various colored paints splattered across her T-shirt and an extremely annoyed expression stood, arms folded and glaring at us. "U-Um," Alex stuttered. "Yeah, so about that—"

"You have twenty seconds to tell me why you guys are skulking outside my house or I'm calling the cops."

I pushed Alex aside. "Are you Ashley?"

She narrowed her eyes. "If Carl sent you, you're wasting your time. It's over. I don't do cheaters."

I smiled. "Neither do I. See? We have something in common already. My name's Dez." Hitching my thumb over my shoulder, I said, "The perv is Alex. We need to talk to you."

She didn't look like she was in a conversational mood. Glaring from me to Alex, she asked, "About?"

When Kale and I hunted for the Sixes on Denazen's hit list over the summer, I'd developed a whole spiel to break the news gently, and for the most part, it worked. But this situation was a little different. We didn't have a lot of time, and every second I wasted here was another I wasn't looking for Kale or the cure.

It was probably a little selfish, and a part of me felt bad, but I decided the best thing to do was dive right in. "We're here because if you don't let us help you, you're going to die."

"Oh, Jesus," Alex groaned.

Ashley blinked. I thought maybe I'd scared her silent, but when she yanked out her cell phone and I heard a distinct three-number call, I knew maybe I'd approached this the wrong way.

Alex swiped the cell from her and held it out of reach when she made a move to take it back. "Okay, so Dez is lacking decorum today—more so than usual, anyway—but what she said is true. We *are* here to help you."

I rolled my eyes. Since when had he been Mr. Compassion? "Do you know what a Six is?"

She sucker punched Alex and grabbed her phone, dancing out of reach as he tried to steal it back. I liked this girl more and more every passing second. Hitting me with the evil eye, she took another step back and said, "Six? Yeah. It's a number. Comes after five and before seven."

"It's a person, actually," I corrected. "A *kind* of person. Like you and me."

She looked me up and down and snorted. "Sorry. I don't think we're exactly the same brand of crazy, girlfriend."

"No one is her brand of crazy. Trust me." Alex chuckled. "But we *are* like you." He waved his right hand and Ashley's cell shot from her grasp. It hovered for a moment between us, then zoomed straight up and landed on the roof with a clatter.

She gasped, staring after it, and turned to Alex. "How— how did you do that?"

"The same way you can do what you do," I said, nodding to the house. "Are your parents home? Can we talk for a few minutes?"

The wonder drained from her face, replaced by caution. "Now you want me to let you into my house?"

"It won't take long," I prodded. "I promise."

She was still wary, but after a moment, she nodded up to the roof. "As soon as I get my phone back."

"Sure thing." With another wave of Alex's hand, her cell shot off the roof and back into his palm. He handed it over.

Ashley led us around to the front of the house and up to the door. Every few steps she'd glance over her shoulder like she was afraid we might tackle her or something. Mainly, she watched Alex. I didn't blame her. To anyone who didn't know him, he came off kind of shifty. Maybe it was the spiky white-blond hair or the weird happy face labret bead we'd named Fred.

When we got inside, I had to tell myself not to stare. Her place reminded me of my old house. Pristine hardwood floors, ugly furniture, and a fireplace mantel complete with pictures to make it look nice and homey. A part of me wondered if this was standard Denazen issue. The cookie cutter mold used to raise their crazy little army.

"You can sit if you want," Ashley said, sinking into the couch. I didn't miss how she settled next to the telephone or how there was a plate on the table next to it with a fork and knife waiting conveniently. "But don't get too comfortable. My dad will be home soon."

Since meeting Kale, I'd become more aware. Some of it was his coaching, while some was simply observation. The fingers on her right hand twitched as she spoke and her foot began to tap. Her dad wasn't on his way home. If I had to guess, she'd be here alone for hours. It was winter break. School was on hold, but people still had to work. It was all an act.

Alex settled in the armchair across from her, but I stayed standing. Like she said, there was no reason to make myself comfortable. I had no plans of hanging for chips and dip. "I'm not gonna beat around the bush, 'cause honestly? There's not a hell of a lot of time. We were sent here today to warn you. I'm gonna give you two choices and the truth. What you do with it is your call. No one's here to force you to do something you don't want to."

"Dez," Alex warned.

I ignored him. During the summer, Kale and I had to literally drag a couple of the Sixes, kicking and screaming, back to the hotel for their own good. I was over it. If they wanted the help, then great. We'd be there. If not, we had no right to force them. Denazen was all about taking away free will. I wouldn't do the same.

"This thing you can do—the ability you have to see things happening someplace else—has made you a target. Before you were born, your mother—your real mother—was given a drug. It was supposed to enhance your ability so you'd be stronger. More powerful. She was part of a science project called Supremacy just like my mom."

"The problem is," Alex cut in with a harsh sidelong glance in my direction, "it has a nasty side effect that eventually leads to death."

"Or murder," I added. Ashley looked a little green. Good. She needed to understand this wasn't a game. "What do you know about your parents?"

She picked up something on the table next to the couch and began fidgeting with it. A paintbrush. "My real parents? Nothing. I was adopted two weeks after I was born."

How was I supposed to tell this girl her adoptive parents were probably going to kill her in her sleep? It wasn't something that rolled off the tongue. "Think of this house as— as a zoo."

"A zoo?" she whispered, pale.

"You were raised in captivity by people hoping to breed a monster."

Her eyes bugged out and she dropped the paintbrush. It hit the floor and bounced, ending up under the coffee table between Alex and her. "Breed— Wha—?"

I thought my analogy was pretty sharp, but Alex didn't agree. In hindsight, it might have been a *little* too graphic. Accurate, but graphic. He shot me a look that threatened violence and continued in a more neutral tone. "We think your parents—the people who adopted you—work for a company called Denazen. They're supposed to watch you for signs of development."

"Development?" she squeaked, fingers gripping the edge of the cushion. "What are you talking about? My mom is an artist and my dad works in construction."

"Have you noticed anything strange about your abilities lately? Anything abnormal or new? Maybe something you couldn't do before but can now?"

Her eyes narrowed and the fingers on her right hand started picking at the fabric on the couch cushion. Bingo! She'd given herself away.

"Look, I wasn't kidding. There's no time to play games. Not for you and definitely not for us. Cut the crap and just be straight."

"Dez—"

"Sorry, Alex. No one coddled me when I found out. It's like ripping off a Band-Aid. *Just do it.*"

"That's the Nike slogan, not Band-Aids," he said with an exasperated sigh.

I always knew I was different from everyone else, but it wasn't until I met Kale that I learned *how* different that was. The truth of it had turned my universe inside out. But I adapted. I had to. It was the only way to survive. Ashley was either going to sink or swim.

"Whatever good-cop-bad-cop routine you two have going, I'm not really interested." Ashley stood and pointed to the door. "I think you guys should go."

"There's no good-cop-bad-cop. Only the truth. And if you don't let us help you before it's too late, you're going to die. Maybe it'll be a stranger. Maybe it'll be your own *parents*. But you've been scheduled for termination. You and me—we've officially become obsolete."

"You know you sound insane, right?" She threw both hands into the air. She might not believe us 100 percent, but we'd planted a seed. Sometimes that was all we could hope for.

"We know how this sounds, but it's the truth," Alex said. He flashed her a smile that, at one time, would have made my heart stop. He'd always been good at putting people at ease. Maybe it was the way he looked at you. Like you were the only one in the room and he was totally absorbed in anything and everything you were about to say.

"These people want to use your ability to do some really messed-up things. The problem is, the drug they used to boost your power is toxic. As you get older, your body can't handle it." He tapped the side of his head, frowning. "Screws up your mind. The signs come on slowly, but they probably would have started by now. You turn eighteen soon, right?"

"A little more than four months."

"Humor me for a sec," I said, balancing myself on the arm of the couch as she sat back down. "Hallucinations, paranoid delusions, unsteady mood swings... Any of that ring a bell?"

Ashley's brow furrowed. "As in, have I experienced any of them?"

"These are just some of the more common warning signs. There are others," Alex said. "Please. Just give us a few more minutes?"

From the way she kept looking from Alex to the door, I didn't think she'd agree, but after a moment, she nodded. "How can you even be sure I've got one of these—"

"Abilities?" Alex flashed her his patented Elvis smile and leaned a little closer. "We know you can see things that are happening in other places. It's called remote viewing."

She hesitated for a moment before sighing, then stood.

"You showed my yours, so I guess I could show you mine…" Ashley bent over and pulled open the red backpack on the end table. She rifled through, withdrawing several loose pieces of notebook paper. Handing one to Alex, she said, "I did this a week ago."

I leaned over to get a better peek. It was a pencil drawing—if you could even call it that. It *looked* like two guys arguing in traffic. The figures were borderline stick with overly large heads and exaggerated features. All it was missing was the big, yellow, smiley face sun, and it would take first prize in the kindergarten refrigerator art awards. "It's, um, *nice*."

Ashley rolled her eyes and snatched the picture back, cradling it protectively. "It's horrible." She flopped on the couch beside Alex. "I've been drawing and painting since I was eight. The only thing I've ever wanted to do was become an artist like my mom." She waved the paper back and forth. "But I suck. No matter how much I practice, I suck."

"I wouldn't say *suck*," Alex said encouragingly. "You might need a little more—"

"Practice? No." She thrust one of the other sheets at him. "Not anymore."

Alex stared down at the paper, mouth falling open as Fred, the happy-faced labret bead, wobbled from side to side. Holding it up so I could see, he asked, "Dez, do you see what I see?"

This drawing was nothing like the first. It was shaded in black and blue ink, giving it an eerie noire quality, with crisp lines and flawless, almost photographic, detail. "*You* did this?"

The difference in skill wasn't the only noteworthy thing about the drawing. One of the people in it was of interest. *Serious interest.* "Able," I whispered. She had the details down so perfectly. I could see the subtle shift in his nose—one of the only ways I could tell apart him and his twin brother, Aubrey. From the picture, it looked as though he stood at her front door talking to a man I guessed was her father. "When did you draw this? When did it happen?"

"That's where things get even weirder. I did this drawing two days before it happened—"

"Before it happened?" Alex asked. "But you said—"

He was hung up on the *how*, which was stupid. Wasn't it obvious? It was the Supremacy side effects kicking in. A surge in ability right before we went over the deep end. I was more interested in the *what*. "When did this guy come here? Do you have any idea what they said?"

She shook her head and took the drawing, returning it to the safety of her pack. "I only caught enough of a glimpse to know it was the same as my drawing. I was too freaked to stick around."

"The guy in that picture is dangerous." Alex lost his grin. "You're in a lot of trouble. You've got to let us help."

She hesitated before coming back and settling next to Alex on the couch. "I know something's not right. I've had a feeling for a while now…" She turned to me. "But my parents love me. They're not going to let anything happen. Before I do anything I need to talk to them."

"That's a bad idea," Alex said, standing. "They could—"

I grabbed his arm and reached past her to rip off the corner of the newspaper on the coffee table. Snagging the pen beside it, I jotted down both our cell numbers—Alex's and mine—and handed her the piece of paper. "Like Alex said, we're not here to force you into anything, but I strongly suggest you think about this—fast. These are our cells. If you change your mind or need anything, call."

Then without looking back, I walked out the door.

After Alex and I made it back to the cabin, Ginger gave us the next name. Conny Delgeto. The information said the girl could manipulate sound—which I thought was kind of vague. Did that mean she could throw her voice? Or possibly mimic someone else's? Was she just really good at animal calls? I found it annoying, not to mention dangerous, not knowing exactly what we were walking into. Just because Ginger had an inside line to the future didn't mean I wanted to stumble around blind.

Brandt was awake, and I suggested he come with me instead of Alex, but Ginger insisted she had something else for him to do. I didn't buy it. The old woman seemed to live to make me miserable.

Conny's house was several towns over, and it ended up taking us almost three hours to get there because about twenty minutes after we left the cabin, it started sleeting. After he'd gotten his license in ninth grade, Alex had a pretty nasty accident in the snow. Ever since, wintertime driving was something he approached with the utmost caution, which was funny, since he was hell on wheels the rest of the year. There was a growing collection of tickets threatening to overflow the glove box, and I was certain that somewhere out there was an officer with a bench warrant for his arrest.

"Please try and be a little less aggressive with this one," Alex said, slamming the driver's side door. He'd been quiet since we left Ashley's this morning, and I knew he was annoyed with how I'd handled things.

I didn't answer. I hadn't been aggressive; I'd been honest. If I were her, I would appreciate not having the whole thing sugarcoated.

Then again, not many people were like me.

We stopped at the foot of the driveway. The Delgeto house was a sprawling Victorian with a perfectly manicured lawn riddled with holly bushes. There was a large pine in the middle decorated with red and blue balls and sporadic tufts of tinsel, topped with a gaudy angel dressed in gold. "No cars. Maybe no one's home?"

"Place does look deserted, but it's almost four. They're probably still at work." The house was dark, the only source of light coming from a single bulb above the front door. Alex inclined his head toward the garage and stuffed his cell into his back pocket. The door sat off the ground several inches. "Shall we?"

"And if someone *is* inside?"

He shrugged and shuffled down the drive. "We'll deal."

The door opened with a shrill squeal, gears in desperate need of oiling announcing our presence like a fire siren in a library. There were no cars in the garage, but it wasn't empty. On the far wall there was a series of shelves, each stacked with cardboard boxes of varying sizes and colors. Some were labeled in black marker, noting kitchen or bedroom, others said living room—one simply had a smiley face with its tongue sticking out.

On the floor against the walls were various types of yard equipment. A lawn mower, weed wacker, shovels, and other assorted gardening tools. Pretty much your typical variety of garage inhabitants.

Typical…except for the blond girl hanging from the door track in the middle of the room.

"Shit," Alex cursed, taking two steps inside.

I turned away, not wanting to see the vacant, dead look in the girl's sallow eyes, but it was too late. I'd seen it—and it was something I'd never forget. "We can't just leave her like this. You have your cell?"

He hesitated, looking from the girl to me, then back again. "It's in the car."

"I'll wait here. Go call Ginger. See what she wants us to do."

He stepped in front of me, strong hands latching onto my shoulders and holding tight. "We knew we weren't going to get them all, Dez. Why don't I wait here and you go back to the—"

"I'm fine," I snapped, pulling away. I didn't need to be babied. He should know that. "Just go call Ginger. I'll be out in a sec. I just—I just need a minute alone."

He hesitated but knew better than to argue. With one last look, he ducked back under the door, leaving Conny and me alone.

One dead Supremacy girl to another.

"I'm sorry we didn't get here in time," I said, turning back to face her. Whoever she'd been, she deserved that much. I didn't know if she'd done this herself or if someone helped her to her end, but either way, this wasn't her fault.

She had short blond hair and a pixie-like face, and I found myself imagining what her laugh might have sounded like and what kind of jokes she thought were funny. Her eyes, wide and unseeing, were a vibrant green. Had she been the popular girl? The loner? Maybe she was the quiet, artistic type with a small, close circle of friends that had been together since kindergarten. The kind who expected to grow up and old together, neighbors until they were wrinkled and gray.

That would never happen now.

I dragged over a large crate, climbed up so we were eye level, and ran my hand along her forehead and over her eyelids to close them. She was ice cold, indicating she'd been like this a while. Even if we'd gotten here sooner, she probably would have been gone already. "Whoever you were, you didn't deserve this. None of us do…"

I heard the door connecting the garage to the house open as I stepped down from the crate. "She can't hear you."

Kale.

I didn't bother turning around. Looking in his eyes would only make this ten times harder than speaking the words. "Did you do this?"

His footsteps echoed against the concrete, the sound bouncing off the garage walls as he came around to stand between Conny and me. "No."

Today Kale was dressed in black jeans and a dark purple T-shirt. He was wearing a leather jacket and for some reason, the sight of him almost sent me into hysterical giggles. I'd seen Kale in a leather jacket once. For the costume party at Sumrun. It was a good look for him, but now it looked wrong. So out of place…

I knew I should be afraid of him after what I'd seen at

the Nix rave, but the idea that Kale could—*would*—hurt me seemed so absurd. Even now, with his movements stiff and expression so cold. "But you came here to kill her?"

"If the opportunity presented itself, I was supposed to take her out. Obviously I wasn't needed." His tone was neutral. Not angry or aggressive. If one were to ignore the actual words, someone would simply see two people casually talking.

"And how many have you killed so far?" I took a deep breath. "How many innocent lives have you taken?"

"The Supremacy experiments are not innocent."

And that's where my control started to slip. "Do you even hear yourself? They're people, Kale. Not experiments." There was a lump forming in my throat. The guy in front of me was wearing Kale's face. He had Kale's voice and his amazing blue eyes, but everything else was alien. "This isn't you."

"How do you know?" He stepped forward. There was something in his eyes that screamed of eerie familiarity. Something dark that reminded me of the day we first met. Kiernan and Samsen attacked us at the amusement park. Kale tried to hide it, ashamed over his lack of regret for Samsen's fate, but that look was in his eyes again. Back then, I'd seen it—and hadn't cared. I had a fairly good idea what he went through at Denazen—feeling anger and wanting revenge was only natural. But now? It scared me because the good parts of Kale seemed to be buried and I wondered what that left exposed.

"I know more about the real you than you do," I whispered. A spark of boldness washed through me and I stepped forward. Closer to him. Closer to danger. "They're lying to you. Everything they've filled your head with isn't real."

"And you want to set me straight. Is that right?"

I didn't miss the hint of mockery in his voice. It was the same tone I'd heard him use a thousand times when ribbing Alex. I ignored it. A seed. That was all I needed. Enough of a seed to get him thinking. I was sure once I started the ball rolling, his mind would do the rest.

It had to, right? This was Kale.

I squared my shoulders and sucked in a breath. "That's right."

He stepped back and folded his arms, expression amused. "Go ahead. I'm listening."

I knew he was just playing with me, but a small voice inside my head begged me to try anyway. "That girl you keep calling Roz—*she's* Kiernan McGuire. She and Marshal Cross are using you."

He didn't say anything, so I took it as a good sign and kept going, hopeful and on a roll. "You're not the monster they're trying to make you think you are."

"Or," he said, taking another step closer, "you're Kiernan McGuire—the girl who tried to kill me, resulting in the loss of my memory." He poked me hard in the shoulder. "My family, my friends—*my life*—all gone because of you. Roz and Marshal are trying to help me. I love her."

His statement pushed the limits of my control. It was one thing to see the lip lock—but to hear him profess his love for her? I couldn't deal. "You love me!" I screamed. Even stomped my foot for dramatic effect. It didn't make a difference.

Kale threw himself forward, knocking us both back against the wall. "I *hate* you," he breathed, face inches from mine. In his eyes was all the rage and anger he had for Denazen. All channeled at me. "You *destroyed* my life."

Tears stung the corners of my eyes, and for once, I didn't care. The weight of his words came close to suffocating me. "I *saved* your life," I managed. "And you saved mine."

"Dez?" Alex called from the other side of the garage door. "You okay?"

Kale looked from me to the door. For a second his brow furrowed, almost as though he recognized the voice and was trying hard to place it. When he turned back, his expression was different. Not warm, but not the same kind of cold, either. This was something else. Uncertainty. War. A thought or feeling—something—was fighting for his attention. I could see it in his eyes. He was in there. My Kale wasn't lost.

I just had to find a way to pry him loose.

He shook his head as if to clear away the cobwebs. "You're…on my list."

My arm was pinned awkwardly between my back and the shelf. Fingers splayed, I felt around for something— anything—I could use as a weapon if need be. *This is Kale*, that small voice inside said, horrified. *He'd never hurt you.* While another voice disagreed. *No. It's not. Not really. Be smart. Be ready for anything.*

"On your list?"

He opened his mouth, then closed it. "They want me to bring you in," he said, voice barely a whisper. "To question. And test…"

"Then get on with it." I leaned closer than any sane person would have.

I was an adrenaline junkie by nature. But this was different. Taking risks for a cheap thrill was one thing. Standing in front of a ravenous bear with no place to run was something else. Courting death, Brandt called this. Fitting, considering Ginger, long before he was born, had dubbed Kale the Reaper. So here I stood. In front of Death, daring it to take me.

"Do it. If I'm on your list, then go for it."

"I…" He brought his hand up, running a finger along my cheek from chin to ear. His touch, so soft, sent goose bumps dancing across my skin. I'd missed it so much and found my dreams hadn't done it justice. It was far better than I remembered, the slightly calloused tip of his finger skimming my skin and leaving a trail of longing in its wake. Even like this, with him crushing me to the wall, possibly contemplating my death, I couldn't get enough.

There was something seriously wrong with the way I was wired.

"Dez?" Alex called. "You coming out?"

"Kale?" a voice yelled from inside the house. Kiernan.

At the sound of her voice, he shook his head and backed away a few inches. I could see his entire face now. Beautiful but deadly. He watched me with a curious expression, eyes never leaving mine. For an insane moment, I was sure he'd lean down and kiss me—but he didn't.

"There's no one here." Kiernan was getting closer. "Kale? Where'd you go?"

He opened his mouth to answer, but I interrupted. "Don't. Please. Just let me slip out the door…"

"I… Roz will… No. I can't."

"Kale?" Kiernan was starting to panic. Inside, I could hear doors opening and slamming closed again.

"Please," I said again, begging.

"NO!" he screamed and one word came to mind. Unstable. My Kale would never have such an emotional reaction. Anger was something he learned to keep in check at a very young age in order to survive. Whatever they'd done to him, it had shaken something lose. "No," he repeated, calmer. "No. I'll save you for last. I owe you for what you did to me. I'll make you suffer like I did, then I'll bring you in."

And just like that, the fragile patchwork of hope shattered, stealing my breath and bleeding me dry. My hand closed around something—I had no idea what, but it was heavy. That was all I cared about. "Good," I said, resigned. I loved Kale and I'd do anything to get him back, but I wasn't stupid. "Then that gives me time."

"For what?"

I whipped the object—it turned out to be a wrench—around and slammed it into the side of Kale's head as Alex yanked up the garage door. "To knock some frigging sense into you."

I raced toward Alex as Kale went down and Kiernan burst through the door.

"Is this blood?" Mom had my T-shirt in her hand. I'd caught the sleeve on the way out Conny's garage, gashing my shoulder in the process. Alex and I had gone straight back to the cabin after leaving Kale—something I felt horrible about doing. I'd hit him hard, and I had no way of knowing if he was all right.

"Figures. One of my favorite shirts, too." I pulled a clean shirt over my head and turned back to Mom. She stood in the doorway, the ruined shirt still in hand, and looked uncomfortable. It was easy to forget sometimes—especially lately—that she, too, had been a prisoner of Denazen. She had been there just slightly less time than Kale, having been imprisoned after becoming pregnant with me. "I don't suppose we've gotten any leads on that Penny chick, huh?"

"Nothing solid," she said. "But Dax and I did manage to find one of the Supremacy kids."

This was the first I'd heard. "And by find you mean—"

"Alive," she confirmed with a smile. "We convinced her to

come back with us, too."

"Seriously?" Maybe Alex was right and I'd been too aggressive with Ashley. Dax had mellowed her out a lot, but Mom still tended to be on the scary side if you didn't know her. If *they*'d managed to talk someone into coming back, I'd screwed up big time. "Who did you find?"

"Her name is LuAnn Moore. Ginger has her in the new wing—on the other side of the pool. She's keeping that area reserved for any of the Supremacy kids we find and bring back."

Reserved. Meaning quarantined in case they went bonkers. I wondered how long before they suggested a change of address for Brandt and me.

Mom hesitated, then said, "How…how are *you* feeling?"

"What you're really asking is if I've started seeing any signs, right?"

She kept her expression neutral, but I did catch a small twitch of her lip. For Mom, that was equal to an emotional outburst. She wasn't the most touchy-feely person out there—unless of course you were Dax. I still hadn't figured that one out. "That, and how are you taking the Kale situation?"

I pulled a hoodie over my T-shirt and sank onto the bed. "There's nothing yet," I said in response to the Supremacy question, even though I was pretty sure it was a lie. I'd stubbed my toe that morning and screamed like a baby because it'd hurt so badly, but the other night when Kiernan slashed me, I hadn't felt a thing. It seemed to be sporadic—and I didn't know if that was good or bad. "As for Kale, I'm dealing. It hurt seeing him like that. The way he was talking—it was hard. But I'm going to fix it. He's in there—I know it. I'll make this right."

She tossed the shirt into the pile of dirty clothes on the floor. "And if you can't?"

I lifted my head and met her gaze head-on. "That's just not an option for me."

A small smile tugged at the edges of her lips. She nodded, and right before she turned, said, "That's my girl."

"Hey," I called as she disappeared around the corner. I'd almost forgotten the reason I'd called her in.

"Yes?"

"That list. The one Brandt gave us with the Supremacy names. Where is it?"

"Why?"

I shrugged and tried to play it cool. "No reason. Thought maybe I could take a peek. See what's ahead. Might help to get an idea of who else is still out there and what we'll be up against."

And just like someone flipped a switch, Mom's demeanor changed. She went from normal Mom to I-have-a-secret Mom. It'd taken me a while, but I finally had her moods down—not that there were many. "Ginger has it. She's keeping the names a secret for now."

"Really," I said, folding my arms.

She started inching to the right. "I have to find Dax. I promised I'd spar with him." If I'd blinked, I would have missed it. She was gone.

"You'd think she'd know better by now," I said to myself. I mean, she'd basically *dared* me to go find the thing. If Ginger was keeping the names a secret, then there had to be a reason. I had a duty to myself—and to the other Supremacy kids—to find out what that reason was.

I waited a few minutes to be sure Mom was gone before heading out of my room and down the main hall.

Dax was our own resident Bruce Wayne Six, and he had financed the entire underground community to keep us safe. I didn't know it when I first met him, but apparently Dax had money. *Lots* of it. And at the rate we brought in new blood, we'd have to expand soon. That is, unless some of us started dropping off.

I hurried through the pool room, pinching my nose against the stench—I'd never liked the smell of chlorine—and made my way toward Ginger's room. She was at the end of the hall, away from everyone else. She said it was because she liked the quiet, but if you asked Dax, he put her there because she snored loudly enough to wake the entire complex.

When I got to Ginger's door, I leaned close and held my breath, pressing my ear up against the wood. I counted to ten and waited. Nothing. The room was empty. Good. Next step— getting inside. The door was locked, of course, but something as silly as a lock hadn't stopped me since my ability surged.

Truthfully, a locked door had never stopped me.

"Dez, right?"

I whirled around, guilty, and found myself face-to-face with a brunette girl. "Um, hello, person who I've never met. I'm not doing anything wrong."

She extended her hand, smiling. "Ooookay. I'm LuAnn— call me Lu, though. I saw you come down this way and I wanted to say hello. Your mama just brought me in. She was with that really handsome man."

"Dax." I nodded. "But hands off. They're kind of a thing." A quick glance over my shoulder told me the coast was still clear, but standing here out in the hallway—in front of Ginger's room—probably wasn't the best idea. "So how did you know who I was?"

"You look just like your mama. She told me all about you on the drive over." She had on a baggy green sweatshirt with a picture of a snowman—Frosty if I had to guess—roasting over an open fire and a small pin of a Christmas tree with flashing lights on her right shoulder. Long, straight hair with no real shape, no makeup, and odd fuchsia jeans. She was the kind of girl the guys at school would have made fun of—slightly overweight, with a quirky fashion sense and a thick accent.

Me? I thought she was kind of awesome.

Taking her hand, I returned the warm smile, and in an attempt to get her to move along, said, "Well, welcome to the funny farm. Lemme know if you need anything."

But she didn't take the hint. "So I know I just got here, but I wanted to see how you were. Your mama said we were in the same boat. This whole thing is a little—"

"Crazed?" There was a noise at the other end of the hall. Someone was coming. My time was up. "Lu, is it? Let's get to know each other." I placed my hand over Ginger's door and instead of the brass handle pictured one made of Nerf. The texture changed—and unfortunately so did the color. I'd been thinking of Alex's old Nerf ball. The damn thing had been neon yellow.

"Holy hound dogs. Did you just—"

I pushed open the door and tugged her inside. "Nothing says bonding like a little breaking and entering."

"Whoa," she breathed as I closed the door behind us. "Do y'all do stuff like this often?"

I shrugged, made a beeline for Ginger's desk, and pulled open the top drawer, yanking things out one by one. "Depends on the day."

Lu stood by the door and shuffled from foot to foot. "Mind if I ask you a question?"

Bank statements, an ancient-looking address book, and about a hundred old food store flyers—but no file folder. On to the next drawer. "Go for it."

"When do you turn eighteen?"

"My ticker is up on February first." Crap. Nothing in the second, either. "What about you?"

"My birthday is on March sixteenth."

"Bites the big one, eh?" I slammed the third drawer closed and dove for the fourth—the last. "So how did they convince you to come back here?"

"No convincing needed." She stepped farther into the room, seeming to relax a little. "I knew they'd be coming. Six perk. I was all packed when they showed up this mornin'."

"What about your parents?"

"They won't miss me. I wasn't theirs, after all."

That made me stop and look up. She was still smiling, but it was sad somehow. "So you knew? For how long?"

"I've known about it since I was twelve. We lived in Kansas most of my life, but last week we moved here."

"I don't understand... If you knew, why stay? Why come with them to Parkview at all?"

She smiled. "I knew your mother and her friend would come for me."

"If it'd been me, I would have jumped ship and run as far away as possible."

She shook her head and stepped around the desk. "No you wouldn't have." Shifting the contents of Ginger's desktop around, she uncovered a yellow folder. "Is that what yer lookin' for?"

In her hand was the yellow folder Ginger had earlier in the common room. "You are the very definition of awesome, Lu!" I dove for the folder and yanked it open. Several sheets in, I found what I was looking for. "Gotcha."

Lu leaned over my shoulder. "Who're all those people?"

I tapped the page, flipping through a few more. "They're

like us. The rest of the Supremacy kids."

"There are so many."

"Twelve of us total," I said. Names, addresses—some sheets had pictures. Some didn't. Nothing struck me as super secret and I couldn't imagine why Ginger wanted to keep this hidden—until I got to the fifth page and it all made sense. "Holy shit."

Lu jumped and spun for the door. "What? What's wrong?"

"This is why they didn't want me to see the list." I pulled my cell from my back pocket and snapped a few pictures.

"Ben Simmons," Lu read aloud. "Who's he?"

I e-mailed the pictures to my account and pocketed the cell. "It's not so much who he is but what he can do." I tapped the page again. "It says he's a memory thief. If he can steal memories, maybe he can fix broken ones."

Her expression turned sympathetic, and she reached across, awkwardly patting me on the shoulder. "Did you lose a memory?"

I closed the file and pushed it back underneath the stack of papers. "Not me. My boyfriend. These guys who did this to us? They took him. Messed with his head. He doesn't know me anymore…"

"I'm sorry," she said.

"It's cool. If anyone can beat this, it's him and me." The words came out strong and sure, but deep down I still had my doubts. Every time I remembered the way Kale looked at me in Conny Delgeto's garage, my fragile hope slipped just a little. But maybe I didn't have to wonder. Knowing what she could do, I couldn't resist. "I don't suppose you know how this is all gonna turn out?"

"My gift only allows me to see things about my own life. I wish I could tell you what you want to know, but I only know what's going to happen to me. Moments I'm in, events in my life. It's sadly limited."

"And it's always been like that?"

"Yep."

She turned eighteen in about three months. Maybe there was hope for her. If nothing had changed, maybe her body wasn't rejecting the drug. "You might be all right, then. One of the earliest signs the body is starting to reject the drug is a noticeable change in your ability. If there hasn't been any change, and you're this close, then you might be okay. My ability changed back in the beginning of summer."

I had what I'd come for. Staying longer would be pushing my luck. As I started for the door, I turned back and asked, "You said you knew how it was going to turn out for you. Are you going to start showing side effects?"

She shrugged and, with a sad smile, followed me out of the room. As I changed the knob back to its normal metal state, she said, "I'm not sure. I don't make it long enough to find out."

• • •

Lu's confession haunted me the rest of the night. I was tempted to tell someone but decided it wasn't my place. Her future. Her choice. That was my new motto.

I lay in bed, brain whirring two million miles a minute as I tried to come up with a plan of attack. Somehow, I needed to get to Ben Simmons. The address in his file was just over the Connecticut border, but getting there without letting the others know would be tricky. With the word out to terminate the Supremacy kids, the chances of Mom and Ginger letting me skip around on my own were slim.

I knew Ginger would send someone to get him, but she

wouldn't make it a priority, which seemed stupid. Denazen had the same list we did. If Ben were still alive, Denazen would make it its business to get to him ASAP to keep him from reversing what was done to Kale—unless they knew it couldn't be done.

I'd almost slipped into dreamland, thinking about Kale and our last trip to Gino's—a little Italian restaurant several towns over we liked to sneak out to—when something shook the bed. Without rolling over, I swatted the air. Ginger had taken in a stray cat and the damn thing, for some reason, loved my room. More specifically, my bed. I warned her that the first time I found a dead animal of any kind between my sheets, the cat was history.

"Stupid cat. Go away," I mumbled into my pillow.

"Dez?" Huh. Cats didn't talk. It took a second to shake the impending sleep from my brain before I figured out who it was.

"Alex? What the hell—"

"Dez, we don't have time. Wake up."

"Time?" I untangled myself from the covers and twisted to see the clock. Two a.m. "You realize it's the ass-crack of sleepy time, right?"

"We need to go. Now."

I bolted upright and threw off the covers, sliding my feet into the sneakers at the base of my bed while flipping on the lamp. "What happened?"

"Ashley. She called my cell. After we left, she did a drawing. It showed her parents—"

A rush of guilt crashed through the room. "Where is she? Is she someplace safe?"

"She called from her room. She was close to hysterical, Dez. Kept going on about how sorry she was for not coming with us earlier."

She was sorry? Great. Now I felt worse, if that were even possible. "Even if we leave now and with no traffic, it'll still take almost an hour. And that's doesn't include waking everyone—"

"There's no time. It's just you and me. We're the cavalry."

Right. He was right. I shoved Alex from the room and threw on a pair of jeans and the first sweater I put my hands on. Ashley was terrified and alone and it was only a matter of time before the bad guys closed in.

This was all my fault.

8

I was sure we were going to get our asses handed to us for going alone—but we could deal with the verbal fallout later. I didn't think I'd be able to forgive myself if something happened to Ashley. Alex had been 100 percent right to rib me for the way I'd acted. If I'd been less bitchy and more understanding, she might have come back to the cabin with us in the first place or, at the very least, been a little more careful.

We were on the way to the elevator and were up and out the top front door no more than five minutes after Alex woke me up. It was going on two-thirty in the morning, and thankfully, the roads were empty. Unfortunately, a new, thin layer of snow had fallen in the last few hours, making travel a little slower than expected. The salt trucks hadn't been through yet, and the car kept slipping and skipping all over the road. Alex refused to drive, so I took the wheel as he sat in the passenger's seat looking pale. I was so focused on keeping the car steady on the road that I almost missed the exit.

A half block away, I tucked Alex's recently refurbished Chevy behind an old rusting Volkswagen van and we hoofed it the rest of the way. I'd rushed, not bothering with socks, and the snow had started to seep through my sneakers, numbing my toes. By the time we got to Ashley's, I was convinced I had frostbite.

Alex handed me the keys, then rubbed his hands together. "Keep the car running. I'll be right back."

He turned toward Ashley's and I grabbed his arm. "Um, excuse me?"

"Dez, we have no idea what we're walking into. And think about it. You were kind of a bitch yesterday. If Ashley's scared, do you really think your face is the one she needs to see right now?"

Wow. Ouch times ten. I took the keys from him and nodded like a good little girl. Not that I had any intention of letting him walk in there on his own, but if he needed to think himself the big bad savior, I could give him that.

I counted to twenty once he'd disappeared around the bushes, then approached the front of the house with caution, keeping my eyes peeled for any signs of Denazen. The neighborhood was quiet, the soft sounds of light snow falling like miniature footsteps all around. I moved forward, alert and ready for danger. The front door was ajar, making me wonder if Alex had walked right in and left it that way or someone else had.

A little voice inside my head told me to turn around. Run to the car and don't look back. I couldn't do it, of course, but I was human, and despite what Mom might think, I did have some small sense of self-preservation. But Alex was in here somewhere, and Ashley needed help. There was a good chance none of us would be in this position had I just approached things differently the first time we'd been here.

I pushed through the open door, cringing when it creaked, and froze. The living room looked the same as it had earlier, shadows of the couch and lounge chair casting oddly shaped figures on the wall. With each step I took, the feeling of dread in my chest grew heavier and heavier.

"Ashley?" I dared to whisper, but I got no response. "Alex?"

Through the living room and into the hall, I stopped at the base of the stairs and held my breath to listen for movement. Other than the falling snow—now pounding against the tin awning outside—everything was still.

I took the stairs, hesitantly stepping down on each one. If there was a creaky board within a thousand miles, inevitably my foot would find it. Sure enough, halfway to the top, I hit one that let out a squeal and caused my heart to skip several beats. I waited, but no one came rushing, so I continued.

At the top of the stairs, there was a long hall with three rooms to the right and one to the left. Left first. Process of elimination. That would be Kale's logic. Start with the smaller side and rule it out. I opened the door to find a bathroom—empty—and began moving carefully in the other direction.

The first was the master bedroom. The lamp on the nightstand was on, casting a soft glow through the empty room. The bed was still neatly made with a light blue bathrobe folded at the foot. Next looked like a computer room. There was a large flat-screen monitor mounted to the wall above a cherry wood desk, with the keyboard on the surface below. Plush carpet. Uncomfortable-looking desk chair. Half-full bookshelves. No Ashley. No Alex.

The next room was hers. I had no doubt. Other than the multiple easels and painting supplies strewn about, the fact that it looked like a tornado hit the room was a dead giveaway.

The mattress was turned over and leaning on its side up against the wall, the sheets in a tangled pile at its base. I stepped up and picked the pillow off the floor. Tossing it on the dresser—the only thing still upright—I started to turn, but froze when I noticed a shadow fall across the floor.

"I told them you wouldn't come alone. Yet here you are," Kale's dark voice said from the doorway. "You're an odd one."

"You don't realize it, but coming from you, that's kinda funny," I said, swallowing hard and turning to face him. The light from the hall lit the entire right side of his face, leaving the left cloaked in darkness. Two sides of the same dangerous coin. I wanted to back away but resisted, meeting his gaze straight on. My Kale was in there somewhere—and he could sense weakness. "And who says I came alone?"

"You're alone now," he said, taking another step closer. At his side, the fingers of his right hand tapped against his leg. One. Two. Three. One. Two. Three.

"Did you kill her?"

"She's dead."

"I figured as much," I said, jaw tense. Another step closer. "But I'm asking if *you* did it."

He cocked his head to the left and I could see his expression. Confusion. "You asked the same thing about the other girl. Why does it matter?"

"Because it does. It matters to you, too. You just don't remember."

He took another step. Inches. He was inches from me now, the warmth from his body radiating like the sun. Every one of my muscles plunged into an all-out war with my heart. Common sense screamed for me to match his steps forward with ones away. *Keep your distance—he's dangerous!*

My heart wanted to move closer.

"Why did you do it?"

"Because she needed help," I said, inhaling. He still smelled like Kale.

"No. Not come here." He tilted his head a bit farther, a lock of midnight hair falling into his eyes. He studied me with clinical interest. "I'm asking why you attacked me."

"You attacked me first." My fingers itched to touch his temple where a small bruise fanning from the thin gash had formed. I wanted to trail tiny kisses and apologize for hitting him.

I wanted this to all be nothing more than a bad dream.

"Does it hurt?"

He touched his temple and leaned closer—the movement taking him out of the thin beam of light from the hall and into the shadows of Ashley's room. When he spoke again, his voice was different. Unlike anything I'd ever heard from him before. It made my legs itch to run, kicking my survival instinct into high gear.

It scared me.

"I feel like…when I look at you—" He shook his head and placed a hand on either side of me, up against the mattress, and brought his face close to mine. For the longest moment all he did was stare. When he did speak, there was so much rage in his voice. "You stabbed me. When that didn't do the trick, you pushed me from the bridge. I'm asking you *why*?"

"I never did that, Kale. No one's ever pushed you from a bridge as far as I know. I promise. As for the scar, yeah. You were stabbed. Alex did it."

"You're lying, Kiernan."

"I'm not. And my name is Dez," I said, voice cracking under the weight of his words. *"Deznee."*

Through my jacket, the sharp jut of an out-of-place spring dug into my skin. Right hand remaining flat to keep me in place, he brought his left up and ran it down the side of my face. A surge of pain ignited in its wake, stealing my breath and nearly bringing me to the ground, a mass of blubbering goo. It was like being pulled apart on the most basic of levels. Cell by cell and vein by vein, the sting worked its way along my skin and in seconds, it encompassed my entire body.

"All it would take is a single touch. I could kill you and it would all be over. No discomfort. But that's too easy after what you've done." He withdrew his hand and pulled away a few inches. "If you think that hurts, you should consider what it's like for me not to remember my life. My friends. *My family*."

I could tell him that most of the life he had wasn't worth remembering or that *I* was his friends and his family, but the look in his eyes told me that at the moment, he was beyond words that might bring reason.

Still, I wasn't ready to give up, so I went with what had always worked for me. Something insane.

Pushing forward, I crushed my lips to his, wrapping both arms around his neck to lock him in place. He didn't resist and, to my surprise, didn't shove me away. Instead, after a moment, he responded, his lips moving fervently with mine.

The kiss only lasted a few moments. I was the one who broke it, pulling away as the clouds passed, allowing the moonlight to shine through the bedroom window once again. For a second, neither of us said a word. His cheeks glistened with my tears, making it look like he'd been crying, too, as he stared—eyes wide and mouth agape—like he'd never seen me before.

For a crazy, insane moment, time froze. I thought maybe

the kiss had done the trick. That this time the princess had woken the prince. He looked at me with a mix of shock and awe, the tiniest hint of my Kale gleamed through. My heart pounded so loudly I could barely hear anything else. It was there. I could see the spark in his eyes. "Kale?"

But it didn't last. Or maybe it hadn't been there at all. Maybe I wanted to see it so badly that I imagined the whole thing.

His lips parted and the corners tilted upward just a hair. "Roz is right. You *are* crazy."

I pushed him hard and ran.

Down the stairs, through the living room, and out the still-open front door. I tripped down the icy steps, catching myself just before planting face-first into the edge of the decorative wrought iron railing. My knee skimmed the slush-covered concrete, the fabric ripping—along with a nice chunk of skin—as I dragged myself up and bolted for the car. But that was a no-go. In the moonlight I saw the silhouette of a tall, broad-shouldered figure waiting by the front bumper, so I changed directions.

I slipped into the woods through the neighbors' yard, following the rock wall as a guide. I was many things—and directionally challenged was one of them. Without some sort of guide and in the dark, there was a good chance I'd get myself lost in the woods—but at least I had some small amount of cover.

"This is more like it," Kale called from somewhere behind me. The noise his footsteps made in the snow announced he wasn't far, motivating me to run faster.

I quickened my pace, lungs reaching combustible levels as I struggled to keep up the speed. Before going back to Denazen, Kale had run three miles every day. I'd gone with him once and five minutes in was convinced he was trying to kill me. I hadn't run since, and at this particular moment, regretted giving it up.

A fresh coat of freezing rain had fallen, making the entire forest one big, uneven ice rink. I was running blind, at the mercy of the constantly moving clouds and intermittent moonlight, while doing my best not to fall on my ass. Add a tornado or some other type of natural disaster and my night would be utterly complete. Sometimes I was sure my existence was simply entertainment for some higher power who got off on seeing people suffer.

I stopped beside a thick pine tree for a second and scanned the area to get my bearings, but in the confusion lost my sense of direction. The rock wall was nowhere in sight and I had no clue which way Ashley's house—or Alex's car—was. And where was Alex? Please, God, let him be okay.

Something behind me snapped—a tree branch or something—and I started moving again. I dug the cell from my pocket but fumbled when I slipped on an icy root. Going down hard, the phone flew from my grasp.

"Shit!" I hissed, dragging myself off the ground. I thrust my hands through the layer of ice and into the slushy snow to find the cell. After a few seconds, my hands closed around the familiar plastic and I pushed off the ground and kept going.

"You're fast," Kale called, voice bouncing off the trees. "But you won't get far." There was no mocking in his tone. Only a painfully familiar, matter-of-fact pitch.

Ahead I caught sight of a large clump of rocks. Hoping it would lead me back to the house or at the very least give me a place to hide, I banked hard and turned the corner into total darkness. I got two steps, maybe three, before someone grabbed me, hand clamping down hard over my mouth, and spun me away from the path.

"Shh!" the voice hissed in my ear.

I stopped struggling, my attacker maneuvering us behind the side of the rock as someone else—assumedly Kale—raced by. Then he let go and stepped away. At first a rush of relief flooded me, thinking it was Alex, but then the person spoke. "Are you crazy?"

"I'm getting really tired of people asking me that," I fired back, slightly surprised. The moon moved behind the clouds so I could barely make him out, but it didn't matter. I knew that voice. "Is it just you? Or is your creepy other half lurking somewhere?"

"It's just me and Kale," Aubrey whispered. "And keep your damn voice down."

"Ashley Conner. Is she—"

"She's gone. The parents got her." He leaned back and crooked his finger at something. Alex stepped out from behind the rock.

Relieved to see him in one piece, I threw myself forward and hugged him. He returned the embrace with a low chuckle. "Jeez, Dez, if I knew this was what it would take to get you to put your hands all over me again, I would have done it sooner."

"Jackass," I said, pulling away and turning to our unlikely savior.

The last time I'd seen him, Aubrey had *technically* saved me from a violent and excruciatingly painful death at the hands of his brother, Able, but that didn't mean he was now batting for the home team. They were twins, and their ability—a freaky joint thing—allowed one to poison you while the other could heal. Kale had sacrificed himself by making a deal with Dad. Aubrey would be allowed to heal me if Kale went back to Denazen, but Dad never planned on keeping his end of the deal. Aubrey's orders had been to heal the poison and bring me back—or let me die. Instead, he chose to cure the poison and let me go, leaving with the promise that he would look after Kale.

"What did they do to him, Aubrey?"

"This isn't really the time or place—"

I grabbed the lapel of his coat and gave a good shake. He was taller than Kale—probably six foot four—and I had to throw my head back to look up at him. "*What* did they do to him?"

"He's been given Domination. It's the—"

"Working version of Supremacy." Alex rolled his eyes. "Yeah, yeah. I know. I think she means his brain. What did they do to his *head*?"

"He thinks I'm Kiernan. And he thinks Kiernan is…" I couldn't finish, the memory of the way he'd kissed her back at the party still slowly eating a hole through my soul. "Was it the drug? Did it have a side effect?"

And please tell me it can be fixed…

Aubrey shook his head, long hair loose and blowing in the breeze. "It wasn't Domination. A Six did it. They didn't want to give him the drug unless they were sure he could be controlled. They went in and altered his memories—almost killed him doing it, too."

My stomach clenched. "What?"

"You, Dez. It was you. The harder they tried to wipe you away, the more he fought the process. In the end, they couldn't do it without killing him, so they had to swap you and Kiernan."

In a truly screwed-up way, Aubrey's confession made me happy. It was exactly like Alex said. If I was that deeply embedded in Kale's subconscious, then whatever the Denazen

Six had done, we could undo. Somehow, it could be fixed. "Anything else? Anything that might help?"

"The only thing I can say is Cross is worried the swap won't stick. He has Mindy, the Six who did it, working with Kale daily. She tells him she's trying to help recover his memory when really, she's ensuring they don't lose control over him."

This was great news! "So if we keep him away from this chick, he'll start remembering?"

Aubrey hesitated, peering around the corner of the rock. When he turned back, his expression was grim. "It's a possibility—but *not* a guarantee. I've seen people wiped once who never revert, but Kale's different. They're really not sure what will happen without Mindy reinforcing the wipe. Honestly, I think they're more worried about him going apeshit."

"What's that supposed to mean?" Alex asked. He cupped his hands to his mouth and blew out, sending a stream of smoky breath into the air.

The moon danced out from behind the clouds again— just in time to showcase Aubrey's sad expression. "The other thing they couldn't wipe out was all the anger he felt toward Denazen. Kale's normally in control of it, but by stripping things away and messing around inside his head, they kicked a hornet's nest. The guy has some serious issues. He spent most of his life at Denazen. You must know the things they did to him. He may keep it in check, but trust me, it's there—and Cross is worried it's a ticking time bomb."

I remembered the way Kale looked at Samsen. There was so much rage in his eyes. So much hate. Everyone had a dark side. Thoughts and feelings they kept hidden from the ones they loved. I knew he thought he was a monster for the things he'd done during his time with Denazen, but maybe there was more to it than that. Maybe he didn't know what to do with the anger. Feelings like that couldn't be controlled forever. They needed to be dealt with. "I need to get him alone."

Aubrey shook his head. "Stay away from him. He's not the same guy you knew."

"No," I said. "I saw something. A spark. My Kale is still in there."

"*Parts* of your Kale are in there," he corrected. "And trust me, they're not the parts you want back." He stuffed both hands into the pockets of his trench coat. "Besides, they rarely let him out alone. If Kiernan isn't glued to his side, Cross has me with him."

"Then I need your help. Tell me where he's going to be next. Make sure you're the one with him."

"This is suicide, Dez. He was dangerous before they gave him the drug. Now he's ten times worse. Time away is no guarantee he'll remember."

"Maybe not, but one of the Supremacy kids might be able to help."

Aubrey didn't look convinced. "You're assuming you'll find any of them alive—and still possessing the ability to spell their own name. I've seen the decline. It's not pretty. These kids turn into drooling psychos—" He paused as Alex made a face. "Oh. Yeah. Sorry."

"I have no intention of drooling, thank you very much." I sucked in a deep breath. "Why did you help us? I mean, I kinda get why you saved me a few months ago, but why help us tonight?"

Aubrey was silent. Just when I was sure he wouldn't answer, he sighed. "I made Kale a promise. He may not remember it, but I do."

Alex narrowed his eyes. It was no secret he didn't trust Aubrey—not that I did 100 percent either—but I was willing to give him a chance. Judging by the tone in Alex's voice, he wasn't. "A promise? What kind of promise?"

Aubrey shook his head. "Doesn't matter. Just know that I understand how you feel, and I wouldn't wish this on anyone." He took a step away. "So what do you plan on doing? Asking Kale to go on a nice little road trip with you? There's no way you'll be able to take him anywhere he doesn't want to go."

He was right. Kale wasn't going to be *led* anywhere, but I had a plan. I fished my cell from my back pocket and handed it to Aubrey. "Then I'll make him come to me."

9

We made it back to the cabin by five a.m. I was soaked and limping from a twisted ankle. I was also numb. Ashley was gone, and although Alex tried convincing me on the ride home that it wasn't my fault, I knew better. There were a million other ways I could have handled things. I let my anger over the situation, as well as my desire to bring Kale home, interfere with common sense.

Mom, Ginger, and Dax were sweet enough to welcome us back by waiting in the doorway, expressions full of concern and gratitude that we'd taken the initiative and gone to help Ashley.

Not quite.

"I know this is a redundant question with you, but what the hell were you thinking?" Mom stalked from one end of the kitchen to the other, hands stuffed into the pockets of her flannel penguin pajama pants.

"Why wouldn't you wake anyone up?" Dax asked, glaring

right at Alex. He looked like he was still half asleep. "Going alone was stupid—even for you two."

"There was no time," Alex seethed. "We went together. We came home together. Everything is fine."

Shortly after the hotel burned down, he'd abandoned his apartment and moved into Dax's complex. Some days—okay, most days—I wished he'd stayed put. Living under the same roof with someone like Alex was bad enough—but add to that the fact that he was my ex? Can you say *awkward?* At least this time, he had my back.

"Alex is right. There was no time." I whirled on Ginger. Everyone else had expressed an opinion; I wanted to make sure she got a say, too. "Your turn. Tell us how stupid we were for going to help her."

The old woman's lip twitched, but instead of jumping on the bandwagon, she simply stared. Not good. A Visionary, she saw people's life path when she looked into their eyes— she probably knew for months that we'd do what we did. The catch was, by some freaky code of her own, she refused to tell anyone about the things she saw. It was selfish, in my opinion, and had resulted in the death of her daughter and imprisonment of her grandson—twice.

I held my breath, sure she was about to call me on breaking into her room and getting into the file, but to my surprise, she simply asked, "Did you find her?"

Alex frowned. He shot a quick glance my way before turning back to Ginger. "Didn't make it in time. Aubrey said her *parents* got her. There was *nothing* we could have done."

"Aubrey?" Dax asked, surprised. He grabbed Mom's hand as she passed and tugged her into the chair beside him. Thank God. She was starting to make me dizzy. I was a pacer, but when someone else did it, it drove me nuts. "Why would you believe anything he says?"

"He's no saint—but he did save me. Twice. He helped us avoid Kale last night, too." While I probably wouldn't give him my home address and e-mail password, I did believe he wanted to help.

"Kale?" Mom leaned forward. Her voice rang of worry, but her eyes sparked with hope. "Kale was there, too?"

Ginger leaned back in her chair, unfazed. "And what else did Aubrey have to say?"

"He confirmed what Alex suggested earlier about a Six switching Kiernan and me in Kale's memory. Some chick named Mindy. They're making him see her every day so they don't lose control of him." If I could convince them getting Kale away from Denazen sooner rather than later would benefit us all, then I was going to do and say whatever it took. "He's in there, Mom. I saw him. He's messed up and confused, but he's in there."

The expression on her face was somewhere between regret and pity, and it took a second until I realized why. She didn't believe we'd get him back. None of them did. Mom loved him, but she didn't believe he'd ever come home.

"Dax and I are heading to the airport," Mom said. Dax stood and tugged her to her feet. "One of the names on the list, Andrea Marko, lives in California. Our flight leaves in three hours. We confirmed with a contact in the area she's alive and living on her own in an apartment in SoHo. Hopefully we can convince her to return with us."

"We're not going to find the others alive," Alex said. He looked at Dax with an expression that caused my chest to tighten. "I think we should focus on finding this Penny chick and dealing with Kale. We all know how Cross works. He's a twisted fucker. He'll send the freak after Dez."

"I have people following leads on Penny Mills," Ginger said. "Until something comes of it, we continue chasing the Supremacy offspring. We won't save them all, but we *will* get some. I'm not giving up on them."

We will get some.

It was the closest thing to a revelation since she'd told me the worst was yet to come and that Alex and I would pay the biggest price. I probably should have been standing around waiting for the sky to fall, but if I did that, I'd never get anything done. The sky in my world always seemed to be coming down. My biggest issue with her plan was that we were wasting time chasing down people she might already know were gone when we could be focusing on Kale.

"Since everyone is up, we might as well get started." She fished into her pocket and pulled out two small slips of paper. Handing one each to Alex and me, she said, "Get ready and head out. These are the next two semi-local names. The last two, actually. The rest are out of state and Dax and Sue will deal with them."

I took my slip, but Alex didn't make a move for his. He glared at her hand like she'd asked him to cuddle a cobra. "Different names? This doesn't seem like the brightest move."

I gave him a sideways glance, begging him to be quiet. He'd sided with her on everything lately and he picked *now* to open his mouth?

"Yesterday you said no one goes alone. Today you're changing your tune?" he continued. "What the hell?"

"You won't be going alone. You'll be taking Jade," Ginger said.

"Because that's so much better than going alone?" he quipped, snatching the paper from between her fingers. "And what about Dez?"

"I'm sure she's touched by your concern, but she'll be fine."
Ginger slammed her cane against the table. "Now get moving!"

Grumbling, Alex stood and stalked from the room. If I had
to guess, he was off to wake up Jade. Last time, he'd dumped a
gallon of ice water on her head. She, in turn, hit him with a jar
of cold tomato sauce the next morning. It was a good match-
up. Denazen wouldn't dare attack them—they'd be too afraid
to get in the middle of their squabbling.

When I turned back to the room, Mom glared at me. "Can
I trust you—"

"To behave?" I finished for her. "Not likely."

"Behave?" she balked. "The most I can hope for is that
you exercise some amount of common sense."

As Mom settled into her new role in my life, it had become
obvious we were a lot alike. I got my strength and stubbornness
from her, as well as my gleaming sarcastic wit. "I'll be careful,"
I said.

She nodded, but beside her, Dax didn't look convinced.
They left without another word, leaving Ginger and me alone.

"Who are you forcing me to take? And if you say the kid
who can read minds and smells like mothballs, deal's off."

"You can go alone," she said after a moment.

"Can?"

"I leave it up to you."

"Well, that's stupid. You know I'm going to choose solo—
but why? You made Alex take Jade."

She didn't answer and I understood. Bait. She was using
me as bait. "Kale is going to be there, isn't he?"

"It's a possibility," she responded, expression neutral.

"And that's code for yes—not that you'd actually tell me."

"It's *code* for maybe. The chances of him being there are
good. And no. If I knew for sure I wouldn't tell you, but the

truth is, I don't know for sure."

I wasn't sure I bought that. "So you're on the fritz, then?"

She looked insulted. "Most certainly not. You accuse me of knowing every little detail about your lives and keeping it a secret for my own personal gain, Deznee, but I don't know how many times I can tell you that's not the way it works."

I rolled my eyes. *Here we go.*

"I don't know what cereal you're going to wake up and eat. I have no idea what garish outfit you'll put on or what crazy color your hair will be from day to day. I only know the key points—the defining moments in your life. The things in between are hidden from me."

"And my going to check out this name isn't one of them."

"No."

"But you still think there's a chance Kale might show up?"

"I believe it's possible, yes."

"Why?"

She hesitated, fidgeting with the handle of her cane before lifting her gaze to mine. "I knew you would go to Ashley's last night."

"So last night was one of those *defining* moments?" I thought back to the woods. Nothing really stood out as epic.

"It was. But not for you."

That's when I understood. She hadn't seen me there through my path—she'd seen me there through Kale's. "So you're using me as bait, then. Correct?"

Ginger wasn't one to apologize for her actions or the way she viewed the world—and that was fine with me. "Essentially. Is that a problem?"

"It's Kale. It's no problem. And what's the big, right? You just said this wasn't one of those life-defining moments. That means I'm not gonna bite it, because that's pretty defining in my opinion." I waited for her to correct me, or at the very least, twitch, but I got nothing. "Plus, this makes you feel a little more human."

Her brows shot up, and for the first time since we'd met, she looked genuinely pissed off. "You think I don't want to find my grandson? That I don't care?"

I made my way around the table and stopped for a moment in the doorway. She loved Kale in her own way, but Ginger was single-mindedly focused on ripping down Denazen. She believed that since her family was responsible for its creation, it was her job to see it destroyed. I had no delusions that all of us weren't considered possible collateral damage.

"I know you care, Ginger—but you don't care nearly as much as I do."

10

Ginger was kind enough to let me shower and shove a breakfast bar down my throat before practically shoving me into the elevator and out the front door. I'd been tired when Alex and I got back, but now, knowing my shot to fix things with Kale might be right around the corner, I had a renewed sense of energy.

This time I was on my way, in Ginger's decrepit car, to see Thom Morris. His birthday was three weeks from yesterday, so I didn't have much hope. Even if I found him alive, would what was left even be salvageable? Or would I find someone like Fin? Spouting gibberish and almost past human.

Before I left, I snagged Alex's cell from the kitchen counter. He'd probably kill me for it later, but I didn't want to be without a phone and I'd given mine to Aubrey last night.

I got to Thom's house at eleven.

Semi-local, Ginger had said. Well, her idea of semi-local turned out to be nearly a four-hour drive. I was betting the only reason they let me do it on virtually no sleep was the fact that she already knew I'd make it there in one piece.

I loved a road trip as much as the next person, but sitting still for that long with so many other things on my mind was agony. Add to that a broken radio, and I was ready to beat my head against the wheel ten minutes into the trip.

Thom's mother, a worn, frail-looking woman, informed me her son had been missing for the last month. The police were still looking but they were convinced he'd run away. He could have, but I was betting he had a little help. Judging from Mrs. Morris's swollen eyes and red-rimmed nose, I figured if there was an agent in the house, it was her husband. The woman was clearly distraught. Definitely not the behavior of someone responsible for offing her teenage son. I gave her Alex's cell number and asked her to call should she hear from him, then trekked back to the car, which I'd parked two houses down.

I sat in the car for an hour, hoping that Kale would show. But each vehicle zoomed past, never slowing. He knew we were searching for the Supremacy kids, and Thom was one of the last locals, so it made sense that I'd be here.

I started the engine, fingers numb, and cranked the heat to full blast. It had started to snow, and as I watched the fluffy flakes fall to my window, an ache bloomed deep in my chest. We'd made so many plans, Kale and I. His first Christmas and snowfall. I'd told him all about sledding and we'd planned to hit Memorial Park at the first sign of powder. They had the best sledding hill in the county.

As I sat there rubbing my icy hands in front of the vent, Mom's question bounced around inside my head. *What if you can't?* Aubrey said they had done a lot of damage. If that meant Kale could never get his memories back, I'd have to start over.

Fine. Then that's what I'd do. Jade's appearance in September had proven Kale and I were solid as a boulder. She'd presented him with the chance to touch anyone he wanted—including her—and he'd still chosen me. His words echoed through my head.

If I had the ability to touch anyone else in this world, I still don't believe I'd want it to be anyone but you.

I closed my eyes and let out a breath. I would never— *could never*—give up on him. We'd missed out on a lot, but I was determined to give him his first New Year's kiss.

A few minutes later, the door opened and a burst of cold wind followed someone inside.

"A little far from home, aren't you?" Kale asked as the door clicked shut.

A jolt of excitement mixed with unavoidable fear filled me. I opened my eyes but kept them front and center. If I avoided looking at him it made this easier. "Could say the same thing to you."

"Drive."

I didn't hesitate or ask questions. Something like this was what I'd hoped for, right? Another chance to get him alone. If he was here, then Aubrey had done his part. Shifting into drive, I pulled away from the curb and tapped the gas. The car skipped a little on the ice, tires spinning for a second before lurching forward.

"Take a right at the end of this street, then go three blocks and pull into the parking lot."

I did as instructed, focusing all my energy on keeping both eyes on the road. The lot was empty, so I pulled in and put the car into the spot at the very end, up against a chain-link fence. "Planning on bringing me in or offing me?"

Something slammed against the dashboard, sending me

about a foot into the air. "Explain this."

Slowly, I turned, still trying to avoid looking directly at him, and saw my cell on the dash between us. With a satisfied smile, I said, "I seem to recall going over this with you several months ago, but that's a cell phone. You use it to call other people."

"Pick it up," he growled.

I did as I was told and reached for the phone. After I'd given it to Aubrey last night, I told him to make sure Kale saw it—particularly the pictures I kept stored. It was on, the screen opened to my picture folder. More specifically, to a picture of him and me.

Aubrey had come through for me again.

"Explain this," he repeated. "Who is that in the picture with you?"

A sarcastic retort did its damnedest to push past my lips, but I swallowed it and sighed. "There's nothing to explain, Kale. It's you. And me. Our friend Dax took these pictures right before school started. Well, Ginger's twisted idea of school."

In the picture, Kale and I were huddled together, huge grins on our faces. We were sitting in the common room at the Sanctuary hotel—before it burned down. I remembered the whole thing like it was only yesterday. We'd talked for hours that day about Thanksgiving and Christmas and made plans to decorate our rooms with as many colored lights as we could possibly fit. Of course, that had never happened. Thanksgiving came and went. So had Christmas. For the first time in my life, I didn't touch a string of lights or kiss someone beneath the mistletoe.

Kale ripped the phone from my hand as it started to ring. Glaring at the thing, he said, "This is a trick. You wanted me to see this."

I tried to take it back—it was probably Mom or Ginger looking for an update on Thom—but he held it out of reach. "What I *want* is for you to wake the hell up." I yanked off my seat belt and twisted to face him. "They messed up your head. Another Six did this to you. There was no *accident*. There's no *Roz*. And Denazen is not trying to *help* you!"

He returned my glare with a steely one of his own. "And why would I believe you?"

I wanted to reach across the car and shake him. All the pain and anger I'd bottled up since seeing him walk away with Dad and Kiernan churned in the pit of my stomach, ready to explode. "Look at me and tell me there's nothing. That you *feel* nothing."

He stared at me for a long time. Something flickered in his eyes, but it was fleeting. There and gone in half a beat of my heart. "There's... I only feel anger."

"Good. That's a start." Mainly because it wasn't just anger in his eyes. There was also confusion—and more importantly, curiosity. That's what I'd aimed for.

He leaned against the passenger's side door, brows askew. "It's directed at you. You find this *good*?"

"You *should* be angry at me, Kale," I said. The words came out before I could even think about them. I'd never given it much thought, but they were true. "I might not have stabbed you, or pushed you from a bridge, or *whatever* it was they said I did, but this *is* my fault."

He didn't say anything so I continued. "I was sick. Dying. My dad—*Marshal Cross*—had the only way to save my life. He said he would only give me the cure if one of us agreed to go with him. You went."

The memory of that day had played in my mind ten thousand times on repeat. I couldn't help feeling like I'd missed something. Like I could have done something more and taken control of the situation.

Like I could have prevented it.

"I should have tried harder to stop you. I should have *made* him take me instead."

"You're lying," he said simply.

"I'm not."

He grabbed my arm, stubby nails digging into the skin. A few moments later, a wash of cold hit me, starting in my arm where Kale's fingers rested, then spread through my entire body. I refused to look. Keeping my eyes on him, I locked my jaw and waited for the pain.

It didn't come. I wasn't the only one surprised by this. Kale's eyes widened, alternating between my face and arm. "What—"

It went against every one of those little voices in my head, but I forced myself to look down—and wished to hell I hadn't. The skin beneath Kale's fingers was blackened, darkest at the center, getting lighter as it fanned down my arm. Just under the surface, a mass of black twitched and churned, making it look like a swarm of *something* moshed to a death-metal symphony beneath my skin.

"You should be screaming," he said matter-of-factly, and a small part of me wanted to smile. It was the kind of simple statement that my Kale would have made. Blunt and to the point.

"It's part of the Supremacy drug's side effects. It just means I'm going to end up like the others." It was the first time I'd admitted it out loud. There was something freeing about it. "Crazy, then dead."

"Why haven't you tried to run? You wouldn't get far, of course. The only reason you got away from me last night, and in the garage, was because I let you. Your actions are confusing. You may not be able to feel it, but you must know I can kill you. Dead is dead." He removed his arm, the expression on his face one of genuine interest.

I watched, relieved when the black mark faded. "I'm hoping you don't kill me."

"But why would you risk it? Do you have a death wish?" He shook his head. "There are easier ways to die."

"No death wish," I said. "I guess the truth is I really don't believe that you'll kill me."

"I've been told to." He unlocked the phone and stared at the picture of us on the screen. With his index finger, he traced the outline of my head, frowning. "At first they wanted me to bring you in. Marshal was convinced you would tell them what they wanted to know about the Underground. They changed their mind, though. I was given the order this morning that you needed to be terminated immediately."

"Why do you think that is, Kale?"

He looked up from the phone, eyes burrowing straight through me. "Stop saying my name."

"Why?"

"Because, I… *Just stop it!*"

I held both hands up in surrender. "Okay."

He took a deep breath, then settled back in the seat and glanced at the cell. "They think you're going to jeopardize what they're doing."

"Why are you telling me this?"

The question seemed to confuse him, which in turn made him angry. "I'm not sure."

I gripped the steering wheel tightly. The leather was peeling at the top and I picked at it with my thumbnail. "So by jeopardizing what they're doing, you mean killing innocent kids?"

"These people are anything but innocent. Some are dangerous and lack self-control. The others will soon be the same way. They're a menace and need to be stopped."

"Not long ago, you lacked control," I fired back. "They considered you a menace."

He looked at me like I'd just recited the alphabet in Elvish. "I've always had control over my gift."

Gift? If he could only see the wrongness of what he'd just said. Kale never considered his ability anything other than a curse. Something that kept him separated from the rest of the world. "The ones who have become dangerous are only that way because they're sick. They don't need to be killed. They need to be cured."

"Marshal said there was only enough to cure Roz."

More than anything, I wanted to shake him and scream that there wasn't a Roz. She was a figment. A thing made up to blot me out. But there was no point. Not yet, at least. Nothing I said would get through the wall they'd created. "There isn't much, but we're sure there's more."

He was silent for a moment. "And what if there is? What will you do with it?"

"Cure them," I snapped. "What else?"

"You said there wasn't much left. How will you choose who lives and who dies? There are several left. Surely there isn't enough for everyone."

I didn't know if Mom and Dax would have any luck with their names, but we hadn't found many alive. Still, there were bound to be some. Ginger confirmed at least that much. If we didn't find this Penny person but managed to get our hands on Dad's reserves, there *wouldn't* be enough for us all.

"*I* won't have to choose. You were told to terminate me

immediately, remember? Speaking of which, why haven't you?"

His lip twitched with the smallest hint of a smile. There and gone. Boom. "I thought you said you *didn't* have a death wish."

"I don't, but you said you had orders. You've made it clear you don't trust me—or believe what I've told you. So why not just do it?"

He looked back to the phone in his hand. The picture of us on the screen was still open. Pocketing it, he said, "I need to find out what this is first. I need to be sure. Consider your sentence extended until I am."

It wasn't much, but it was something.

I could work with *something*.

11

"So, is this like a hijacking?" We had been driving for more than an hour now, and Kale still hadn't told me exactly what we were doing—or where we were headed. The only thing he'd said was to pull out and take Interstate 90. This was exactly what I'd hoped for. The longer I kept him busy with me, the longer he'd be away from Denazen—and the brain-busting Six Aubrey mentioned. Hopefully time away would clear some of the cobwebs from his noggin. "Because if you're holding me hostage, shouldn't there be, I dunno, demands?"

He sighed, and from the corner of my eye, I saw him pinch the bridge of his nose just like Mom did when she was annoyed at me. "You talk a lot."

"You like the sound of my voice. You told me so—on several occasions."

He snorted. "Now I know you're lying."

I let several minutes pass before I prodded again. "So we're going…where?"

"We're going to get to the bottom of this. The truth."

"And we're going to find the truth by driving aimlessly? Because that's a new kind of approach, and I'm not sure it'll get us very far. Besides, the car's almost out of gas and I'm starving."

"Just drive. Get off at exit twelve."

I followed his directions, and ten minutes later I pulled the car off the interstate by way of exit twelve. In his jacket pocket, my cell had gone off three separate times. If I didn't get him to let me answer it soon, Mom might have a coronary.

Once we were off the highway, it was farmland as far as the eye could see, which reminded me of the cabin. Peaceful. None of the chaos and bright lights of the city. Until recently, I'd been a noise and chaos kind of girl. But after spending some time at the cabin, I was kind of growing to love the peace and quiet. "Okay. Now what?"

He scanned the area, and then pointed to the side of the road. There was a long white fence—and nothing else. "Pull over and get out."

"The road to revelation is a picket fence? Who'da thunk it…" I opened the door and swung out a leg. A burst of icy air kicked in, sending tremors up and down my spine. "Where are we?"

I closed the door. It creaked in protest, and I was sure if I got in and out too many more times it would simply fall off. I leaned against the fence and peered out into the field. Six fat brown cows grazed in the distance. "Cow tipping doesn't really seem like a productive use of our time right now."

He turned to me, eyebrows high. "*Cow* tipping?"

"Really?" I tapped the side of my head, frowning. "You'd think if they were going to swirl things up in there, they would have added some reality along with the bullshit."

Kale rolled his eyes and stepped to the fence. "More talking. Don't you ever get tired?" Hefting himself up, he threw a leg over and propelled his body to the other side in true ninja fashion. At least that hadn't changed. "Follow me."

Although the barking-orders thing was getting old pretty damn fast.

We trekked through an open field—around the cows and without tipping any—until we came to the edge of a steep cliff. A narrow wooden bridge that hung over a raging river about twenty feet below connected our side to the other.

"This is it," he said, sounding surprised. He spun slowly in a circle, taking in every inch of the area. "This is where it happened."

A sign posted on a short wooden stake said, DO NOT CROSS. Kale either hadn't seen it or didn't care, because he stomped out onto the middle of the bridge and leaned over the edge. I followed him, trying hard to ignore the not-so-subtle creaking the wood made with each step and the extra breeze as the planks swung from side to side. Stopping beside him, I watched tiny bits of pebble and dirt loosen, break away, and plunge into the water below. Wonderful. One wrong move and that would be us plunging to our deaths. "Where what happened?"

"This is where you pushed me over the edge." He spoke the words, but they didn't sound right. It was almost as if he were asking a question, not making a statement. At his sides, his fingers started to tap again. One. Two. Three. I'd noticed it at Ashley's.

"I've never been here before. You have to believe me." I backed away from the edge and the boards underfoot creaked loudly.

He whirled and pinned me with a look that, while deadly, was full of sadness. "Believe you? I *don't* believe you. I don't

believe them. I don't believe her." He brought both hands up
to tug at his roots, backing away from the edge. "I don't believe
me."

This entire time, I'd kept going over how hard this was
for me. How much *I* missed him. How much *I* wanted him
back. Sure, I'd thought about the long-term impact this whole
situation might have on him, but I'd never stopped to think
what it might be like for him now—especially with me trying
to shake things up. "We can figure this out, Kale. I promise."

He froze, hands falling slack at his sides. A second later, he
was on me. "You did this to me."

"Me? I swear I've never been—"

Bending me back against the rickety wooden railing, he
pinned me tight with his body, face hovering inches above
mine. More cracking. I didn't know how much more this bridge
could take before we both plunged into the river. "That drug
gave you an ability they don't know about—didn't it? You did
something when you kissed me last night. Confused me!"

"No," I promised, unable to hold it together any longer.
The tears fell and for the first time since we'd met, I was truly
afraid of him. Aubrey was right. There were parts Kale kept on
a short leash in order to conquer the darkest parts of himself.
All the anger over his past and the dark emotions that went
with it. Denazen shook it all loose. "Please, Kale. Stop and
listen—"

"Stop!" he screamed. "Stop talking. Stop trying to confuse
me." His weight pressed harder, and I was sure we'd both end
up going over the edge. The old railing whined in protest, and it
moved behind me. Flexing and ready to give.

"Calm down," I said. "I have an idea. A way to fix the mess
in your head."

He eased off a little and the creaking stopped, allowing

my heartbeat to return to some small level of normalcy. "I'm listening."

"One of the Supremacy kids. Ben Simmons. I think he can help you."

He pushed back again, eyes darkening. "You're lying. There is no Ben Simmons on the list."

I pushed against him, trying with no luck to slide out from under his weight. "Yes, there is—but it's not surprising that you don't know about him."

"What do you mean?"

"I'm willing to bet all my fingers and toes that Dad isn't planning to let you within a million miles of the guy. His ability has something to do with messing with memories."

"So now you're telling me it was a Supremacy subject that did"—he tapped the side of his head—"this to me?"

"No, but it was definitely another Six—a Denazen Six—with the ability to mess around up there."

"And you want me to believe there are *two* Sixes out there who can do the same thing—a thing that conveniently suits my situation?"

"I've learned that when it comes to Sixes, there are a lotta different shades of the same color out there. The Six who did this to you has a similar ability to Ben Simmons, but not the exact same, I'd guess. I'm betting having been given the Supremacy drug makes Ben Simmons way more powerful—at least until he dies."

"You're lying," he repeated, but with slightly less conviction. "There's no Simmons."

"But what if I'm not?" I could see the crack in his armor. It was small, but if I could slip in a sheet of doubt, I might have a chance. He wanted so badly to make me pay for what they'd told him I did, but more than that, he wanted his life back. If I could keep him away from them a little longer, I might be able to give it to him. "If he can mess with the inside of a person's head, with the help of the Supremacy drug, maybe he can fix what someone else messed up."

Kale didn't answer.

"You said you wanted your life back, right?" The desire for truth reflected so plainly in his eyes. This could work. I could find Ben Simmons before Denazen, and at the same time, keep Kale away from the Resident sludging things up inside his head. If that didn't work, maybe Simmons really could use his ability to help things along. "Well, I'm offering you a way to get it. Ben Simmons *is* on the list of Supremacy subjects—and that means your boss and his daughter have been keeping things from you. You may not remember much about your life before this all happened, but you must know that secrets never end in happy."

He backed away another step but still didn't look convinced.

That's when I remembered the picture I'd taken of the sheet with Ben Simmons's name and picture. I'd e-mailed it to myself! "I can prove it!"

"Fine. Prove it."

I held out my hand. "I'll need my phone."

He hesitated, then pulled it from his jacket pocket. I reached for it, but when my fingers closed around it, his didn't let go. Eyes on mine, he said, "Don't try anything."

"Wouldn't dream of it." I forced a smile and unlocked the cell. Thankfully, even though we seemed to be in the middle of nowhere, I had enough of a signal to pull up Gmail. "Here. See this? I took a picture of this yesterday. Ben Simmons's file."

He squinted, holding the cell close, then turned it sideways in examination. "This could be fake."

"It could," I agreed. "But it isn't."

Kale stared at the screen, and when he handed the cell back to me, I was sure he didn't buy it. But instead of coming at me again, he said, "Where is he?"

I breathed an internal sigh of relief. "Connecticut. It's not *too* far from here." When Kale didn't say anything, I got nervous and pushed it. "What's the worst that could happen? I'm lying—which I'm not—and you can exact your devious revenge later, rather than now. You've got nothing to lose. Not like I can take you or anything."

He snorted, lips curling into a familiar smile. "Of course you can't."

I held my breath. This was a goose-crapping-golden-eggs kind of opportunity.

He nodded. "Fine. Let's go."

I threw my hands up as he reached for my arm. "Whoa, boy. We can't just go storming the castle. We need to agree on a few things first."

An amused expression slipped across his lips. "Oh? And what *things* would that be?"

"Well, for starters, like I said earlier, the car is almost out of gas. I have no money. Do you?"

"I have plenty of money," he said with a sneer. "But even if I didn't, you could simply make some. Roz told me about your ability. All we need is paper." He gestured for me to walk ahead. Eager to get off the bridge, I complied. He stayed right on my heels, never letting me get more than a foot ahead.

"That's true, but it's not the only problem," I said once we'd reached blissfully solid ground again. "I'm supposed to be back by now—with that rust bucket on wheels. You heard the phone. They've already tried calling to see where I am. If I don't answer or show up soon, they'll come looking for me.

You need to let me call home."

He nodded to the cell. "Fine. Then call them—but be careful what you say."

"Careful? What do you think I'm going to say? That you and I are taking a nice little romantic trip?"

"Don't give away our location."

"No plans to." I stretched to get the kink out of my lower back. The railing had done a number on it. Our location was the last thing I'd give away. Mom and Ginger would never agree with my plan. In fact, there was a good chance they'd chain me to the furniture in my room for the next fifteen years if they found out. "I'll call them and then we'll go find Ben Simmons—but we have to get some food first or I ain't going anywhere."

"Agreed. But only because I'm hungry. And I'm going to check this guy out because I'm curious. You're going because I'm not giving you a choice. I'm in control. Remember that."

12

We stopped at a gas station to fill up and grab munchies. I suggested Kale go in and pay while I finished with the gas to save some time, but he only glared at me and waited, arms crossed, as Ginger's ancient gas-guzzler sucked in fuel.

Some people were just so damn untrusting.

When he was done paying, he stood by while I called Mom's cell—mainly because I knew she wouldn't actually answer—and left a message. I told her I was safe and following a lead. It would piss them off that I was so vague, but it would buy me time and hopefully get Ginger to stop calling. Each time the phone rang Kale grew more and more agitated. In his condition, there was no telling what might push him over the edge, and I had no desire to find out.

We couldn't have been on the road more than forty minutes when an unfamiliar tone rang out. From the corner of my eye, I watched Kale fish in his jacket pocket and pull out a cell. Somewhere on earth, pigs were getting ready to fly. "You have a phone? Seriously?"

He ignored me and held it up to the ear farthest from me. "Yeah?"

I couldn't make out what was said on the other end but I could tell it was a guy, and I did catch Dad's name once or twice.

"Aubrey and I split to follow two different leads. He went to Bakersfield and I went to check on Thom Morris. Morris supposedly left home last month. I spoke to the mother. She says he went to stay with friends. I'm going to check it out before heading back."

A lie. Thom Morris was missing. That's what his mother had told me. She never mentioned anything about him staying with friends. If Kale was lying to Denazen there was a chance Thom was still alive.

The person on the other end said something and Kale's lips twisted into an angry scowl. "Tell her I'll be back later. I'm not a dog. I do not need a leash." He mashed the end button and stuffed the phone back in his pocket with a growl.

"Aww. Trouble in paradise? Lemme guess. Your skank is a little too clingy?"

"Watch your mouth," he said in a low, dangerous voice. "And mind your own business."

"Whatever." I shrugged. "But you may have to drive soon. I can't keep my eyes open over here."

"I don't like to drive."

"Oh, that's right. You don't know how."

"I know *how*. I just don't like to do it."

I took the on ramp and brought us back to the interstate. Connecticut was about ninety miles away according to the sign we'd passed. Since seeing Kale at the Nix party a few nights ago, I'd gotten little to no sleep. Add to that last night's midnight hike and the four-hour drive this morning, and I was running on fumes. It was starting to catch up to me. "When was the last time you drove a car, Kale? Do you even remember?"

He was quiet for a moment, then slammed his hand down on the dash beside the wheel. "When I lost my memories, I forgot. Roz had to teach me again. I'm not very good at it."

"We're probably a couple hours away. If you're not *willing* to drive, then after we find Simmons I'm bunking somewhere for the night. No way am I driving all the way back to Parkview like this."

The rest of the trip went by in silence. I drove under the speed limit, making the drive last as long as possible without arousing suspicion. I'd tried to get him talking a few times. That had been interesting. Even though it hadn't worked, and despite the fact that he wasn't himself and thought I was the enemy, it felt good to be near him again.

Somewhere out there was a shrink salivating to make me a field study.

Seventeen Spencer Drive was a rundown apartment complex on the edge of Burns, Connecticut. The inside reminded me of Alex's old building. All it was missing was Ed, the drunk who sat in the corner of the entryway screaming obscenities at people as they entered, occasionally waving body parts not fit for public viewing.

We crossed the threshold and, without thinking, I passed the elevator and headed for the stairs. It'd become habit because Kale refused to step anywhere near one. But that was the old Kale. This one didn't have the same hang-ups.

"What are you doing? Isn't the apartment on the eighth floor?" he asked. When I turned, Kale was in front of the graffiti-covered double doors, mashing the up button.

The doors gave a sickly *ding* and I opened my mouth to

argue, but shook off the urge, silently following him inside the thing he'd once referred to as a steel trap of death. You'd think I'd be happy. Taking the stairs everywhere was hell on my heels, but I liked Kale the way he was. Blister-inducing quirks and all.

We came to apartment number eighty, and before I could say a word, Kale pounded on the door like a mad man. There was a commotion on the other side and a rush of voices before the door opened and a puff of thick, pungent smoke preceded a mop of messy curls and stormy gray eyes.

The guy coughed and waved a hand back and forth in front of his face in a vain attempt to disperse the cloud. "Yeah?"

I took a step back and pulled a very surprised Kale with me. A contact high was the last thing an unstable ex-assassin needed right now. "Ben Simmons?"

The guy snorted, covering his mouth as a fit of giggles escaped. Oh, yeah. This would be interesting. "Ha, he wishes," he said. "I'm Jerry Watson. His roommate."

Kale mimicked Jerry, waving a hand back and forth to clear the air. "What is that smell?"

Jerry winked. "That's the smell of pure nirvana, man. Want a hit?"

Kale placed a hand on either side of the doorframe and leaned closer. "If you hit me, I'll kill you."

Jerry's eyes went wide and he stumbled back a few inches. I batted Kale's arm aside. He growled in annoyance but I ignored him, flashing Jerry my sweetest smile in an attempt to get the situation under control. "Is Ben home?"

"Nope." He focused on me and thrust his pelvis back and forth, grinning from ear to ear like an idiot. "Dude went to France for the week to see some chick he was cyber-banging."

"Very classy." I cringed at his visual. We couldn't get to

Ben, but neither could Denazen. That was a start. "So when's he back?"

With a wicked grin, Jerry said, "Couple days. You can come in and wait if you want. I'm sure we could find something to pass the time, baby."

Kale reacted before I could blink. One second Jerry was shooting me looks that would have made Curd—Parkview's most well-known player—proud, the next he was rammed against the doorframe, face mashed and distorted as Kale's hovered inches away.

"She's passing her time with me. Is that clear?"

"Crystal, d-dude. C-R-Y-S-T-A-L," he stammered.

Kale eased off, wrinkling his nose and rubbing both hands down the sides of his jeans. "Now *exactly* what time will he return?"

Jerry peeled himself from the doorframe and stepped back across the threshold, putting a safe distance between Kale and him. "Two days from today. I'm supposed to pick him up at the airport at eight p.m."

Without another word to Jerry—or me—Kale turned on his heel and strode back down the hall toward the elevators. I started to follow, but Jerry stopped me.

"Is Ben into something? You're the third ones to come looking for him in the last few days."

"Third?" Denazen must have beaten us to him, but who was the other group?

He shrugged, and I couldn't help noticing how he lengthened the already wide distance between us, occasionally sneaking glances in Kale's direction. "No idea who they were. The first guy was old. Like, in his forties or something."

"He didn't give a name?"

Jerry shook his head. "Nope. Just showed up looking

for Ben." His eyes widened and he stomped his foot twice. Reaching into his back pocket, he pulled out a small slip of paper. "Oh! But he did give me this. Said to have Ben call him and leave contact information. That this was urgent."

I took the paper. It was a cell phone number. "This is better than nothing. You said there were two groups?"

"The second pair was younger. Twins with a kind of goth look and way freaky."

Aubrey and Able.

"Did you tell them what you told me?"

"The old guy never gave me a chance, but I did tell the goth guys." He inclined his head down the hall in Kale's direction. "One of them was like him. Seriously strung out. I just wanted them gone."

"Thanks." I couldn't really blame him. My bet was on Able, and that guy could be scary. Flashing him a genuine smile, I added, "We'll pick Ben up from the airport."

With a half smile, he closed the door and I pulled out my cell. The older guy could have been something completely unrelated. Maybe Ben had a bookie. Or possibly a friend or relative his roommate didn't know about. Just because someone showed up looking for him the same day the toxic twins did didn't mean it *had* to be connected to Denazen. Right?

Dialing the number on the paper, I glanced over at Kale who stood, annoyed, at the other end of the hall. With each ring, I told myself some innocuous voice would answer and put my mind at ease. But the phone rang five times before going to automated voice mail. No name and no voice, which equaled useless—not to mention suspicious. I could keep trying in hopes someone would eventually pick up, but something told me whoever this was wanted to remain anonymous.

Disappointed, I hung up.

"Kiernan," Kale barked, rapping the elevator doors. "Let's go."

And that was about the time I pretty much snapped. I loved Kale more than anything on this earth, but this guy I was road-tripping with wasn't *my* Kale. He was an imposter with a bad attitude, no manners, and a slightly extended vocabulary. My guy was in there, I'd seen hints and sparks, but he was buried deep. I was determined to dig him out, but in the meantime I'd be damned if I let anyone—including Kale—talk to me like that.

I stalked down the hall, stopped a few inches from him, and poked him hard in the chest. "Let's get two things straight, *Kale*. I'm not a dog. I don't obey commands like sit, stay, or *let's go*."

His gaze fell to my finger, then lifted to my eyes, staying there. There was the smallest hint of amusement, but more than that, challenge. With a quirk of his lips, he said, "Is that right?"

"And the other thing? If you call me *Kiernan* one more time I'm going to kick your ass. My name is *Dez*." I grabbed his cheeks and squeezed until it sort of looked like he was making a fish face. In the back of my mind, a small voice screamed that I shouldn't irritate the unstable assassin, but I didn't care. I'd reached my limit. There was only so far I could go before losing my shit. "Say it with me now—D-E-Z. Maybe by calling me by the right name, you'll start remembering who the hell I am."

He stepped away, eyes still on mine, and in a deceptively calm voice asked, "Is the loss of fear one of the Supremacy side effects?"

"Not that I know of."

"Hmm," he said, and turned to push the down button again. "Are you certain?"

Then I understood what he was getting at. Imagine that. The new Kale came with a twisted sense of humor. "You're mistaking fear for intolerance. I don't suffer assholes."

The doors opened with a *ping* and Kale stepped inside. As I followed him in, he turned to me, lip twitching, and said, "Neither do I. We have something in common."

13

I tapped the hood of the car and waited. Kale had the keys. We were just standing there and I was freezing. If we stayed much longer, I was going to lose a limb or two to frostbite. "Well?"

"Well, what?" he said, finally unlocking the car and pulling open the passenger's side door.

"You're the one holding me hostage. What now? We come back in two days?"

"Obviously. I am surprised Simmons exists. I'm interested to see what else might be true."

I rolled my eyes and slid into the car as he did the same on the other side. "We have two days to kill."

"We're killing them together. I'm not letting you out of my sight until I have the truth."

No arguments from me. If there was a chance his memories would return on their own, this would do the trick. Two days had to be enough time if they were treating him to a mind mushtini each and every day. All I had to do was bide my time.

"Then we should get a room. It's after five and I'm ready to keel—but don't get any ideas."

"Ideas?"

"Us. Alone in a hotel room. Time to kill… You know."

He looked me up and down and snorted. "Don't flatter yourself. I have a girlfriend."

I'd been joking—okay, *half* joking. "Yeah, I know. *Me!*"

He watched me for a moment with an odd frown, then fastened his seat belt and leaned back in the seat. "I'm actually starting to believe you're not lying."

A surge of hope welled in my chest. "Really?"

"Yes. I'm starting to think you really believe your own story."

"You're really redefining the whole love/hate relationship thing, here." I turned the key. The engine sputtered several times but finally turned over, and I said a silent prayer of thanks. Being stranded in the ghetto with crazy-Kale was not my idea of a good time. "And I ask again. Where to?"

"I saw a motel when we got off the interstate. We'll stay there for the night."

"And in the morning? Simmons doesn't get back to town for two days."

"I'm sure we'll think of something."

There was a time not long ago when a statement like that from Kale would fill me with excitement and a rush of tingly possibilities. Right now? Not so much.

We drove back to town in silence, but I could see Kale watching me from the corner of my eye. It drove me crazy, but he didn't say anything, so I didn't, either. Let him stew for a bit. Alex was right about one thing. I couldn't force him to remember. All I could do was be there, present the memories, and let the universe do the rest. Hopefully it wouldn't take long. Patience wasn't a virtue I rocked.

We ended up checking into a cheesy nookie motel called Frank's Fantasy Facility, the only game in town.

"Well, this is…" I kicked the edge of the bed. It was one of those extra-large round ones with a full ceiling mirror above it and a collection of obnoxiously bright heart-shaped pillows scattered on top. "…creepy."

"I don't understand the reasoning for the mirrors. It seems dangerous."

"Dangerous how? We don't get many earthquakes in this part of the country so they're not likely to fall…"

"There's no privacy. Anyone in the room can see each move you make if one were to simply look up. It's a flawed design."

I started to tell him that was the point, but the ring of my cell cut me off. Pulling out the phone, I cringed. I'd known it was coming, but seeing Mom's number flash across the screen sent chills down my spine. I couldn't put it off any longer.

Kale leaned closer to see the screen. "Who's Sue?"

I rolled my eyes and stepped away as he made a swipe for it. "When this is all over you're going to realize how stupid you just sounded."

Another swipe. This time he got me. Hand locking around my wrist tight enough to kill the circulation, he asked, "What are you going to say?"

"Nothing unless you let go of me before she hangs up."

He hesitated, then begrudgingly let his fingers go slack and took a step back. "Don't tell anyone where we are."

"Believe me," I mumbled, lifting my head toward the ceiling, then letting it fall to the gaudy pillows and obnoxious pink walls. If anyone ever found out about this, I'd never live it down. "I wouldn't risk my carefully crafted reputation."

He nodded, satisfied. "And put it on speaker."

The second I hit the call button, I had to pull the phone away from my ear.

"What the *hell* do you think you're doing? Get back here. *Now.*" Mom kept going like the Energizer Bunny on speed and I patiently waited for the screaming to stop before holding the phone closer and taking a deep breath.

"Mom," I said as calmly as I could manage. "Listen to me very carefully, okay? And don't freak."

"Dez, do *not* start a conversation like that. It doesn't instill me with any amount of confidence—especially when it comes from you."

"Well, then fair warning. You're not going to like what I have to say—but you need to listen."

I couldn't see her, obviously, but I knew exactly what she was doing. She'd sunk into the nearest chair, eyes squeezed closed with her thumb and pointer pinched tightly across the bridge of her nose. The Sixes at the cabin had dubbed it her *What did Dez do now?* expression. Before everything in my world turned upside down, I would have been proud to have an expression named after me. Hell, if Dad had done it, I would have considered life a victory.

"First, you should know that I have you on speaker." Not that there was anything I expected her to say to cause trouble—I had nothing to hide, since what I'd told Kale was the absolute truth—but better safe than sorry. Head trouble off at the pass. That was my new motto in life. Well, one of them.

"Second, I went to find Thom Morris like Ginger asked. He's been missing for a while. His mother has no clue where he went—but I think he's still out there." I glared at Kale, who sat on the bed staring at me. "I'm making a better than average bet that Denazen hasn't gotten to him yet."

"And why would you say that?"

"Because Denazen showed up looking for him, too."

I could practically *hear* the change in her demeanor. There was a thickness to the air that would require a chainsaw to hack through. "Dez, come home right now."

And *this* is where the fun part of the conversation started. "I can't. I'm—I'm here with Kale."

There was a few moments of silence, and I couldn't tell if it was good silence or bad. With Mom, it was usually impossible to tell. I probably would have preferred the screaming. At least I'd know where I stood. "Are you hurt?"

"I'm okay. I promise. There's a name on the list, Ben Simmons—"

"How—"

"Did you really think I wasn't gonna check out the rest of the names? You made it clear Ginger didn't want me to see the list. What did you *expect* me to do? Telling me *not* to do something is pretty much the same thing as waving it back and forth in front of my face like a bright red, coffee-scented flag…"

"Point made," she said angrily. "And lesson learned. Obviously you know what Ben does…"

A smidge of anger, ugly and sharp, bobbed to the surface. I still hadn't fully forgiven her for taking Ginger's side at the cabin, but knowing Ben was on the list and out there—possibly able to help Kale—and ignoring it? Totally different level of wrong. "And so do you. How could you hide something like that from me? If there was a chance this guy could help—"

"Penny Mills needs to be your priority. If you're dead—or crazy—what will it matter if Ben Simmons can help Kale's memory? Do you think he'd want that?"

"Right now it's a nonissue. Priorities have changed

whether we like it or not."

"Changed? What's that supposed to mean?"

"It means," Kale said, leaning closer to my cell, "that I want the truth. If Ben Simmons can give that to me, I intend to have a talk with him."

Mom was quiet for a minute. When she spoke again, her voice had that tone. The dangerous one that hinted she was about to lose her temper. I'd seen it happen. It wasn't pretty. "And what does that have to do with my daughter?"

"Because if Simmons confirms what your daughter claims, then she is telling the truth and I've been lied to. If he tells me there's nothing wrong, then your daughter is lying. And if she's lying, that means my friends are telling the truth. And that means she and I have unfinished business."

"And what makes you think we won't intercept you?" Mom asked with a hint of amusement. I could almost see the smile creep across her face. "We know where Simmons is, too. We could simply take her back."

"I don't advise that," Kale growled. "Because if anyone shows up, there won't be enough left of Kiernan, or *Dez*, or whoever she is, to fill a paper cup."

Mom took a deep breath. I could hear it as clearly as if I'd been standing beside her. "I love you like you are my own, Kale, but if you hurt her, I'll kill you myself. Slowly." Her voice was like ice, sending a chill through the room cold enough to freeze fire.

Kale stepped forward and picked up the cell. "Then let's hope she's telling the truth." Eyes on me, he jammed the end button and tossed it on the bed. "She called you Dez."

I stared at the phone, thankful it stopped bouncing right before tumbling over the edge. If I told Mom I needed *another* phone, she'd have a llama. This was the third one in two months. I snatched it from the bed and set it safely on the nightstand. "Probably because it's my name. Oh, and this new personality? It leaves a lot to be desired. Alex is right. You're kind of a dick."

Kale didn't answer. Instead, he sank onto the mattress and pulled off his shoes. I could try to get away when he slept. I'd probably have a fifty-fifty chance—okay, more like ten-ninety—but I had no intention of trying. As much as it hurt to see the disgust in his eyes each time he looked at me, this would be my only opportunity to get through to him.

"So…sleeping?"

"What about it?" he said, kicking both feet up.

"You expect me to sleep in the same bed as you?"

"That's up to you."

"How do I know you won't roll over and dust me in your sleep?"

"I don't *roll*."

Hah. Kale, on a good night, would end up on the floor at least twice. Nightmares. Obviously it wasn't an issue anymore. Still, I was worried. I looked from him to the bed, frowning.

He reached across and flipped the light switch, and the room went dark. "As I said before, no need to flatter yourself. You're not my type."

I hesitated, then sat on the opposite edge of the bed. If I could get him talking, maybe I could shake something loose. A memory or a feeling. I wasn't picky. I'd take anything at this point. "And what would that be?"

"My type? I thought you said you knew all about my life. Why don't you tell me."

I twisted around and pulled my feet up, tucking them close. "Nothing I say to you right now is going to get through. You're convinced I'm the enemy."

After a few minutes, he let out a soft snicker. "Okay. Roz is strong. She's confident and loyal. She's there when I need her."

"Congratulations," I mumbled. "Sounds like you're dating a German shepherd."

I felt the bed shimmy, and in the dark I saw the outline of his figure rise. A moment later, his face moved into the moonlight beaming in through the heart-shaped window. "Roz and I fit. I can't explain it, and I don't expect someone like you to understand."

"*Someone like me.* Exactly what is that supposed to mean?"

"You're spiteful. I know you're her half sister. Roz told me how she tried reaching out to you and how you turned away. She offered you help and in return, you tried to hurt her by hurting your father and me. All because you felt slighted."

My heartbeat quickened. "What do you mean, *slighted*?"

A car drove by, its lights streaming into the window to reveal Kale's serious expression. "Roz tells me everything. She said you were bitter about having grown up in foster care. You were in a horrible situation until Marshal finally came to get you, while she lived a good life."

I lay on my back as close to my end of the bed as possible and rolled over to face him. "What else did she tell you about how her sister grew up?" I wasn't willing to say *I*. That would only make him think it was a confession—or worse, a slipup.

"Your foster father was a drunk with a heavy hand."

"I didn't know." What she'd done to me—to Kale— couldn't be overlooked, but I couldn't help feeling bad for her.

Little things started to make sense. Things she'd said when we first met. Comments made in passing during the months she spent at the hotel. Why hadn't she said anything? If she was angry or resentful, why not just yell and get things out in the open? We could have been there for each other. We could have been family. Instead she turned to Dad, and because of that choice, innocent people were dead.

When I yanked myself from thought, Kale was staring at me. "What?"

"I don't know," he said, sliding back to his pillow. He rolled onto his side, facing me, and propped himself on his elbow. "You look…almost sorry."

"It doesn't excuse what she did, but I am. No one deserves that."

Lips parting as if he wanted to say more, he bit down and rolled stiffly onto his back in silence.

Apparently the conversation was over.

I did the same, remembering the first time we were in a hotel together. How I'd gone to sleep thinking of our very first kiss. More than anything, I wanted to go back to that moment. To its perfect simplicity and the promise of things to come.

"Good night, Kale," I whispered.

14

I tried to pull the edge of the blanket up around my shoulders to chase away the chill but it wouldn't budge. That's when I remembered I was lying on top of it, not underneath. Without opening my eyes, I gave an internal groan. Kale. Hijacked. Nookie motel. Memory loss.

Ah, crap.

As sleep faded, I stretched my right leg and wiggled my toes. It was much colder in the room than it had been, and every part of me was freezing. My nose and fingertips were nearly numb. Either someone had moved the bed outside to the parking lot, the heat had gone off—

Or the window was open.

Something thumped from the other side of the room. I fought back an icy shiver as my heart kicked into hyper-speed and my eyes flew open. Kale was on the bed next to me, lying very close, eyes wide with a finger held over his lips. He'd heard it, too.

I nodded to show I understood and took a deep, controlling breath as he carefully rolled over and slipped off the bed. Reaching across, he flipped the light switch several times. Nothing happened. Power. The power could be out. That would explain the cold. No power, no heat. And that would have been an awesome theory—if the alarm clock on the nightstand hadn't glared bright red numbers back at me.

Kale took two steps, then turned and motioned for me to follow. I wasn't nearly as quiet as he'd been. The mattress creaked twice as I eased myself off, and my foot came down on a particularly creaky board. Typical.

When I finally got around the bed and to his side, he took hold of my arm and dragged me toward the bathroom. We'd almost made it when a soft, annoyingly familiar *pop* disturbed the eerie silence.

Kale turned to me. There was a spark of worry in his eyes. His gaze traveled over my face, then dipped lower, catching on my arm. I followed it down and all the air rushed from the room in a single, dizzying swirl.

I didn't know what scared me more. The fact that the dart had embedded itself in my forearm and I hadn't felt a thing, or the fact that the dart had embedded itself in my forearm and I was possibly moments away from keeling over, helpless.

His fingers gripped the dart and, with one smooth yank, pulled it free. We stood there, eye-to-eye, and then I was flying backward. In a blur, Kale's arm shot out, knocking me aside as something flew at us. Another dart.

He wasn't happy about it, either. A feral scream split his lips as the door exploded inward and several agents swarmed the room. Two went for Kale while the third rushed me.

I stumbled narrowly out of my attacker's path, falling backward onto the bed as he tripped over the tacky shag carpet. He recovered quickly and dove again, this time catching my ankle and yanking hard. I slipped from the bed, landing with a jolt on the floor, breath knocked from my lungs as his other arm made a swipe for anything he could grab.

He probably would have gotten me, too, if one of the other agents hadn't careened backward into him. They fell sideways, giving me enough time to scramble off the bed and wobble unsteadily in Kale's direction.

"Ignore her," the one circling Kale snapped. He nodded to my arm. "She's as good as down."

I started forward, determined to help Kale, as the other two regrouped and joined the fight. Kale struck out at the first, gripping a handful of his hair and pulling hard. "What are you doing?" he snapped. "Why are you attacking me!"

When the only response he got was a poorly aimed right hook, he pressed his palm flat against the man's skin. There was a rush of churning darkness and seconds later, the man was nothing more than dust.

The other two were smarter. They teamed up, coming for him from either side. He ducked, and for a minute I lost track of the fight. Everything started to water around the edges. The sounds of struggle were hollow and far off, and my vision snapped in and out of focus.

When things cleared, one of the agents lay still at Kale's feet, while the other was in a pile already blowing away in the icy breeze streaming through the open window.

"Denazen," Kale whispered, face pale. He had one of their guns in his hand and stared at the motionless agent on the floor. "These are agents. They attacked me."

"Welcome back to—" His face zoomed out of focus and the entire room faded away.

Reality. I'd been about to say reality.

• • •

When I came to, everything was stiff. My back had a wicked knot and my arms were pins and needles from fingertips to shoulder. Oddly enough, I was happy to feel the pain.

"I know you're awake," Kale said. "I can tell by the change in your breathing."

Of course he could. I opened my eyes and did my best to stretch. We were in Ginger's car again, parked behind a dark brick building. It wasn't the nookie motel. "How'd we get here?"

Sighing, he said, "I drove."

"You *drove?*" I repeated, then bit down on my tongue to keep from screaming when a charley horse attacked my thigh with a vengeance. Apparently Kiernan *had* taught him to drive. A part of me was jealous. It was something Kale and I planned to do next spring. "As in, the car? How'd that work out for ya?"

His face flushed and he looked away. "I didn't like it— but I had no choice. I managed to get us here and decided to wait for you to wake up. As I said, I'm not very good at it." He opened the door and kicked out his left leg. "The car was making odd noises."

I could have pushed it, but he was obviously embarrassed, thinking he'd forgotten something so elementary. I let it go and slipped from my seat to trade places with him. "What happened?"

He slid into the passenger's seat and closed the door, thankfully cutting off the gusty supply of icy wind. "You're clumsy. You walked into one of their darts." A slight pause. "Tell me how I did that." There was the smallest hint of panic in his voice. It made him sound so much younger.

I fastened my seat belt—or at least, I tried. Ginger's driver's side belt had a habit of sticking when it shouldn't. I hadn't tested it and didn't want to, but I wondered if it would actually stick in an accident. My guess was no. "Did what?"

"Marshal had one of his men teach me a few defensive moves, but that was—"

"Something more?"

His eyes met mine. Intense blue filled up every inch of my vision. "Yes. I didn't think. Only reacted. Like my body was controlled by some greater force."

"You've been a fighter all your life, Kale. It's called instinct. You don't remember, but you've fought like that before. Many times." I snickered and tore my gaze away from his. "You're actually one hell of a badass."

"I think I would remember something like that."

"Obviously not. None of it was familiar? Nothing at all?"

"No," he said, but I could tell he was lying. His eyes flickered from the building to me several times and he began tapping his fingers against the seat. Just like he'd done after our kiss and at the bridge.

"Why didn't you…" I held my hand up, wiggling my fingers. "You know."

"Touch them?"

"Yeah."

He sighed, and for the first time on our little road trip to crazy, he looked genuinely sad. "Because I liked it. I'm not sure how I was able to fight like that, but I liked it. Using my gift, it would have been too easy. Too fast."

The tone of his voice nearly killed me. It was something Kale refused to talk about with me under normal circumstances. I knew he didn't like using his ability to harm people, but I'd seen him fight. Deep down, I knew he enjoyed the rush of it. The surge of adrenalin that came when you were in the thick of it. I knew, because I felt the same way. Maybe not about fighting, but I lived for the rush. Before Kale, it's all I had. Now he was my rush—and I wanted him back. "Where are we going?"

"I'm not sure yet."

Not exactly helpful. I reached across and turned the key—for once, the engine started right up—and turned the heat to high. "How did they find us? GPS on your cell?"

"Aubrey said he turned that off."

I let a few minutes of silence pass between us. Something was bugging me, and when I couldn't stand it anymore, I gave in to curiosity. "You could have left me there. I'm sure there are more on the way." I held both hands over the blower vent in hopes of getting some of the feeling back. The heat in Ginger's old rust bucket was tepid at best, but it was better than nothing. "There are always more."

"I could have," he agreed. Suddenly he looked tired. Like he'd gone days without more than a few hours of sleep.

"So why didn't you?"

"I need to find out the truth."

"Let's be honest, Kale." I threw the car in reverse and backed from the spot. "You don't need me to find out the truth. You know about Simmons and you know where he's going to be. You can't tell me you're keeping me around to exact your revenge on the off chance I've been lying. I think you know I'm not lying—especially after what just happened."

"I don't know what's true."

"This is confusing. I can't imagine how hard it has to be. After everything you've already been through, this is the last thing you deserve." I took a deep breath, letting the car idle on the edge of the lot. My heart wanted me to take an awful chance and ask again. I needed to know my Kale was still in there. "Tell me the truth. Why didn't you leave me?"

I was about to pull from the lot, assuming he wouldn't answer, but he sighed and said, "I'm not sure."

"Not sure? Did you remember something?"

"No," he growled. "Yes. I don't know? Stop asking questions. You're worse than Roz."

That was unexpected. "Worse than Roz?"

A frown slipped across his lips. There and gone in the blink of an eye. "She's always asking me questions. How am I. What's on my mind." He turned to me, expression fierce. In his lap, both hands knotted tightly for a moment before his fingers started to flick. Not tap—flick! "I didn't leave you behind because I *couldn't*. Like, I physically couldn't. I tried. I made it to the door. But when I looked back and saw you lying there, all I could think was that more would be coming and they'd take you. Marshal would finally have you. For the briefest moment, the thought nearly crushed me."

I couldn't help it. A smile crept across my lips. Kale saw it, too.

"Don't. It doesn't mean anything. The thought was there one minute and gone the next. I could push you from the car right now and not think twice."

I shook my head. "No. You couldn't." A short snicker escaped despite my best efforts to rein it in. "You wouldn't make it far. You can't drive well, remember?"

"You did something. When you kissed me. My head's been...wrong ever since."

"It's not wrong, Kale. It's starting to clear."

• • •

We drove until the sun crested the horizon. I didn't know where we were going and didn't ask, instead following the directions Kale would occasionally bark. I was tired but energized by the tiny glimpse of progress. It was enough to keep me going. The road that stretched in front of us was full of possibilities. Despite the situation, I felt more hopeful than I had in months.

Kale had me pull the car off the interstate and into a Sunoco station parking lot. Digging into his jacket pocket, he said, "I'm going to make a call. Don't speak."

"Make sure you put it on speaker," I said, and to my surprise, he did.

It rang six times before a girl's voice, frantic, answered. "Kale?"

"What's going on, Roz."

"Oh my God, Kale. I've been so worried."

It gave me some small amount of pleasure to hear the chill in his voice as he spoke to her. It was all business, tinted with anger. And the expression on his face? Yeah. Obviously, Kale wasn't *feeling the love.* "What's going on?" he repeated. "I was attacked by agents."

On the other end of the line, you could have heard a feather hit the ground.

"How did they find me?" he pushed.

"Are you sure they were Denazen agents? It could have been an Underground tr—"

"They were Denazen. Why would they attack me, Roz?"

"I—I have no idea. Where are you? Come home. Please? You're so close to a breakthrough. Mindy's waiting to do your next session. If you miss it you'll lose all the progress you've already made."

"I'm in the middle of something."

I could hear the panic in Kiernan's voice. Teeth digging into my tongue to keep from saying something out loud, I leaned a hair closer. Kale didn't seem to notice, or if he did, he didn't care. I let myself believe the latter.

"Then tell me where you are. I'll come to you. Whatever it is, we can tackle it together. You don't have to be alone."

"I'm not alone. I have Kiernan with me."

I could almost hear the steam coming from her ears. Her reaction was so epic that for once, I didn't get pissed about him calling me Kiernan. *"What?"*

"I found her outside Thom Morris's house."

"And you, what?" she snapped. There was banging in the background—like she was slamming things around. Typical Kiernan. She was the temper tantrum queen. I'd seen it a thousand times. She'd hummed her cell through one of the windows at the hotel when some guy at Ginger's Six-only rave never called her back. "Thought you'd take her for a ride? Didn't Daddy give the kill order? *Why* is she even still alive?"

"First I owe her for what she did to me."

The tension in her voice eased a little. "But we need you back here. We have to find the others before they do any damage—and your treatments... I want to see you well again, Kale. Why don't you bring her home? Maybe Daddy can reason with her." Then, in a softer voice, she added, "Please...I miss you."

Kiernan was frantic. It reinforced Aubrey's theory about Kale's memories coming back on their own. Every minute I spent with him was another that her control over him might slip. She knew how much he loved me. Spending time with the real thing—and not the phony—was bound to shake something loose.

Dez Cross. Accept no substitutions.

"I can't yet. There's something I need to do."

"What?" she squealed so loudly that I cringed. "What could you possibly have to do?"

"You're going to have to trust me." His eyes darted to mine, then back to the cell. "You trust me, right, Roz?"

"Of course I—"

"Then what's the problem?"

"I don't like you running around with her. She's dangerous."

"I can take care of myself. I'm hanging up now. I'll be in touch."

"Kale, wait. I—"

He looked down at the cell, then up at me. It wasn't a smile. Not really. But it wasn't a scowl, either. "Let's go find the truth."

15

We drove for another hour before Kale made me pull off the interstate again. I asked him twice where we were going and he kept saying he wasn't sure, but it looked like we were headed somewhere specific.

"How much farther? Remember Simmons's plane comes in tomorrow. We can't miss it."

"We won't."

And that was it. It was all he said for another forty minutes. When he spoke again, it was to tell me to pull into the driveway of a small, unassuming ranch with a barricade of firewood all around the front porch and a three-foot lit snowman with a bright red Santa hat by the door.

I killed the engine and unfastened my seat belt. "So obviously we're here for a reason. What is it?"

He got out of the car without responding and started up the walk. I stuck my head out the open window. "Kale?" And when he didn't answer, I extracted myself from Ginger's uncomfortable seat and begrudgingly followed him to the house. "Are we just randomly knocking on people's doors for some reason, or do we have a specific purpose here?"

"I don't know," he snapped, then stopped halfway up the walkway. Sighing, he said, "I don't know where we are or why we're here. I don't know who lives inside, and I don't know why I feel such a pull, but I do."

I put my hand on his shoulder and was surprised when he didn't pull away. "It's okay."

"I feel like I *have* to be here."

"Then let's be here." There was nothing else to say. There was desperation in his eyes as well as fear. He'd spent his entire life controlled by Denazen, having no free will to speak of. Feeling the need to come here, but not knowing why, must have brought up buried fears.

He turned to me and I saw it again. A glimmer of my Kale. "I don't know if you're telling the truth, but I know something's wrong. I can feel it. My own family attacked me, and I keep seeing…"

I had to fight the urge to grab his hands and shake him. "Seeing what? Are you having flashes?"

He looked like he wanted to say more, but he only nodded to the house. "Let's go."

We climbed the steps and knocked several times, then waited. Unfortunately, it looked like no one was home. There was no sound coming from inside the house and it didn't seem as though any of the lights were on.

"That's inconvenient." I sighed. The only chance we had of finding out what had drawn Kale here was getting into that house. I tapped the doorframe and waggled my eyebrows as I turned to him. "We could always do a little breaking and entering. See what's inside?"

"There's no need to break in. Just knock a little louder."

We both jumped, spinning back toward the door. A woman slightly older than Mom, with short black hair and bright green eyes, watched us from behind the screen. She looked from me to Kale and when her eyes fell to him, a brilliant smile lit her face. "You came!"

That was unexpected. "You know him?"

She stepped back, holding the door open, and enthusiastically waved us inside. "Not formally, no. But we've met...in a manner of speaking."

We stepped into the house, Kale more easily than I did. Apparently, along with his memories, he'd also lost his caution to Denazen. My Kale would never just walk through a door in a strange place without checking things out first.

"What are you names?" I didn't miss how she looked from left to right, almost as if to be sure we were alone, before closing the door and clicking all three intricate padlocks in place.

Huh. Someone was a paranoid puppy.

"My name is Kale." He pointed to me. "This is Kiern—"

I shot him a look that would have scared most children and small animals, daring him to finish the sentence.

"Honestly, I have no idea who she is," he finished with a shrug of his shoulders.

I smiled and held out my hand. "I'm Dez."

The women nodded, smile bright as the sun, and shook my hand. "It's very nice to meet you, Dez and Kale. Please. Take a seat. Make yourselves comfortable."

We followed her inside and I settled on the couch, while Kale sat in the armchair on the far side of the room. The woman sat between us, saying nothing. She watched Kale, and I found it a little creepy how she just sat there smiling at him.

"That's a really cool bracelet," I said in an attempt to get things moving. As nice as it was to be somewhere with real heat, we didn't have all day. Things to do. Secrets to uncover. Evil corporations to topple.

"Thank you," she said, holding up her arm. On her wrist was a shiny silver band with a raised red stone. It was simple yet elegant. "It's my good luck charm. A…safety blanket so to speak."

"You seem like you've been expecting me. But you didn't know my name?" Kale fidgeted. Not flicking his fingers but back to tapping again. Sets of three.

One. Two. Three. One. Two. Three.

"Let's start out easy, shall we?" Smile still in place, the woman asked, "Do you know who I am?"

"I don't remember anything about my life," he said, leaning forward, elbows on knees. "My childhood, family, friends—all of it's gone."

She lost her smile. "I thought something might be wrong." Leaning back, she placed both hands in her lap and crossed her feet at the ankles. It was all very *British*, as Alex would have said. "But if your memories are gone, how did you find your way here?"

"I don't know. We just started driving. This is where we ended up."

We started driving? *I* drove, and technically it was more a hostage situation than the leisurely road trip he made it sound like. Granted, I was a *willing* captive, but still, he didn't necessarily know that. "What do you mean, you thought something might be wrong?"

She relaxed a little and faced me. "First, explain to me about his memories."

"A place called Denazen happened," I spat without

thinking. To most people, the name wouldn't mean anything. The company made the news at the beginning of summer when the building burned down, but other than that, as far as the world was concerned, they were a simple law firm specializing in juvenile and divorce cases. This woman, though…this woman knew who they were. Her expression softened, but there was a distinct twitch in her right eyebrow. Fear. "They scrambled his brain," I continued. "Turned him against his *real* family and friends."

"So you're the girlfriend?" she said with a sad smile. "One of the Supremacy children?"

A chill raced through me, chased by a healthy dose of fear. I stood, and to my surprise, Kale rose and stepped close. It was an unconscious gesture. I could tell because after he did it, he stopped and looked down at me, taking a step away, confused, as if he hadn't been aware of his own actions.

She threw up her hands. "Please. I mean you no harm."

"How do you know who I am—and more importantly, who are *you*?" At the mention of Denazen, she'd been afraid—but that didn't necessarily make her an ally.

"I know who you are through Kale."

"Who you've said you'd never met until we showed up on your doorstep," I finished for her. "But *then* you said you thought something was wrong." Shoulders squared, I narrowed my eyes and gave her my most intimidating stare. "You're all over the place, lady. Make up your mind already because you're making me dizzy."

"Answer her questions," Kale said, voice low. "Who are you? And how did you know something was wrong with me?"

"It's true. I've never met Kale in person, but I know you from his memories. You were inside his head—and his heart." She turned to Kale. "And I know you because my blood moves through your veins."

"You're a relative?" His eyes became impossibly wide and just a little bit hopeful, but I knew that wasn't the case. Ginger was his only living relative. If there'd been someone else, she would have told us.

Then again, maybe not. This *was* Ginger.

The woman shook her head. "I'm sorry, no. But you are as you are because of me." She stood and held out her hand to him. "I'm Penny Mills."

16

I couldn't speak. Now that she'd said it, I could see a faint resemblance to the picture Ginger had shown us at the cabin. The eyes were the same, and the shape of her face similar, but not much else. She'd obviously gone to great lengths to change her appearance.

"I can't believe it," I whispered, sinking back onto the couch. Kale took a seat beside me. "My friends are looking for you. Denazen is looking for you."

"Yes, I'm quite popular, aren't I?"

"But how have you stayed hidden? Denazen is looking under every rock in the country right now—and let's face it, those guys have some pretty insane resources."

"I've been extremely careful since parting ways with Denazen. I only managed to maintain my freedom because they believed me dead. It wasn't until recently that they uncovered the truth about my survival. I'm afraid my carelessness in being discovered has led to the current predicament."

"Current predicament? You mean the creation of a working trial of the new Supremacy? Domination?"

"Yes," she said. "They used my blood to make it, but it's not one hundred percent successful. People are still dying."

"Exactly!" I exclaimed—but that *still* didn't answer all our questions. If she didn't stop being so cryptic I was likely to implode. "How do you know all this? Do you have contacts inside Denazen? You still haven't said how you know Kale. The thing about your blood is a little vague…"

"Contacts inside Denazen?" She laughed. "How absurd! No, I have a special connection to the latest trial. Apparently, since my blood was used, I can communicate on a subliminal level with anyone given the new drug. That's how I know Kale. It's how he knew where to find me."

"Wait," Kale said, paling. "You're saying I was given Domination? That's impossible."

"I'm afraid it's true. I wouldn't have been able to feel you otherwise. The drug was administered in late September. I knew you the moment it integrated with your system."

"How many others are there besides Kale? Have you spoken to any?"

She looked at me as if I were insane. "Spoken to them? Of course not. Kale is the only one I've contacted."

Holy crap. Getting information from her was like dragging an elephant out of a mouse hole. "You keep saying that. Contacted. What do you mean?"

"And why me?" he added. "Why *contact* me at all?"

"I'm what Denazen calls an empath. I feel the emotions of those physically close to me. When given the Supremacy drug, my ability became heightened. I was able to focus on a specific person—no matter where he or she was—and use my ability.

In the case of those administered the new drug, the one that contains my blood, I found I didn't need to try establishing a connection. It was automatic. I felt people involuntarily. I also found I could communicate with them while in a rested state."

"Rested state? You mean when they were asleep?"

She nodded. "Asleep or relaxed. Some of my communications with Kale were while they had him semi-sedated, shortly after administering the drug."

"This is very interesting, but it doesn't tell me why you chose to communicate with me and not the others," Kale said flatly.

"You were overwhelmingly sad and frightened after you received the drug—not like the rest. You were so worried not only for yourself but for the girl you loved. A girl from the previous trial."

Kale glanced at me, then quickly looked away.

Penny's eyes teared as though the pain were her own. "Those first few days were excruciating. You felt so alone—but you weren't. I was there with you."

Kale stood and took several steps toward the door. "This is crazy."

"But something changed." Penny stood as well, frowning. "The connection grew clouded and erratic. I could still sense you—could still feel you—but it was pure confusion. I thought it was possibly a new side effect of the drug. That maybe you were somehow allergic but not fatally so. Now I understand it must have been what they did to your mind."

"A Resident did it. They needed to be sure they could control him if he survived," I said.

Kale shook his head and was almost to the door. "You're both wrong," he insisted. The look in his eyes was enough to steal the breath from my lungs. Fury, disappointment, and worst of all, pain. "*No one* controls me."

The ferocity in his voice sent my heart thundering. Kale had been given a taste of freedom—his first—when we met in the woods behind my old house. Until that day he'd been told where to go, what to do, and who lived and died. Once free from all that, he swore no one would ever have that kind of power over him again.

"I showed you where to find me so I could help cure your girlfriend," Penny said softly.

"Your blood," I said, watching Kale. "We have friends who believe they can create a cure using it."

"This is ridiculous," Kale snapped, making both of us jump. "She's not my girlfriend and I wasn't given Domination. This is the way I've always been."

"It's not," I said quietly.

"He knows." Penny took a step closer to him. "I can feel the confusion swirling inside his head. His mind is at war with his emotions."

Kale froze a foot from the door, pinning her with a dangerous glare. "Shut up."

She ignored him and turned to me. "Whatever they did goes deep, but you *are* familiar to him."

"Stop it," he said, this time louder. He took a menacing step toward her, and I jumped between them as, at the tips of his fingers, a black mass started swirling.

But Kale's hostility didn't faze Penny. She gently nudged me aside and stepped closer. "Think, Kale. This is what you wanted more than anything. To save her. You found your way here—against all odds. Denazen buried everything you knew. You couldn't remember your own name—or hers—yet you found me. For her."

"You said it yourself," I added, as the convulsing mass of

black receded. Hesitant, I reached out and took his hand, surprised when he didn't pull away. Instead, he stared down at our twined fingers, mouth agape, tightening them around mine. The sensation sent tingles of excitement shooting through me. "You don't know what to believe. She's right. You found your way here. There has to be a *reason* for that. Maybe you should at least hear her out before making any rash decisions, okay?"

He thought about it for a minute before nodding once in Penny's direction. "Fine. I'll hear you out."

Penny nodded. "Denazen must never get their hands on more of my blood. They haven't been able to reproduce it synthetically and, since they need it for the current successful drug trial, it will run out eventually." She held up her arm. The one with the stunning red bracelet. "Inside this bracelet is a device that, with the push of a button, will destroy this house and everything inside it. I don't ever leave."

I blinked. "You're telling us that you're essentially wearing a suicide bomb?" That was it. Jury was in. Penny Mills was *insane*.

"There is so much you don't know about Denazen. Their influence—their reach—extends much further than you can possibly imagine. If they were able to bring me into custody—a veritable never-ending source of the thing they so desperately need—they could engineer the army they set out to create all those years ago. The economy, world government—nothing would be safe. I am willing to sacrifice myself—and *anyone* else—to ensure they never get what they're after."

A lump formed in my throat. *Anyone*. The message came across loud and painfully clear. She'd said she brought Kale here to help me, but something had changed. "You changed your mind, didn't you? You're not going to give me your blood."

"Quite the opposite, actually. When I first sensed Kale, I had no intention of helping you. I simply intended to make his transition smoother. Please, don't take it personally. But this is a war we're fighting. As with all wars, there are always innocent people caught in the crossfire. Then I realized who Kale was and what you meant to him." She bowed her head and sighed. When she looked up, her expression was resigned. "I have no choice but to help you."

Kale shifted from foot to foot. "Who I am?"

Penny smiled and rested her hand on his shoulder. "The fabled Reaper. The young man who will one day be responsible for bringing the Denazen darkness to its knees."

In all the chaos of the last few months, I'd forgotten the story Kale told me when we first met. The Reaper. The man Mom told him to find if he ever managed to get outside the Denazen walls. It's what brought us to Ginger and the Underground, and ultimately to the truth: *Kale* was the Reaper. Seen through Ginger's ability and spread to the people to give them hope for the future during dark times. We'd looked for someone who hadn't taken his place in the world. A foretold hero.

That story alone should have given me comfort. Kale was destined to take down Denazen and that meant he would eventually see that Dad and Kiernan were the bad guys—but it didn't mean he'd recover his memory. Or that the damage done along the way wouldn't destroy us all.

"I know they've darkened your world, but your love for this girl—for Dez—was enough to make me take a chance. If you let them, I believe your true feelings will show you the way home."

"I—" Kale froze. One minute he was standing beside me, and the next he was on top of me. The breath whooshed from my lungs on impact and we landed in a tangle of limbs and shooting stars on the carpet at Penny's feet as something behind us shattered.

The picture window.

Penny dropped to the ground, too, and I kept trying to twist to see what had broken the glass, but Kale was too heavy and wouldn't let me up. "Penny, is there a back door?"

The only response was the sound of more breaking glass and voices outside getting closer.

Finally managing to twist around, I grabbed her shirtsleeve and tugged her closer. She coughed and grabbed my arm, squeezing until I thought it might pop off. "Penny?"

All the air in the room was gone. Sucked away, right along with any hope for the future.

"No," I whispered. *"Nonono!"*

Spilling to the floor from an ugly hole in her gut was Penny Mills's life — as well as my own. Bullets. They were using real bullets.

She raised her arm, cradling the bracelet in her left hand. "If you want to get out alive, run for your life."

Kale cursed and tried to drag me off the floor, but I pushed him away. "No! We can get you out of here. The hospital — "

She ignored me and, with shaking fingers, popped the small red gem from its prong. Even with the chaos all around us, I could hear the tiny plinking sound as it hit the hardwood and bounced away. Beneath it was a tiny button, and before I could stop her, she pushed it.

"You have sixty seconds. Back door. Through the kitchen," she wheezed. "G-Go!"

There was no telling Kale twice. Despite my struggling, he hauled me from the floor, threw me over his shoulder, and barreled into the kitchen and out the back door. We got several feet from the house before I managed to wriggle free. It was stupid and pointless, but I started back anyway. I had a better chance risking an explosion than I did getting my hands on whatever blood Denazen had left.

But it was no use. Kale tackled me before I got three steps. A deafening roar split the air and a tremor shook the ground beneath our feet as a bright flash of red and orange swallowed the house—and everything inside.

Including my last hope of survival.

17

I hadn't said a word since Kale dragged me to the car. Agents had swarmed the backyard as we climbed to our feet, but Kale, who must have had a moment of clarity, fought them off with practiced ease. Now, with the trees zooming by in a blur of green and brown as my foot fell heavily on the accelerator, I went over the important moments in my life.

The first thing I'd mimicked—a stupid Barbie doll at the toy store with Brandt and Uncle Mark. The time Brandt and I smoked our first—and last—cigarette. The moment Dad told me Brandt had been killed. The first time I saw my mom. The moment Sheltie confessed to being Brandt. And Kale. Thousands of freeze-frame moments with Kale. There were some in-between things. Alex, scenes from parties, holidays with friends… None of it was enough.

When Able poisoned me, I'd been terrified of dying. Still, somewhere in the back of my mind, I'd always believed there'd be a way around it. No matter how low I got and how hopeless

the whole situation seemed, I believed in my soul I'd make it
through. And I had. I'd gotten the antidote and lived to see
another day. This time was different. For the first time in my
life, I truly felt like I had no hope.

"I'm sorry," Kale said as we crossed the border back into
Ben's town. He peeked my way every so often but remained
silent the entire ride.

"Are you?" I intended to ignore him, but the words
slipped from my mouth regardless. I swiveled in my seat as
we pulled up to a stoplight, stomping down hard on the break
and slamming it into park. "And what exactly are you sorry
about?" I unfastened the seat belt and threw open the car
door.

It was late—or early, depending on how you looked at it.
The road was empty, and the storefronts lining the sidewalk
were dark. The world was slipping away. I didn't care about
manners and niceties. The fact that the engine was still running
or that I was standing in the middle of the road in a strange
town and nearly blocking a four-way intersection was of no
consequence.

On the other side of the car, Kale got out as well.

"Are you sorry because you sucked face with my sister?
That you've threatened to kill me several times? Or maybe
you're sorry that you've essentially kidnapped me?"

There was an edge of hysteria to my voice that, while it
scared me, was somewhat comforting. Each day that passed
without Kale was like a cancer that ate away my soul. For
months it built, the pressure coming so close to consuming me,
but I'd kept it together. Now, though, that buildup had finally
reached the breaking point.

"Or," I continued, stomping around the car to stand in
front of him, "maybe you're sorry that you can't remember

me? Could you be sorry because you're too weak to admit you have strong feelings for me—even though you don't understand them? Maybe you feel sorry for the poor, lovesick girl who's sticking around in hopes of getting the most important person in her life back—just in time to die." I smacked my head and stomped my foot hard. "That's it! You're sorry you just condemned me to death? Is that right? Because that's what you did by dragging me from that house *without* Penny Mills. I'm as good as *dead* now. I'm dead. She's dead. Ashley's dead. So many innocent people—dead! Is that why you're *sorry?*"

He waited. Patiently standing there while I raged in the middle of the road like a raving lunatic. The light had since changed colors—several times—but no other cars had come. Once I finished, breath coming in short rasps and heart hammering like the bass in the back of Brandt's old jeep, he pushed off the car and was in front of me. Pinning me tightly between the back door and his body, he leaned close.

Intoxicatingly warm breath tickling my neck, he whispered in my ear. "Maybe I'm sorry about none of it." His lips didn't touch my skin, but I could feel them, excruciatingly close, as he moved down my neck and then back up again, trailing imaginary kisses all the way to my ear. Skimming the edge of my jaw with the tip of his nose, he pulled back, bright blue eyes affixed to mine. "Or maybe I'm sorry about all of it."

How fast could the human heart beat before it exploded? How much could the body take before it simply caved?

There was so much going on in that moment. The fierce, hungry look in his eyes. A look that was at war with the language of his body.

Get closer.

Stay far away.

Touch her.

Don't touch her.

Love her.

Kill her.

I opened my mouth to speak but could only gasp when he leaned even closer. Icy blue eyes kept me rooted as his jaw tightened. It was like he was concentrating. Trying hard to see me—*really see* me. "You're right. I am lying. I have very strong feelings for you. I just don't know if they're good or—"

He never finished. Instead, he mashed his lips to mine, fingers gripping my hips hard enough to guarantee bruises. I could barely move—barely breathe—but I didn't care. If I was going to die, then this was how I wanted to go out. He might not be 100 percent *my Kale*, but Kale was Kale. I would take him any way I could.

One minute we were pressed against the back driver's side door, the next we were scooting toward the trunk, lost in each other. Our lips never broke contact. Not as he hefted me onto the trunk or as I wrapped my legs around his waist, securing him tightly as his fingers wound through the belt loops of my jeans.

The kiss at Ashley's hadn't done my memories justice. Granted, it'd been quick and mainly for shock value, but this... This was the fire I remembered. Even with Kale's thoughts of me buried out of reach, I seemed to have an effect on him. I'd kissed a lot of guys in my life, but his reactions—even now— were unlike any I'd ever experienced.

He kissed me as though I were life itself. Precious and balanced precariously on the edge of everything. With each passing moment it grew more heated. It were as if he was waking up from an eternity of sleep and trying to make up for the time we'd lost. *He* was Sleeping Beauty and *I* was the prince.

God only knew how far we would have taken it if a car hadn't pulled up behind us and the driver hadn't leaned on his horn.

We pulled apart, breath labored. The driver swerved around us, screaming a string of colorful phrases, and peeled away, tires squealing as he disappeared down the road into darkness.

When I turned back, Kale was staring at me. "I... That was..."

Something rattled in the alley behind us. The streetlight on the other side of the road was out, so when I turned to look I almost missed it. The subtle flash of something metallic. "Shit," I breathed. My legs were still wrapped around Kale's waist, and when I threw myself sideways off the trunk of the car, he followed by default. The dart sailed harmlessly above us.

"Denazen," I whispered, peering around the edge of the car. Sure. Someone couldn't drive up now, right? It had to be in the middle of that awesome kiss? It was official. The universe had a grudge against me. Though maybe the driver had done us a favor. If not for him, I was pretty sure Denazen could have danced their way to the car with bells on and tranqued us at close range before we knew what was going on.

Kale dropped to his stomach as something dinged the side of the car. "They're surrounding us. We need to move." He grabbed my arm and shoved me toward the back wheel. "Get underneath."

I slid my body along the blacktop and wedged myself beneath the car as Kale did the same. A small part of me started to panic. If someone came up behind and wasn't paying attention, what would happen if they hit us? Would we be squashed?

"Here." Kale pried the manhole cover off and dragged it to the side. The scraping sound it made against the pavement echoed through the streets. There was no way the agents hadn't heard it. They would know exactly what we were doing—and where we were going. "Hurry. Get in."

I tried to shimmy around, but the way I was angled, it was headfirst or nothing. Fantastic. Sewer diving. My December was officially complete.

I slipped my torso into the hole, grabbing the ladder tightly with both hands, and crept down several rungs, trying hard not to flinch at the icy metal. When my feet were clear of the opening, I kicked off and flipped. The landing was less than graceful, but nothing was broken and there was no blood. Sometimes that was all you could hope for. A few moments later, Kale's feet appeared and the sound of the metal lid scraping the pavement as he pulled the cover back over the opening filled the air.

"Move," he snapped, jumping from the ladder. "They won't be far behind."

We followed the wall for a while. The smell was horrific, and I didn't even want to think about the squishy stuff I was stepping in. For once I was thankful it was freezing outside. If this had been summer, the stench would have been unbearable.

"So…"

"So, what?" Kale didn't turn, but I could see him glancing at me every few minutes from the corner of his eye. We'd been moving for a few minutes and the silence was driving me crazy.

"You don't wanna say anything?"

He stopped walking and turned. "Anything?"

"About the kiss?"

"Oh." He shrugged and started walking again.

"Oh?" I practically squealed. "One minute you hate me,

the next you're sucking the tonsils from my throat and all you have to say is, oh?"

"It was nice."

"Nice? *Oh*, that was better than nice and you know it. But did it bring anything up?" When I realized what I'd said I felt the heat rush to my cheeks. With anyone else—Alex particularly—it would have been a disaster. Ten thousand jokes handed to him on a silver platter. "Memories," I added quickly. "Did it bring any *memories* up?"

"I remember the feeling." He sighed. "Something all-consuming. A need I couldn't get enough of. Someone..."

"Someone?" I asked, hopeful.

He turned, and for a second I was sure he'd lean in and kiss me again. But he didn't. Instead, he nodded into the darkness ahead. "It's not safe to stand still. We should keep moving."

We should keep moving.

Holy crap. What the hell was I thinking? As much as I wanted to know his thoughts on our kiss and if it'd gotten us any closer to a breakthrough, doing it now, with agents so close, was suicide. Worry churned in my stomach, and I tried to push it back. It was getting worse. Each day that went by stole more and more of my focus. Concentration was something that took effort, and it scared me. What if the protein was building faster in my system for some reason? Maybe I'd go over the deep end *before* hitting eighteen.

"Are you okay?" Kale asked when I didn't make a move to follow.

"Oh, yeah," I answered. Not the time to freak out. There'd be plenty of time for that later. I hoped. "Sorry. I turn eighteen soon. I guess the drug is starting to take effect."

He looked like there was something he wanted to say, but instead, he nodded and held out his hand. "I think we're almost at the end."

When we finally emerged onto the street, I was wet, nearly frozen, and suspected my sense of smell might be gone for good.

Kale grabbed my hand to help me up. When I placed my foot on the pavement I wasn't paying attention. Truthfully, I was watching him. The subtle bulge of muscle beneath his hoodie and the generous tilt of his lips. That kiss... In my defense, I'd been Kale-deprived for months, but I knew my timing was a bit on the stupid side.

I slipped on a patch of ice but Kale, quick as ever, caught me before I toppled completely. Our eyes met, and for a second I forgot how to breathe.

"We can't go back for the car," he said. He sounded a little disappointed.

A simple, casual statement with no romantic overtones, right? Sure. The words were general. But the look in his eyes was anything but. Heat flared to life as those beautiful blues stole every ounce of my focus—what little I had—and I wondered what we might do if we *could* go back to the car. The months we'd spent apart vanished. It was us against the world again. There was no *my Kale* and *their Kale*. There was only us.

"Dez, I—" But he didn't finish. Whatever he'd been about to say was lost as confusion set back in.

It was the first time he'd used my name since the night I'd found him at the party. The sound of the word on his lips made the butterflies rage in the pit of my stomach and sent warm tingles up and down my spine. I cleared my throat and stepped away, trying hard not to be disappointed when he didn't continue. Time. It would take time. I was about to tell him how annoyed Ginger would be about the car but a low hum came from Kale's pocket. "What is that?"

He dug his cell out. "I put it on vibrate. Just to be safe." After staring at the screen for a moment, he motioned for me to follow him around the side of the nearest building and answered it. "Start talking."

Speaker was out of the question, but I was able to lean close enough to hear the other end of the conversation. It was Aubrey.

"Not a lot of time, so listen up. She's telling you the truth— Dez. Everything Cross and Roz told you is a lie. They're going to be at the Burns airport in Connecticut tomorrow to get a Six named Ben Simmons. You need to get to him first."

Kale was silent for a moment. His eyes stayed fixed on the ground at our feet, but his shoulders tensed. He took a deep breath and asked, "Why are you telling me this?"

There was a small pause, then a sigh. "We're friends, man. We didn't start that way, but we are now. That's *not* a lie. You don't remember, but we talked before they did this to you. I trusted you with something. Now you have to trust me."

"Denazen attacked me," Kale said, voice dangerous. His free hand balled into a tight fist. "You're with them. Why should I trust you?"

"I'm not with them, man. Not really. I'll be at the airport with them tomorrow, and I'll do what I can to slow them down, but no promises. First things first, though. In your right shoulder there's a chip. They've been tracking you. It's how they found you at the hotel, and how they were able to follow you to Penny Mills's house. You need to get it out now or there's no place you can run that they won't be able to find you." A slight pause. "Look, I know you, dude. You're not sure if you can believe me and I get it, but I'll give you proof. There's a bathroom on the first floor at the airport. It will be marked with an Out of Order sign. Check under the last sink.

There will be something there for you."

And the line went dead.

"Aubrey?" When he got no response, he growled and I was sure he'd toss the phone, but he didn't. He crammed it into his back pocket, and in a single swift movement, he had his jacket off. Shoulder of his T-shirt pulled aside, he turned to me. "Can you see anything?"

"Yeah," I said, backing up so I could see his face. He looked angry, but more than that, he looked worried. Aubrey was right. There was no place we could go that they wouldn't find us. Tugging his collar back into place, I frowned. "I see darkness."

I could have sworn he rolled his eyes. He snatched up his jacket, stuffing both arms through the sleeves, and said, "It needs to come out."

"I totally agree, but it's not coming out here. First off, like I said, I can't see crap. Second, what am I going to do, dig it out with my fingers?"

Kale poked his head around the side of the building and scanned the area. "Okay. They know we went into the sewers. So if we keep moving, we might be able to throw them off track long enough to get it out."

"That's brilliant, but how exactly are we supposed to do that?" I wiggled my fingers in front of him, frowning. "My nails aren't quite that epic."

He nodded across the street with a sly smile. There was a small mom and pop convenience store on the corner. "We'll need supplies."

We dashed across the road and around to the back of the store. The outer door was easy to get through. It was old and the handle was rusted, breaking easily in Kale's capable hands. When we got to the second door, he drew his elbow back, then smashed it into the small window. The sound of shattering glass echoed through the air and I held my breath waiting for the betraying high-pitched squeal of an alarm—but there was nothing. With a twist of his arm, he was able to slip through the opening and undo the locks.

"I'll find a knife," he said, closing the door behind me. "You grab medical supplies."

We dashed in separate directions. Luckily, the medical supplies were close to where we came in, so I didn't need to go searching in the dark. I stuffed several packages of gauze, some tape, and antiseptic into my pockets, then moved a few aisles over to the medicine. It took a minute, but I finally found a bottle of Advil. As a rule, Kale didn't like taking medicine. Pills, liquids—it didn't matter. Mom once said it was because they'd drugged him so often as a child. I couldn't blame him, but I took the bottle anyway. Just in case. I'd never had anyone carve something from my skin, but I imagined it would hurt like hell.

Supplies in hand, I turned back to the door, but something occurred to me. Kale's blood. His abilities were different now, but we didn't know what else the drug might have changed—or not changed. Scanning the shelves, I found a small box of gloves. Better to be safe. Kale's blood had the ability to render Sixes mindless and compliant. Denazen used it to control us.

Kale emerged from behind the counter with what looked like a Leatherman tool and a yellow Sponge Bob lighter. "Time's up. We need to move."

"Where to? It'll take time to get out. Wherever we stop, they'll find us."

"I have an idea." He grabbed my hand and my breath caught. I couldn't help the familiar tingle I felt when his fingers closed around mine.

18

We ran seven blocks to the transportation depot on the edge of town and were lucky enough to catch a train just before it pulled from the station. Kale's plan was brilliant. We'd set up on the train, dig out the tracker, all while staying mobile.

"Here," Kale said, handing me the knife and lighter as he settled into one of the seats at the back of the car. He pulled off his jacket, followed by his T-shirt, and set them down on the bench beside him. "Sterilize it with the lighter before you make the first cut."

It was after 3 a.m. and thankfully, that meant an empty car. Having to explain to other passengers why Kale was half naked and I was performing minor surgery on a moving train with a swiss army knife and Sponge Bob cigarette lighter might be difficult, not to mention disturbing.

Reluctantly, I took the items from him. I knew it was going to have to be me. He couldn't slice the damn thing from his own shoulder. But that didn't mean I was happy about it.

Blood didn't squick me out like it did some people—namely Brandt—but I wasn't necessarily a huge fan of it, either. And hacking into someone's skin to dig something out? Ick factor squared.

I flicked the flint and held the blade over the flame as Kale sat there, patient and bare-chested. I tried hard not to look. Really. But I couldn't help myself.

He noticed, too. "You're going to have to look at me—not to mention *touch* me—if this is going to work."

"I know." I let go of the flint and set the knife down beside me to cool. "Too bad Alex isn't here. He'd get a kick out of it."

Kale took a deep breath and angled his shoulder closer. "Can you do this?"

Digging into my back pocket, I pulled out the handful of rubber gloves I'd taken from the store and wriggled my fingers into the left one first, and then the right. "Not like I have a choice, right?"

Kale reached over and grabbed the knife from the seat. Holding it out, he said, "That's not what I asked."

"Guess we're about to find out." With a deep breath, I took the blade from him and ran my left hand across his skin. With just the slightest bit of pressure, I felt along his shoulder, trying hard to ease the trembling in my fingers. The light wasn't fantastic in here and I felt it before I saw it—the thinnest ghost of a scar. "I think this is it." Pressing down with my thumb, I poked around until I felt something hard beneath the surface.

"Good. Get it out. It won't be long before Denazen figures out what we're doing and where we are."

"Right," I said, and positioned the tip of the blade down what felt like the center of the chip. "Ready?"

His left hand curled tightly around the top of the seat. "Just do it, Kiernan."

So we were back to Kiernan, were we?

I told myself that pushing the blade through his skin was out of necessity and not because he'd called me Kiernan again, but it was probably an even mix of both. He gritted his teeth, muscles tightening beneath my gloved fingers, as I deepened the incision.

"You know…" I spoke as much for his sake as mine. I needed to keep myself grounded. There'd been a lot of crazy messed-up crap in my life, but I was sitting in an abandoned train car zooming through a strange town while trying to dig a tracking device from the skin of my boyfriend who may or may not still want to kill me. It was enough to make anyone dizzy, and I deserved an extra-large cup of coffee and one of those chocolate-covered strawberries the Blueberry Bean had for taking things as well as I was. "I seem to recall telling you my name was *Dez*. Not Kiernan. Aubrey confirmed what I told you. I heard him—not to mention what Penny said."

I dug the tip in a little farther and Kale flinched. "Penny could be lying."

"You're unbelievable. You even called me Dez not an hour ago!" The tip of the knife clipped the chip. I flicked the point in an attempt to move it closer to the surface, but the blade slipped and Kale hissed in pain.

"Easy," he snapped, gripping the edge of the seat. "And so could Aubrey—but I believe him. I don't know why, but I have this feeling…"

"I don't suppose you remember what he trusted you with, huh?" The night in the woods behind Ashley's house rushed back. Aubrey telling me that he'd made Kale a promise. Now this. My curiosity was going wild.

"I don't," Kale said. He gripped the edge of his seat, knuckles turning white as I flicked the point of the knife again.

"Why?"

"Just wondering. Aubrey is... He's a little hard to pin."

Kale tilted his head to the side, thoughtful, and sighed. "No. I trust him. I'm very curious about the proof he said he'd supply, but I believe what he said."

I didn't know what to say to that but thankfully, Kale didn't give me much of a chance.

"I don't belong with them," he said after a moment. "I've felt it from the moment I woke up in the hospital bed."

"If you felt that way, why did you stay? And why fight so hard against what I told you?"

"Have you ever been blind?" He closed his eyes and took a deep breath as I continued to probe his skin with the tip of the knife. "Have you ever walked into a room, closed your eyes, and tried to find your way?"

"Can't say that I have."

"Do it. Do it and you will know what my life has been like since I woke up in that hospital bed. Blind. Imagine that you've been blind your entire life. Then one day you can see. Someone tells you that the color of the sky is called purple." He opened his eyes. "You don't feel like it's purple—you feel like there might be another name, a *better* name, but no matter how you try, you can't remember what it might be. It haunts your every waking moment but you can't remember. What choice do you have?"

"I guess," I said, swallowing a lump. "I guess I'd have to go with purple." I was blue and Kiernan was his purple.

"Correct."

I swallowed and flicked the point again. This time, the edge caught the chip and it moved a little closer to the surface. "Can you... Would you tell me what happened? After you woke up, I mean?"

"There's not much to tell. At least not much I remember. I woke up and Marshal was there. He told me I'd been in an accident and that I'd gotten hurt trying to save my girlfriend—his daughter. Roz."

The chip moved another centimeter. "And you knew who he was? Cross?"

Kale shrugged to cover up another flinch. Typical boy. "It was hazy. I remembered his face and that he was somehow a large part of my life. Other than that, there was nothing." Another flinch.

"What about her?"

"He told me her name. It sounded familiar, but I couldn't place it. When she came in and I saw her, it was strange... I didn't recognize her. Not really. But little things screamed familiarity."

"Like what?" With one last flick of the blade, I finally saw the chip. Gripping the edge between my thumbnail and pointer, I took a deep breath and pulled. The gloves made it difficult, but after slipping a few times, I was able to wriggle it free.

Kale still hadn't answered the question, so I looked up from my work to find him staring. "Amazing," he said, reaching out to finger a strand of blond hair. "This. I saw this crazy hair—blond with black tips—and somehow I knew everything was okay."

I had a much better handle on my ability than I had several months ago. Right before Kale went back to Denazen it changed, becoming uncontrollable. I mimicked parts of myself at random without trying. Specifically, my hair. It still happened once in a while when I was under a lot of stress or feeling overly emotional. Now was obviously one of those times, since a moment ago it'd been brown.

"I change my hair a lot—normally with dye. This is how I had it when we met in June."

"I like it," he said, letting the strand slip between his fingers. "This is silly, but it makes me feel calm."

I dropped the chip to the floor and smashed it with the heel of my shoe, then dumped some of the antiseptic over the wound and recapped the bottle. Bandage held securely over the incision, I ripped a long piece of tape from the roll and slapped it across. When I was done, I stepped back and sank into the seat next to his. Kale was still staring at me. It was like he'd never seen me before, while at the same time there was a spark of something raw in his eyes. Something familiar. "I think it was my fault."

"What?"

"They gave the order for your retirement. It was only after I started asking questions that they changed their minds about wanting you brought in alive. I believe that's why they used real guns at Penny Mills's house."

"Of course," I said, feeling sick. Penny was dead because Kale saved me. The bullet that killed her had my name on it, not hers. "They didn't want her dead—they wanted me dead. I wouldn't be a threat to your memory if I wasn't breathing anymore."

"They've been keeping tabs, and they guessed your next move based on the names left on the list. Two others were sent to one location, while Aubrey and I were sent to Thom Morris's. We were instructed to kill you on sight."

"I didn't see Aubrey."

"At the last minute, he said he'd found another lead." Kale picked up another strand of my hair, shaking his head in wonder.

"And you decided to hijack me." I couldn't help the sarcasm

in my voice—which was stupid, really. Hijacked was better than dead any day of the week.

"I saw you come out of the house and get into your car—"

"You saw me? I sat there waiting for you to show for hours."

"I know. I was just watching you."

I forced a smile. "That's a little creepy."

"Marshal's last words to me before I left kept replaying in my head. Over and over. 'Kill her. Make it fast.' I tried a thousand times to move." He moved away and held up his hand. A churning black mass gathered at his fingertips. "I didn't even have to come any closer. I could have done it from where I stood. There was no need to speak or look you in the eye. You would have been there one moment and simply gone the next."

"But you saw the picture on the phone and wanted the truth." I pulled off the gloves and grabbed the empty, discarded Starbucks cup rolling on the floor at my feet. Depositing the bloody plastic, as well as the remnants of the chip inside, I put the cover back on. More than anything, I would have loved to toss it out the window but, since we were in a moving train, that wasn't an option.

"Aubrey said he found the phone in the woods. I saw the photograph and it confused me, but it was more than that. I kept thinking about that kiss at Ashley Conner's house."

I threw the cup down and kicked it across the car. It rolled until it hit the wall, then slipped under the last seat by the door. "I *am* an expert kisser."

"I thought I loved her—Roz. That's what they told me, anyway. But when I kissed you back there on the street...I never felt like that with her."

Standing, I handed him his shirt. "Stop right there. This is starting to border on TMI and to be honest? The last thing I want is to hear about you sucking face with my sister."

I started to step away, but he grabbed my arm and pulled me back down. "You're not the only one who feels this," he said softly. "If everything you've told me is true, then I lost just as much as you did." He let go of my arm and yanked his shirt over his head. Rotating his arm, he nodded. "That's pretty impressive."

"What is?"

"The fact that you just preformed minor surgery on my shoulder. Most wouldn't handle it as well. You seem surprisingly calm."

"I'm not most."

"I'm starting to understand that." He pulled on his jacket. "Roz would have passed out."

While I didn't necessarily revel at being compared to Kiernan, I did get some small amount of satisfaction that she wouldn't have been able to hack it. She hated the sight of blood. We'd gone to a Nix party after Kale and I had returned from our trip to warn the others, and two testosterone-fueled man-monkeys ended up throwing each other through a glass door. She'd puked for an hour straight.

The train slowed, about to come to a stop. Hopefully we weren't far from the airport. "If you compare me to Kiernan one more time — Roz isn't her real name, by the way — I might dig into the other arm. Just for fun."

A slow smile spread across his lips, and he threaded his fingers through mine. "I can see why I like you."

19

Ben Simmons's plane was scheduled to land at ten a.m. That didn't leave a lot of time to plan.

"I don't like this," Mom said on the other end of the line. We'd settled in the field behind the airport and the sun was almost up. There wouldn't be enough time for backup to get to us before Ben landed. They were too far away.

"I'm open to other options," I said, waiting for someone—anyone—to give us something better to work with. Mom, Dax, Ginger, and Vince were on speakerphone, and Kale sat across from me. The only plan we'd come up with so far was for Kale to distract Kiernan and for me to mimic her, getting Ben out of sight before Denazen could get him out of the airport. But there were too many variables, and that made me nervous. Not to mention the idea of slipping into my sister's skin made my stomach turn, and the physical cost of mimicking an entire person was hard on me. Normal stuff had become a piece of cake, but an entire person sapped my energy and left me vulnerable.

"Are you sure you can trust him?" Dax asked. "What if this is a ploy so Cross can get his hands on you?"

Kale laughed. "If I wanted to give her to Marshal, we wouldn't be having this conversation. Besides, I know all about you, Daxil Fleet. You can hear my voice. What do you think?"

Dax's ability worked through sound. If Kale planned to double-cross us, Dax would know. "He's telling the truth."

Mom let out an audible sigh.

"You won't make the flight, but if you guys leave now, you can be here not long after the plane lands. If this works, we're gonna need a ride."

"A ride? What did you do to my car?" Ginger growled in the background.

"Relax, its fine. I just…don't have it at the moment."

"We had to run," Kale interjected. With a sidelong glance my way, he added, "Unfortunately, the car was probably impounded by the local authorities."

"The car isn't important at the moment," Mom snapped. "We can leave now, but I need to know you'll be all right. Do you think you can do this?"

Everyone asked me that lately. *Do you think you can do this*. The truth? I wasn't sure, but I'd never let fear and doubt get in my way before. No reason to start now.

• • •

Ben's flight was slightly delayed, and I still hadn't decided if that was good or bad. Kale was pacing the room, the proof Aubrey promised—a CD he'd taped to the sink—now in his hand. He waved the thing back and forth, angry. "How is this supposed to show me the truth?"

I grabbed his arm. He was making me dizzy. "There's information stored on it, I imagine. Something that will shed some light on things."

Kale looked down at the disk in his hands with nothing short of pure suspicion. "Information?" He turned the disk over several times before sighing. "I suppose you know more about it than I do. I'll have to take your word for it."

We were camped in the out-of-order men's room, conveniently right by the terminal where Ben was set to arrive. So far the coast was clear, but we didn't have a good view from in here.

"I promise. As soon as we get back to the cabin, we'll find out what's on there." I stole another peek around the corner, impatient. Doing nothing was making me crazy. "This is ridiculous, and I'm sick of waiting. There's an easier way." Closing my eyes, I took a deep breath and concentrated on the flight attendant I'd seen getting ready to board one of the planes. The familiar tingle at the back of my neck and the shift in clothing—from comfortable jeans to restricting nylons and a stiff pencil skirt—told me the mimic was a success. When I spoke again my voice was different. Not entirely foreign, but it had more of a rasp to it.

I braced myself against the wall as a wave of fatigue washed over me. It only lasted a moment before passing, allowing me to stand on my own. "This way, I can go out and have a better look around. They could be out there somewhere, and we'd never see them from in here."

I turned and started for the door, but Kale grabbed me. "What am I supposed to do?"

Kale could easily move through the room unseen if he wanted to—he just didn't remember. "If you have to ask, then you're probably safer staying put and waiting for me."

He lifted his free hand to my face and ran his index finger along my cheek. "I get the feeling that you find trouble often."

"How do you know it doesn't find me?"

Finger trailing down to my chin, he tilted my head toward his, frowning. "No. I think I was right the first time."

I slipped free and made my way out to the floor. The crowd was thicker now, which would make it easier for Denazen to hide. Passengers were coming down the escalator and I took the spot at the end of the hallway, following the lead of another attendant as she thanked passengers and wished them a safe trip home.

Clumps of people came and went, filing down the gangway and embracing their waiting loved ones. I waited as the crowd thinned and, after a few minutes, caught sight of a familiar mop of long dark hair and a weathered leather trench coat.

Aubrey stood in the back, and a few feet in front of him, Kiernan stood to the side. Looming on the outermost edge of the crowd were three additional agents. It wasn't easy, but I was able to pick them out due to their trademark blue suits. If not for their clothing, they would have blended perfectly into the chaos.

When the last of the passengers trickled down, I started to panic. I'd seen a blurry picture of Ben next to his name on Ginger's list, and no one even remotely resembling it had exited the plane. And I wasn't the only one getting edgy. Kiernan rose on her toes, shooting Aubrey a worried look. He shrugged in return and started forward. He had a choice between me and another airline employee. Luckily, he made a beeline for me.

"'Scuse me," he said, Kiernan coming up beside him. "We were waiting on a friend. Is everyone off the plane?"

"Is it possible your friend took another flight? Or maybe

he's already been through. Could he have been picked up by someone else?"

"Over my dead body," Kiernan mumbled.

I pretended not to hear her and turned back to Aubrey. This was my opportunity to get them to leave. "You might want to check with the gate agents. They'll know more than I would, I'm afraid."

Aubrey nodded and turned, but Kiernan stayed put, staring down the hall. "You *sure* they're all off?"

"I'm certain, yes," I replied, fighting the urge to physically shove her in the other direction. It said a lot about my self-restraint—to be so close and still be able to resist decking her.

She hesitated, then turned to follow Aubrey, but it wasn't fast enough. A hair-curling scream rocked the terminal, freezing everyone—including Kiernan and Aubrey—in place. The three of us whirled toward the gangway where two burly security officers escorted a tall guy in a bright red hoodie down the gangway.

A guy who looked freakishly like the picture in Ginger's file.

"Let go of me," he screamed, pulling against the taller officer's grip. "I didn't do anything!"

"What happened?" I asked when they reached the end of the hall. Kiernan and Aubrey waited off to the side for their chance to pounce.

"He went nuts halfway through the flight from Paris," one of the officers said. "Started yelling about blood and brains or something."

"Sent the entire cabin into an uproar. Everyone panicked," the other said with a sneer. He gave Ben a good shake. "Police are on their way to have a little chat with him."

They turned and started down the hall, and I followed. No

way was I letting Ben Simmons out of my sight. With a quick glance over my shoulder, I saw Aubrey and Kiernan trailing behind. They obviously had the same idea I did.

Stopping, I turned to them and flashed my sweetest—or the attendant's sweetest—smile. "We'll take care of your friend and let you know what's going on. There's coffee and cookies in the lounge. Feel free to make yourself at home."

Kiernan looked like she wanted to argue, but Aubrey put a hand on her shoulder and pulled back. I doubted they'd given up—or that there were any cookies to be had—but I needed to stall them. Hopefully this would buy Kale and me the time we needed to get Ben out of the building and to safety.

Security led Ben down a side hallway and into a room at the end. I hovered in the doorway as they cuffed him to a bar beside the small table and closed the door. "You boys seem to have this under control," I said with a smile. "Call the office if you need assistance."

I turned on my heel and started walking, headed in the opposite direction we'd come. Think. I needed to think. I was fairly confident I could take out one, but in order to do that I needed to get rid of the other.

Slipping inside the first door I came to, I found myself in a small waiting area. There was a couch and coffee pot as well as a slew of outdated garden magazines—no cookies, though. There was also a bathroom. I ducked inside and looked in the mirror. First thing that had to go were the clothes. The material hugging my skin twitched and changed, morphing from nylons and pencil skirt to the sturdy leather of combat boots and an itchy black police uniform.

It would have been easier to mimic an entirely new person, but it was too soon. I'd pushed myself recently, curious about my limits when it came to mimicking other people, and found that doing too much too soon would hurl me into the equivalent of a coma for two days straight. Crossing my fingers, I hoped there was still enough juice to change a few key features of my face and clothing.

No one particular in mind, I imagined it a bit puffier, lengthened just a smidge, framed by short dark brown hair and dark blue eyes. As I watched the mirror, my skin began to stretch and morph, taking the shape in my mind. I let out a breath I hadn't realized I'd been holding. My eyebrows were uneven, but no one would notice.

I hoped.

Now, instead of the flight attendant looking back at me from the mirror, there was a petite raven-haired woman with chipmunk cheeks and a chin that came to a bit of a point. Her eyes were blue—darker than Kale's—and held a hint of mischief, her police uniform starched and clean. I sighed. Showtime. "Let's go bag us a Supremacy kid," I said to my new law enforcement reflection.

Out the door and back into the hall, I walked slowly but steadily back to the room where they were holding Ben. Just before I got there, I saw Kiernan stroll slowly past the other end of the hall. They knew where he was and were beginning to circle like vultures. I had to act fast. If it were possible, Kiernan was even more impulsive than me. Where I tended to stop and think things through, she would just charge in.

"Officer Debra Morgan," I said before even thinking about it. Crap. That's what I got for watching reruns! Dad never bothered with cable, and with Kale gone, I'd soaked up seventeen years' worth in record time. Everything from disaster flicks to soaps. I'd moved onto Netflix and was currently working my way through the first season of *The Walking Dead*.

I held my breath and waited, hoping to God neither man was a *Dexter* fan. Casually glancing at the nametag of the man closest to me, I asked, "Which one of you is Spitz?"

He nodded and stood a little straighter. "That would be me."

"My captain wants to see you. He's waiting in the security office."

He nodded again, once to me, then to his partner, then trekked down the hall toward the main terminal. I breathed a sigh of relief. I had no idea where the security office was, but hopefully it wasn't too close. I needed a few minutes to get in and get out.

I inclined my head toward the door, hitching my thumbs through my belt like I'd seen the officers at the Blueberry Bean do a million times. Squaring my shoulders, I cleared my throat and said, "He in there?"

The remaining security officer waved me ahead. "Go for it. He's bonkers. One minute he's normal, the next he's crazy. PCP if you ask me. Kid's higher than a kite."

Wonderful. Supremacy crazies were setting in. That would make things *so* much easier.

I held my breath and ducked into the room. Ben was sitting in the same place, forehead resting atop the table. When he heard the door, he twisted around without lifting his head. "Fantastic," he groaned. "Don't I at least get a phone call or something?"

I closed the door and crossed the room, kneeling beside him. "We don't have a lot of time, so while this is going to be a sort of crash course in reality, I need you to listen. 'Kay?"

"Um, sure." He picked up his head, attention divided between the door and me like he was waiting for the camera crew to bust in. Not long ago I'd felt the same way.

He seemed lucid, and I didn't know how long it would last, so I took a deep breath and launched right in. "I know who you are—what you are." I grabbed the chain of the handcuffs as he started to protest and slapped my other hand across his mouth. "Listen, remember? I know because you and I—we're the same."

In my hand, the cool metal chain grew lighter. More flimsy. My ability used to be limited by similar mass and size. Lately, I'd found the same laws didn't apply. The metal chain-turned-paper crumbled in my hand and tore as I gave a good yank.

Ben gasped. "What the fu—"

I dragged him from the seat and covered his mouth. "Shh! Still talking here. Somewhere skulking around this airport is a handful of people looking to make you their bitch because of the brain-busting thing you can do. We have to get out of here before they find us because, trust me, you don't want to meet them."

He blinked, looking from his wrists to the door, and nodded. I removed my hand. "So you're not a cop?"

I ignored his question and pointed to the corner of the room behind the door. "Get over there and stay out of sight. I'm opening the door."

He hesitated but finally crossed the room, wedging himself into the corner like he was hoping this was all some bad dream.

I pulled open the door and leaned around the frame into the hall, motioning for the remaining security officer to come inside. When he did, his eyes traveled from the empty table to me with a slightly panicked gleam. He made a move toward the door, presumably to call for help. I darted forward to stop him, but something sent him flying back into the room. A second later the door slammed closed…

…and Kiernan appeared.

20

"Whoa!" Ben breathed, sliding farther down the wall. His eyes were wide as Frisbees and he looked a little pale. I hoped to God he wasn't going to puke.

"Back off," Kiernan growled in my direction. "My friend and I are leaving. If you don't want to get hurt, just leave us be."

I snorted and stepped between them, letting go of my mimic. There was a slight tingle, and suddenly I was nice and comfy, back in my own skin. "Over my better-dressed body."

Her eyes widened, and for a fraction of a second, surprise froze her in place.

Then she was on me.

Kiernan's lip curled up and she lunged forward. Fingers extended toward my throat, she wore an expression that defined pure fury—then nothing. "Crap," I spat, spinning in a full circle with my arms flailing. Kiernan wasn't an expert fighter—last I knew of, anyway—but being able to move through the room unseen gave her a serious advantage.

Something connected with my jaw, rocking my head back and sending the room into a swirl of watery color and blurry shapes. I thrust my arms out in front of me, trying to back myself against the wall to narrow down possible areas of attack, but I was too slow. She hit me again, this time from behind, and sent me sprawling to the floor.

From somewhere to my left, I heard her laugh. "What's the matter, *sis*? Feeling a little unbalanced?"

Getting my ass handed to me by an invisible girl was embarrassing and certainly not the best impression to give the new guy. In the corner, Ben watched, wide-eyed, clearly having no intention of leaving his hiding place. Obviously he wasn't the help-a-damsel-in-distress type.

Then again, *I* wasn't the damsel type.

Taking a deep breath, I held it and really paid attention. There was no sound. When Kiernan used her ability, she essentially created a bubble around herself, making her body and anything she touched, as well as any sound she might make, undetectable.

But as helpful as that was for her, it didn't stop me from noticing the ends of my hair flutter on the right side as she geared up for another attack.

I threw myself sideways as hard as I could and a painful howl filled the small room. Kiernan appeared behind me, left arm cradled in her right. I didn't waste time. Bringing my leg up, I caught her in the stomach, and when she doubled over, I struck again by bringing my elbow down hard between her shoulder blades.

There was a point in my life, not long ago, when the actions that followed might have horrified me. But so much had changed—with my reality and my life—that I didn't even think twice. Dropping down beside her, I slapped my hand over her mouth, making sure to cover her nose.

It took a moment but she started thrashing, desperate to shake me loose. Desperate for air.

"Holy crap—you're killing her!" Ben said, finally crawling out from his corner.

As soon as she stopped struggling, I let go, hoping it wasn't an act. "As much as that would have made my year, I only wanted to knock her out." I stood. "In case you didn't realize it, she's with those people I told you about."

"I—" Ben started as the door burst open. Assuming it was someone belonging with Kiernan, he swung without asking questions.

The recipient of his blow—or miss, as it turned out—was less than thrilled with the reception. Kale stepped into the room, artfully dodging Ben's punch, and shoved him hard against the wall. "Do *not* do that again."

"Easy," I said, stepping over Kiernan's still form and wedging myself between the two boys. "You took him by surprise, that's all. Kale, this is Ben Simmons."

He looked at Ben for a moment as if sizing him up, then turned to me. "We need to go. I took care of two agents, but not before one was able to call for help. They know we're here. They'll come prepared."

I followed his gaze to Kiernan, lying motionless on the floor. Her head was at an uncomfortable-looking angle with her right arm wedged beneath her. I was betting she'd wake up with one hell of a stiff neck. "She's fine," I said, a pang of jealousy shooting through me.

He tore his gaze from her and met mine with a look that sent the butterflies in my stomach moshing up a frenzy. "I don't care about her."

"Right," I said with a nod. He didn't care. I was reading into every little thing he did, and that needed to stop. Creeping to the door, I opened it a crack and peered around the frame. The hall looked deserted. If we were going to make a break for it, now was our chance. I waved to Ben. "Come on."

He shook his head, skin slightly pale and eyes alternating between Kiernan and me. His hand rested atop his stomach and, judging from the expression on his face, there was a good chance he *was* going to be sick. "You go ahead. I think I'll wait here for the cops."

Kale moved toward him. "If you don't start moving toward the door, Supremacy will be the very least of your problems."

I grabbed Ben's arm and pulled while giving Kale the stink eye. "What he *means* to say is the cops won't get here in time. If you don't come with us now, there won't be a later to worry about. Trust me on this; we're trying to help you." I'd done the hardass routine with Ashley, and she ended up dead. I wasn't going to make the same mistake twice. "Please, Ben. Trust us."

His eyes widened, then kind of glossed over. Suddenly his breath came in short, shallow pants. "The bloody people. That's who you're talking about?"

I had no clue what he meant, but I nodded with great enthusiasm. I would have told him Santa Claus was real and rented an apartment with the Easter Bunny in sunny California if it got him moving. "Yes. Bloody people. Bloody people who want to *kill* you."

Technically I wasn't lying to him.

Ben's expression was a mask of utter panic, but he followed me to the door and out into the hall. Before starting forward, I gave Kale a neener-neener grin and couldn't help the spike of happy I felt when his lip twitched in amusement.

We were a few feet from the end of the hall when an angry

voice came from behind. "What the— Stop!"

A quick peek over my shoulder told me the security guard I'd sent to the office had returned. He stood in the doorway of the room with his radio out, presumably to call for backup. "Great," I snapped, pushing Ben forward. "Just great."

As the three of us wove our way through the crowd, trying hard to stay at its thickest to avoid detection, I dialed Mom. "Please tell me you're almost here," I huffed when she answered. In the background, a horn blew and Dax's muffled curse, along with the distant squeal of breaks against blacktop, rang out.

"About ten minutes away," she replied. "Why? What happened?"

"We had a little hiccup." Beside me, Ben kept pace, but he didn't look good. Sweat beaded against his brow, and his eyes darted back and forth. He'd wrapped both arms around himself like he was terrified to touch anyone and had started whispering incoherent things under his breath. I couldn't catch much of what he said, but I did hear the words *spike*, *death*, *harpoon*, and *space*. "Actually, it's more like a stinky butt burp than a hiccup."

Mom groaned. "Can you make it outside? We'll pull up right in front."

I looked to Kale for confirmation. "Front door?"

He shook his head. "Blocked by security."

A quick look over my shoulder showed more guards fanning out to canvass the room. They were getting closer. "I'll have to call you back," I barked and ended the call, almost dropping the cell. "If we can get someplace out of the way, I can try mimicking us and we can walk right out the front."

"No," Kale said. "Three people? That will take too much out of you."

Of course it would. Focus, Dez! Focus.

It was stupid, considering the situation we were currently in, but I froze, staring at him like he'd just spouted the lyrics to a Powerman 5000 song in ancient Greek. "What?"

"You've already mimicked yourself twice in the last hour. The attendant and the police officer. You won't be able to change all three of us and walk out of here on your own. If I have to carry you it will attract too much attention."

When my brain was functioning on all cylinders, I knew that, but memory-impaired Kale didn't. I'd never told him. "How did you—"

"My head," Ben said, stopping short and crouching low to the ground. We were in the middle of the crowd, and several people slowed to stare. "My head is going to float away!"

"Oh, shit." The guard said they restrained Ben during the flight because he'd become delusional and violent.

"Is...is he okay?" a tall woman asked, pulling her small child behind her. The boy wouldn't be pushed aide, though. He shrugged her off and pulled back the legs of her pants to get a better look at Ben.

"Yeah, he's fine. He just doesn't—"

"They're inside my head!" he cried, curling tight on the floor.

People didn't pass slowly anymore. They stopped. The woman jumped back, startled, and pulled her son into the crowd as others joined her.

With each word, Ben's voice grew louder and louder, overcoming the noise of the terminal. "Inching their way through my gray matter and trying to eat out my eyes!"

"What's he talking about?" Kale asked, trying to drag him off the floor. But Ben kept going limp, folding like overcooked spaghetti.

"He's having an *episode*. His symptoms are further along," I whispered, bending to help Kale pick him up. "Worst timing *ever*."

We managed to get Ben upright, but he wasn't responsive so I kind of panicked. Taking a deep breath, I backhanded him. Sprained my middle finger doing it, too. He stumbled backward into Kale, eyes wide.

"What the hell?" he snapped.

"Seriously?" I blinked down at my hand. "That actually worked?" Huh. Chalk one up for melodrama in Hollywood!

Kale grabbed my shoulders and spun me toward the door. "They've seen us."

They had us surrounded—at least five at our back and three in front. Kale on one side of Ben and me on the other, we dashed forward.

Agents hovered around the edges biding their time, and security charged full-speed ahead. Typical Denazen. Let someone else jump in and get their hands dirty while they waited on the sidelines to swoop in. There wasn't much time to think, much less get out of their path. We separated, Kale tugging Ben to the right and around a large pillar to avoid two of the men coming at our front. The third was on me.

The crowd shrank back, giving us a wide berth as a collective gasp rolled through the room. Kale decked one guard square in the head and sent him crumbling to the floor as the other made an inelegant swipe Kale easily danced away from.

Kale was fine. He had Ben, and he'd make sure he stayed safe. I needed to focus on the guard flying toward me. I waited until he was several feet away, speed never decreasing, before bending low like Mom had shown me in one of our training sessions. I angled my shoulder just below his waist and jumped up with every ounce of strength I had. The movement sent him flying headfirst over my shoulder to the ground.

I stopped for a second, shocked it'd actually worked. I'd tried it several times on Dax, and the most I'd managed was a sprained shoulder and a ton of embarrassment. My lips twisted into a goofy grin, thrilled over my accomplishment, before I realized I was doing it again. Losing focus. But it was too late. One of the guards came running up from behind and threw his arms around my torso, pinning both arms stiff at my sides. Head back in the game, I didn't hesitate. In one of our training sessions, Dax showed me a trick to throw an opponent off balance. I drew my knees up, forcing the guard to support all my weight as well as his own. He didn't anticipate it, and the move sent him teetering—as planned—and stumbling forward.

We hit the ground in a heap and I wriggled free, but he refused to give up. Clutching a handful of hair, he yanked back, and a painful scream built in my throat. I couldn't remember the last time someone pulled my hair. Kindergarten maybe? And definitely not a guy.

I twisted and kicked out, catching his shoulder with the heel of my sneaker. I couldn't hear anything above the noise the crowd made—people were screaming and talking all at once—but I felt something give, accompanied by a sickening crunch. The guard released my hair and let out a scream that would have done an opera singer proud.

"Oh, man. I'm seriously sorry," I said as I scrambled to my feet. He was just doing his job, and I felt bad. He didn't understand what was going on.

The Denazen agents, on the other hand, did.

I made it to the edge of the crowd as they closed in. Four of them, one approaching from each corner of the mob.

"Everyone calm down," the one to my right called out and

the crowed hushed. "We're Homeland Security. We've got this under control."

Homeland Security? Were people really that stupid?

The crowd shrank back ever farther, quieting, and I had my answer. Yes. Yes they were.

The agents came within four feet, and the one who had addressed the crowd spoke in a voice only loud enough for me to hear. "Where's Ben Simmons?"

"Ben Simmons," I said, tapping my chin. "Simmons. Hmm. Doesn't ring a bell. What's he look like? Is he hot?"

"Don't play games, little girl," he growled. "Simmons is dangerous. You're not doing yourself any favors by helping him."

I shrugged. "I like danger."

"Do you?" He took a step closer, grin stretching to remind me of a freaky clown I'd seen as a child. Good thing Kale wasn't seeing this. He hated clowns. "Do you like pain as well? This is your last chance. Tell me where Ben Simmons is."

I was about to tell him to check all the spots the sun didn't shine when a woman from the crowd let out a horrific shriek. Everyone's attention went from me to the front of the room. I didn't see it at first and wondered what the big deal was as the crowd scampered to either side of the room like the floor was on fire. But when I did, I was filled with an even mixture of fear and elation.

On the other end of the room, crouched low by the door, was Kale. Moving away from him—and speeding toward us— was a dark, churning thing just below the tile floor. It reached the brim of the crowd and separated into four distinct trails, zooming around me and settling beneath each agent.

As an entire room full of fearful Nixes watched, the agents exploded into puffs of dust, sending the crowd into a crazed panic. Suddenly the door—the place *we* needed to get to—was the place *everyone* wanted to get to. The entire room rushed the exit, screams erupting. One woman behind me shrieked something about aliens, while a younger man called out a warning about terrorists.

Seriously?

I didn't know how we were going to explain what happened, but I wasn't worried at that moment. One disaster at a time. I propelled myself from the building, along with the crowd, and made a beeline for Dax's waiting car.

21

Ginger hobbled around the table and set the glass of water down in front of Ben. "Feeling better?"

He grabbed the glass with both hands but didn't bring it to his lips. Instead, he sat there staring over the rim of the cup, mouth open slightly like he expected the liquid to boil and fizz.

"Mr. Simmons?" Ginger tried again, taking the seat across from him.

At the mention of his name, he started, looking up from the glass and flashing us an apologetic smile. "Sorry. I've been having a hard time focusing lately."

"That's the drug," I said, tapping the side of my head. "Same thing's been happening to me."

Ginger didn't say anything, but Mom's head swiveled like a woman possessed. "What?"

"It only just started," I admitted, focusing back on Ben—I didn't like the look on her face. Somewhere between fear and anger. Now wasn't about me. This was about Ben. "What else is different?"

We'd been sitting at the table in the kitchen for the last two hours now. By the time we arrived back at the cabin, Ben was calm and seemed to be more himself again. He'd wanted to rest, saying he felt wiped, but Ginger had to explain things while he was lucid. We didn't know how long it would last, and if there was any chance he could help things along for Kale, we needed to find out while there was still time.

Ben must have decided the water was safe because he lifted the glass and took a tentative sip. I got the impression he didn't like being the center of attention because he kept his head down, not looking any of us directly in the eye.

"When I was a kid, I found I could see into people's heads. Not hear their thoughts or anything like that, but I could get a peek into things that had happened to them. Like, events and stuff."

"Like memories?" I asked, hopeful.

He took another sip and nodded. "I broke this model my dad kept in his office. Some scale replica of his favorite car. My mom found out. Of course, she planned to tell him when he got home that night and I was terrified. My dad was hardcore. I wanted nothing more than to make her forget the whole thing."

Ginger leaned back in her chair. "And she did?"

Ben's gaze rose from the glass. He didn't look directly at her but focused on the table in front of where she was sitting. "It was like it'd never happened. When Dad came home he found the car in pieces on his desk and flipped. We're talking nuclear meltdown at Chernobyl—but Mom had no idea what had happened to it. They had this huge fight. I felt guilty and somehow, I gave her memory to him." Ben snapped his fingers. "Just like that, he knew everything."

Kale sat at the end of the table, away from the others, watching Ben intently. He hadn't said anything to anyone since we'd arrived, and vice versa. Truthfully, I think everyone was a little nervous having him at the cabin in his current state. Mom kept sneaking glances his way, hopeful and cautious, while Dax was less subtle. Thankfully Alex was nowhere to be seen. The last thing we needed right now was his snarky barbs and digs.

"A few months ago, I found that not only could I take and transplant memories, I had access to everything. Emotions, reflexes—there was this bully at my little brother's school. For the big stuff I need to make physical contact, but for little stuff I just need to be in the same general area." He laughed. "I made the kid piss himself."

He was talking about a little kid so I shouldn't have found it funny—but I did. Plus, he was a bully. I hated bullies. "So you're saying it's kind of like mind control?"

"I guess you could look at it that way, but it still revolves around memories. For that kid, I made him remember a time he had to take a leak—badly."

I started to ask about Ben's parents, but Kale finally spoke up. "The memories you steal—are they gone? Can you return them?"

"Steal is the wrong word, man. I don't really *take* them. Think of my ability as a copy machine. I make a copy and black out the original. I can unblock the original or wipe it out completely."

Kale stood. "Try."

Ben actually looked up and met Kale's gaze. The poor guy took one look, jumped from the seat, and visibly paled. "You want me to wipe your head clean?"

"That's not what he means," I interjected. "Someone else messed with his head. We were hoping there was something you could do to help him. Maybe unblock what they blocked."

He relaxed some and sank back into the chair. "I'm sure I can figure out what they did, but I'm not one hundred percent sure I can fix someone else's work."

"Would you be willing to try?" Mom asked. She motioned for Kale to come forward and pointed to the empty seat beside Ben. "Please?"

Ben didn't look too sure of himself, but he nodded.

Kale hesitated, like moving closer to the group might be some trick, but finally relented, eager for Ben to work his magic. "What do I need to do?"

Ben twisted so he faced Kale. He looked uncomfortable, and when he spoke, his voice had a slight wobble to it. "I guess just relax. Try to clear your mind."

The room held its breath as Ben pressed his right hand across Kale's forehead and closed his eyes. Moments ticked by, feeling like an eternity. Even Kale was restless, tapping the fingers of his right hand against the tabletop. *One. Two. Three. One Two. Three.*

"Wow," Ben breathed, eyes still closed. "Who did this?"

"What did they do?" I was out of my seat and around the table, hovering over Kale in the blink of an eye. "What can you see?"

Eyes still closed, his lips twisted into a confused scowl. "It's a little hard to decipher. I think… Wait. Say something, Dez."

"Huh?"

"Talk. Anything. Working with a theory here. Just speak."

"Um, okay," I said. "Is this a good theory or a bad one?"

Ben's hand slipped from Kale's head, and he opened his eyes. Kale did the same. "Well?"

"It's like burned pea soup in there, man."

"That's not encouraging," Kale growled. His fingers

stilled, wrapping tightly around the edge of the table until his knuckles went white. "And it also doesn't tell me anything."

"When I peek into someone's head, any memories I see usually have this kind of faint glow. Like a backlight."

"A halo?" I asked.

"Yes!" he exclaimed. "Exactly like a halo. So like I was saying, normal memories have this whitish halo. The ones in Kale's head are dark. Almost black. There are others—the ones with the white glow, too—but they're dim. Like the dark ones are pushing them out."

Kale looked away from Ben, eyes falling on me. "Why did you have her speak?"

"I noticed when she spoke, the white ones got a little brighter. It was like something was fighting to break free." Kale seemed vindicated by this answer, and nodded, "Can you make the dark ones go away?"

"No way, man. Like I said, someone else's work. But I think they might fade on their own." He nodded in my direction. "If the sound of her voice makes the real ones fight for dominance, I'd say just keep her talking. Think of her as your North Star. It looks like they'll fight their way free eventually."

Aubrey had been right. The daily meetings with Dad's Six had been to maintain control over Kale. By keeping him away from her, we were slowly breaking the hold.

• • •

Kale crossed the room to Dax's computer, then stopped, staring at the machine like he'd never seen it before. "I— What do— Where…" The CD clunked to the desktop, and Kale brought his hands to his head, fingers wrapping in his dark hair.

"What is wrong with me? Why can't I remember how to use this thing?"

I didn't know what was on the disk, and that scared me. All I wanted right now was to curl up in oblivion and sleep till next spring, but Kale was antsy because of Aubrey's claim for the truth. The minute we left the others, he asked about playing the disk. As much as I wanted to, I couldn't put it off.

Gently, I pulled his hands away and picked up the CD. "Because you've never used a computer, Kale. Your vocabulary is…different. You've spent time with Kiernan and the others so you've picked up some slang, but I guess they couldn't imprint practical knowledge. You remember watery things about people and events, but this is different. You don't remember because it's something you've never done."

I dropped the CD into the drive and gave the door a small nudge. It closed, the computer monitor blinking to life as the disk started spinning.

The moment the picture flickered to life, I knew we'd made a horrible mistake.

On the screen, Kale was chained to a wall in a small room. He wore black sweatpants and a dark gray T-shirt wet with perspiration. Weary eyes trained ahead, he stared at something off-camera with unadulterated hatred. Bruises decorated the right side of his face, and he was exhausted—it was evident in his half-lidded stare and slumped posture—but there was still a spark of fierceness to him. Determination.

To his right stood a man I'd never seen before. Wearing a white lab coat and standing impossibly tall, he had salt and pepper hair and cold, dead eyes. He motioned to someone off-camera, and a slip of a girl stepped into view. She stopped in front of Kale and cupped his face on either side. If not for the chains, it would have looked like a loving embrace. The softest touch of two people with deep feelings for each other.

Kale's eyes met hers, and his lips moved, but whatever he said was too low for the microphone to catch. A smile followed and then his eyes squeezed closed, lip twitching and body going rigid. He tried to pull away, but the chains prevented him from moving out of reach.

"Tell me the name of the girl you love," someone on the other side of the room, out of the camera's eye, said in a commanding voice. I didn't need to see him. That voice, so full of vile and lies, was embedded in my memory as sure as my own name.

Dad stepped forward, his back to the camera as Kale's eyes opened. With a taunting smile and a sigh, he said, "Deznee."

"You're making things harder on yourself by fighting the process. Mindy tells me this can be quite painful."

"Then I have nothing to fear. If there's one thing you've taught me over the years, it's to deal with pain. There's nothing you can do that will take her away from me, Cross," Kale said, voice low. *"Nothing."*

Dad's anger was evident in his stiffened shoulders and fists clenched tight. "Again," he barked. "Do it again."

I didn't realize who he was talking to until the girl took Kale's face in her hands again, this time with more force.

"What is the name of the girl you love?"

"Dez," Kale spat, eyes still closed.

The girl's fingers twitched, knotting through his hair.

"What is the name of the girl you love?" Dad asked, rage dripping from every word. I'd never wanted to physically harm anyone as much as I did him in that instant.

"Dez!" Kale screamed. A tremor ran through him, body trembling.

Mindy let go for an instant, eyes wide with surprise, but

had him back in her hands in seconds. "He shouldn't still know her," she cried. "This is impossible —"

Dad kicked a small rolling cart to his right. It wobbled, toppling to the ground with a loud clatter as metal instruments — sharp-looking ones — spilled from its insides. "Again!" he screamed. "The name of the girl you love is...?"

The sound of Kale's voice as he bellowed my name stole all the air from the room. The reason we were here, the possibility of someone walking through the door, all vanished as I fought with the picture on the screen in front of me. His voice broke, throat more than likely raw, as he screamed it. Over and over. *DezDezDez*. The force of it sent the girl backing away and made the man in the lab coat cringe.

Beside me, Kale's eyes stayed glued to the screen. I made a move to remove the disk from the drive, but he grabbed my hand, fingers wrapping tight.

Onscreen, Dad and the man huddled in the corner with the girl, who had to be Mindy. Kale had slid down the wall. He would have fallen to his knees had the chains stretched that far. Instead he was hanging, the metal cuffs digging into his already battered skin and making me sick.

"Any more and I risk destroying his mind," the girl said. She'd turned toward the camera. Long straw-colored hair and innocent brown eyes. On the outside, a normal-looking girl. On the inside? A Denazen bastard with no soul. "I could easily kill him by accident."

"Ninety-eight cannot be given Domination until I know this can be fixed. I can't risk him remembering Deznee. If he survives the drug, he'll be even more dangerous afterward than he is now."

"Are you sure you want to risk his life?" the lab-coat man asked. "One forty-three expired last night. Incompatible with the drug. He was quite strong."

Dad ignored him and nodded to the girl. "Make it work."

The screen flickered, and when it came back, everyone was standing in a different place. Dad was directly in front of Kale now, hand on his chin, tilting it toward the light. There was a glazed look in Kale's eyes. "What is the name of the girl you love?"

Kale didn't answer right away, and my heart gave a small squeeze. Eyes rolling back, his head lolled to the left as the fingers of his right hand twitched. "Blo—blond hair. Black pieces." He tried to stay upright but his knees wouldn't hold the weight. He collapsed, sending a rattle through the chains that echoed in the room. "Brown eyes…beautiful…ez…"

"This will have to do," Dad snapped, pulling his hand back. Kale's head jerked to the side as my dad stepped away and turned to Mindy. "I think I can make this work. Follow the rest of your instructions and come find me when it's done."

The screen went black.

"Kale?" His eyes hadn't moved from the screen even though the picture was gone. The look on his face scared me. "Kale, tell me what's on your mind."

Slowly, he turned to me, expression nearly ripping my heart in two. "I *remember* that day."

Hope was a fragile and dangerous thing. It had the ability to build you up higher than the clouds—and then drop you. A free-fall at a million miles an hour headed straight for solid, crushing ground. Still. I couldn't help it. "You remember?"

He stepped away from the computer. "There was someone they wanted to take away from me. Someone important. Someone *essential*." Turning to me, he frowned. "I know that I would have died for this person. To keep her safe. To keep her happy—and I know that it was you."

I reached for his hand, a swell of relief flooding through my veins, but he pulled away.

"I *know*," he continued, thumping the side of his head, then his chest directly over his heart. "But I can't *remember*. I know you now—and I have very strong feelings for you—but I don't know you from then. That part of you is a ghost, Dez. A shadow that keeps moving just out of reach. And it's driving me crazy."

22

After seeing what was on the CD, Kale was agitated and moody. I understood his frustration and hoped maybe seeing his old room might help.

"This is your room." I pushed open the door and stepped aside, a funny feeling fluttering in my chest as I realized we'd never been in here at the same time. When we moved in after the hotel burned to the ground, Kale hadn't been around long enough to actually use the room. Everything had happened so fast.

Kale followed me in and closed the door. His eyes fell to the bed, the sheets still a tangled mess from the last time I'd slept here. It'd only been a few nights ago—the same night I saw him at the Nix party in town—but it felt like years. "When was the last time I slept in here?"

I moved to the bed and pulled the edge of the blanket off the floor, then straightened the pillows. "Honestly, I don't know that you ever did. We moved in right before you—right before

I got really sick. You spent most of your time next door with me."

"Who's been staying in here?"

I felt my cheeks flush. "Me."

He sank onto the bed, eyes never leaving mine. "You were amazing tonight. Is it always like that? With us, I mean? This is going to sound insane, but it was *fun*."

I sank down beside him and nodded once, trying not to laugh. "We're a team. Our life is made of crazy, but we kinda like it that way."

He was quiet for a minute. "This is hard for me, but I can't imagine what it's like for you. I feel…something for you, but I don't really understand it. You remember me completely."

I blinked back the tears threatening to spill over and took a deep breath. "It isn't easy."

A quick glance to my right and I saw him watching me. Under normal circumstances, that kind of scrutiny from Kale would have sent shivers of anticipation through my body. Now, all I had were my memories. He quickly turned away and sighed. "Your friends don't seem too happy that I'm here."

Mom and Dax had forced Kale to cover his eyes as we approached the cabin. It was all very Batcave of them, but I could understand their caution. They couldn't take any chances. Too many innocent Sixes had taken up residence in Dax's underground shelter.

"It's not that, really. Things are tense. They're just nervous, since you've been living with the enemy for the last few months." I forced a smile. "And they're your friends, too."

He leaned closer. So close that I felt his breath against my cheek and the warmth of his skin radiating against mine. "And you?"

I swallowed. "Me?"

"Do you trust me?"

"I trust you."

"Marshal brainwashed me." He reached across and ran his index finger along the lines of my jaw. The touch brought a rush of heated memories that sent tremors through my body. But it wasn't just the physical contact. It was the sound of his voice. Deep and rich like warm caramel coffee, each word a soothing sip that sent the endorphins in my brain jumping. He could have recited the alphabet and it would have affected me just the same. "I could've faked a recovery just to get inside."

"I trust you," I repeated.

Leaning close, lips brushing my right ear, he whispered, "Then can I kiss you again?"

Can I kiss you?

I remembered a dream I'd had not long before Kale went back to Denazen. Kale and me at the top of the crane. He'd asked me the same thing right before turning into Able. I closed my eyes to keep the tears from spilling over. This wasn't me, this constantly bawling, blubbering mess of a girl. But the memory was like a shot to the heart, turning the air to sludge and making it impossible to breathe. "Please don't ask me that."

He pulled back a bit, genuinely surprised by my reaction. "I'm sorry. I—"

I leaned forward and pressed my lips to his. It was short, and bittersweet, and when I pulled away and stood, he stared at me with eyes full of wonder. It reminded me so much of that day at Curd's. When he touched me for the first time. "It's not your fault. I had this dream once. It— Know what? It doesn't matter."

I was almost to the door when he called out. "Wait."

My feet stopped moving, but I didn't turn around. I was

afraid if I looked at him again, well…I didn't know what I'd do. Cry, kiss him again, scream…

"Why don't you stay?" he said.

The invitation pulled at so many different, warring emotions. I wanted to stay. More than anything, I wanted to be by his side and never let him out of my sight again. "I'm beat. I'd only fall asleep."

The mattress creaked and I relented, turning around. He was standing now, looking between the bed and me. "So sleep here. I promise I won't try anything." He stepped around so he was in front of me. For a moment he simply stood there. Eyes on mine and lips pressed in a thin line. When he did speak, his voice was different. So much more the Kale I knew. "The truth is, no matter how much it scares me to admit it, I feel better when you're close. I don't understand it, and I can't begin to explain it, but I'm more relaxed."

How could I argue with that when I felt exactly the same way? Silly considering the situation, but still the truth.

He placed his hand over his heart, frowning. "I'm angry. I can feel it inside, eating away at me like poison. I—I don't know who or what I'm angry about, but it's easier to forget when I'm with you."

Maybe Aubrey was right. In messing with the bits inside Kale's head, they kicked a hornet's nest. "You told me once that I was your lifeline. That I calmed the storm in your head."

"I think it's true." There was so much emotion in his eyes right then. Fear and sadness. Anger. And something else. Something familiar. Kale had a way of looking at me. It was like I was the only person on earth. "Please stay?" he prodded. "I'd like it if you would talk to me. Ben is right. When I hear your voice, my head feels…lighter."

"Okay." I kicked off my sneakers as Kale did the same, and

crawled into bed, burrowing under the covers. Behind me, the mattress dipped as Kale climbed in.

"Is it okay if I hold you?"

"Sure," I said, throat thick. A moment later, the light went out and all I could hear was the soft sounds of our breath as Kale wrapped his arm around my waist and snuggled close. During the months he'd been gone, I'd lie in his bed and imagine him with me. Sometimes, in the middle of the night, I'd wake and swear I could feel him lying there beside me. Now that he was, a part of me was terrified that any minute I'd wake up and the whole thing would be nothing more than a dream.

"Tell me something. About me. Tell me your favorite thing."

I thought about it for a moment, but it didn't take long. "You have the most amazing soul." Rolling, I turned onto my other side so I faced him. Even though it was dark, there was a small red glow from the alarm clock on the dresser behind him. It gave off just enough light for me to see the outline of his face. "This anger you feel? I think it's because of everything that happened to you. You went through hell. Denazen took you not long after you were born. They treated you like an animal. They used you as a weapon. And you know what? You still turned out to be the most amazing person I've ever met."

I took a deep breath, struggling to keep my voice even. "You see yourself as a monster, Kale, but you're not. You didn't let what happened to you change who you were on the inside. You asked me once what it was about you that I loved. And I'll say it again. It's your soul, Kale. It's unlike anyone else's."

"I don't remember any of it," he said softly after a few minutes went by. "The only memories I have of Denazen are hazy but don't involve anything like that."

"They're fake. If you remembered what they did to you,

you would have killed them all. That's probably why you're having such a hard time dealing with the way you feel. The anger is still there but you don't know where to aim it."

"Maybe it's better that I don't remember, then."

I'd never thought about that. In all this mess, Kale not remembering his life at Denazen was sort of a blessing. I knew he'd still had nightmares. To be free from that was something I wanted for him. But if Ben Simmons was right and this would all fade, then those memories would return.

And deep down, I knew they should.

"I was at a party one night with some friends. We were tipsy and playing some oddball drinking game—Twenty-seven Questions, it's called. You're asked a question and you either answer or drink. One of the questions my friend asked me was if I could change one thing in my life—*anything*—what would it be. I gave it some thought, and when I saw her at school the next day I told her there was nothing I would change."

"Why?"

"Seems stupid, right? I mean, hell, we live in a world where there could very well be a Six that could turn back time or something. It wasn't as crazy a question as my friend thought. I fell asleep that night thinking about it. I had a horrible relationship with my dad. I thought my mom was dead. Alex and I had just broken up... There were a million things I could have—should have—wanted to change."

"I don't understand why you gave the question this much thought. It was for a game, right?"

I smiled. "See, that's the kind of thing you'd say. You're getting better already." I took a deep breath. "There was a point to this, though, and that point is, no. You *wouldn't* be better off not remembering. I won't lie. The time you spent at Denazen was horrific."

"You care for me, correct?"

I draped my arm across his waist, letting my index finger slip into the back loop of his jeans. "I do."

"Then why would you want me to remember?"

"Because it made you who you are. It's the same reason I gave my friend the answer I did the next day at school. I wouldn't want to change anything because I was perfectly happy with the person I'd become. To change even the tiniest detail of my life would ruin the balance. I wouldn't be me."

"That is a very wise answer," he said softly. "But I wonder if you would have the same response were you asked now. Is there still nothing you would change?"

"It's funny. In those first few days after you left, it's actually all I thought of. What would have happened if I hadn't confessed that I was dying? If I'd just gone straight to Dad. You wouldn't be sitting here looking at me like I was a stranger."

"And you wouldn't be sitting here," he said sagely.

"Touché."

"Tell me how we met."

I couldn't help the smile that slipped across my lips. "I was on my way home from a party, and you had run from Denazen agents. You fell at my feet, then took my sneakers."

"I took your sneakers?"

"In your defense, you were barefoot and leaving a trail of dead dirt through the forest. It made you easy to track."

"Trail of dead dirt? I don't understand."

"Your ability used to be…different. Before they gave you Domination you had no control." I shifted so I could lean on my elbow and ran my other hand from his shoulder to his wrist. "The only way it worked was through skin-to-skin contact—and there wasn't any way to shut it off. Until we met, you'd never touched another living person."

He, in turn, reached out to trace the line of my jaw. "But *we* could touch?"

I was thankful for the dark because I felt an involuntary flush rise in my cheeks as I remembered those first moments in Curd's basement, and then many more after that. "Yeah. We could. I was the first."

For a moment he didn't say anything. Then the warmth from his hand disappeared, leaving an icy chill as a growl cut the silence. "When we're together, it always feels like there's something being held just out of my reach." He sat up, facing me. "My insides tell me I know you. The way you set me at ease by simply being close. But my mind can't *see* you. I can't remember anything about our life together."

"That's not true," I said, sitting up as well. "Back at the airport you said something to me—you probably didn't even realize it at the time. When I said I would mimic the three of us so we could walk right out the front door."

"And I knew you couldn't. Not without..." He let out a frustrated hiss. "Not without something. I can't see it. I can't *remember*."

"I know how you feel. It's frustrating and painful."

He raised my hand and held it tight against his face. I bit back a sigh as his warmth coursed through me. "Even if Simmons is wrong and the memories never come back, it doesn't matter. I'm already falling for you, Dez." He pulled me back down to the bed and wrapped his arms around me. "Whatever it was I did to steal your heart when we met, I'll do it again. I swear."

I didn't bother correcting him. He never lost it.

23

"Where is he?" Alex asked as I settled on the couch with an oversize cup of coffee. Mom sat across from me next to Dax, and Vince had his nose buried in the business section on the other end while downing a colossal stack of pancakes doused with an unhealthy amount of maple syrup. I'd never seen anyone eat as much sweet stuff as him. My teeth hurt just being in the same room.

"In the gym. He's dealing with a lot of...anger." I sipped the coffee. There wasn't nearly enough sugar, but I'd left the jar on the counter in the kitchen. I was too lazy to go back and grab it, so I sucked it up.

Kale and I had fallen asleep in his room and stayed that way clear until eight the next morning. We'd talked for a while—mainly about the way things had been before he went back to Denazen. He questioned me extensively about his early years there but was disappointed when I couldn't give him any details. I suggested he talk to Mom, but he didn't seem eager. I was pretty sure it had to do with the slightly cool reception he'd been given upon arrival.

I woke to find him watching me with an odd expression. When I asked if he remembered something, he simply replied *not exactly* and excused himself to the gym.

"Where's Ben?" But what I really wanted to know was, *How's Ben?* Sane or raving nut job?

Mom rested her elbows on the table—something she only did when Ginger wasn't around. For a cranky, jagged old woman, she took table manners seriously. "Ginger's with him now. We also managed to find Andrea Marko and Kayla Dean."

"Kayla Dean is showing signs of decline," Dax said through a mouthful of bagel. Apparently everyone took advantage of Ginger's absence. Last time someone talked with their mouth full, Ginger whipped out her cane. "Not as bad as Ben, but it seems to be increasing. We're gonna have to do something soon."

"What about the others? There were twelve on the list, right?"

"We have Henley Walker—Brandt—and Sarah Milburn has been confirmed dead by a contact in Kansas. The only ones we have no solid information on are Thom Morris and Mark Wells."

"Wells is dead," Kale said from the doorway. Everyone looked up as he stepped cautiously into the room. Turning to me, he said, "The night at the party. The guy outside. That was Wells."

The couple. The first time I'd seen Kale's newly improved ability at work.

"Then that rounds out the list," Dax said. "Now we need to focus on finding Penny Mills."

Crap. After the chaos at the airport and then coming back here to crash, I'd never gotten a chance to tell them about Penny. Or maybe I was trying to avoid it. If I didn't say it out loud, then maybe I could pretend it never happened. "Yeah... about that."

All eyes in the room swiveled to me. Even Vince looked up from the paper, stopping mid-chew on a particularly large mouthful of pancakes. A drop of syrup fell from his lips to the plate.

"Kale and I found Penny Mills."

There was a collective gasp, followed by everyone speaking at once.

"She's dead," I finished, thankfully shocking them into stunned silence. The admission was like swallowing a mouthful of glass. I managed to get the words out with a straight face, calm and without breaking down, but inside the guilt was crushing me.

"And she was dead when you got there?" Mom asked.

"No. She was killed shortly after we arrived. When they used her blood to make the Domination serum, it connected her to everyone who got it. Before they messed with Kale's head, she showed him where to find her. Kale, unfortunately, led them right to her. Denazen implanted a tracker—"

Dax jumped from his seat. "Shit!"

"It's fine." I waved my nearly empty cup. Really? Did he think I was that stupid? "We got the tracker out—*obviously*. He's off the radar."

Dax sat down and seemed to relax a little, but not Mom. If anything, she looked more worried. "That doesn't make sense. They needed her. Why would they kill her?"

I took a deep breath. "They didn't do it on purpose. They were aiming for me." I glanced over at Kale, still standing by the door, and remembered what he'd said about asking questions. "They got paranoid, I think. Dad was probably worried that if I was with Kale, he'd start remembering—which he has. I guess they figured it was safer if I was just dead. But Kale pushed me out of the way and Penny was standing behind me. She's dead because I'm alive."

Dax frowned. "It's not your fault, Dez. Denazen is to blame for this, not you."

It was sweet of him to say, but the facts were the facts.

Mom let out a breath and tapped the table twice. "This means it's going to be ten times harder." She turned to me, and I had to look away. I couldn't stand the fear in her eyes. She was worried I wouldn't get the cure in time—if at all. "With Mills dead, our only chance is the blood Denazen has. Finding it in time is going to be—"

"Kale knows where it is." Ginger appeared behind him in the doorway, expression grim. Brandt was with her, looking bleary-eyed and rundown. He'd slept a lot since arriving at the cabin and it worried me. I knew he technically couldn't die, but I also knew he didn't want to jump again. When he jumped, the person whose body he took over, was just... gone. "It's in a lab under a facility called Zendean Industries. It's a pharmaceutical company about an hour from here that Denazen is using as a front. Like the law firm."

"Zendean is where the Henley suit came from," Brandt said, pushing past her and into the room. I didn't miss how he nudged Kale forward as he went, forcing him to step inside. Brandt took a seat on the couch next to Mom. "That's where I was undercover, trying to find a cure. I'm still in contact with someone there. I found out that a week after I left, Cross and some of his Sixes took over the facility. It's where Kiernan and Kale have been staying."

"Since Brandt is on the outs with these guys, I suppose *Kale* can conveniently get us in, right?" Alex said. He leaned back in his chair, eyes affixed to Kale's, and grinned. "Pick a side, Reaper. This back-and-forth shit is giving me a headache."

Kale's eyes darkened and he turned to me with a sneer. "Are he and I friends?"

"Not even close."

"Good." In one swift move, Kale shot forward and kicked the legs out from Alex's chair, sending him to the ground with a loud *thud*. "Don't talk to me."

Brandt snickered. "Huh. You're right," he said to me. "It *is* funny." My cousin and Alex had been friends until he *cheated* on me. After that, things between them turned icy. Now, even though the truth behind what Alex had done was out, Brandt hadn't really forgiven him.

Ginger sighed and pushed past them, settling in her armchair. Eyes trained on both boys, she said, "I didn't miss the bickering."

I did my best to stifle a giggle. She might not have, but I sure had.

Kale made his way around the coffee table and settled next to me on the couch. "We talked to Ben again this morning," he said, glancing at Ginger. The expression on his face said it all. "He has sporadic moments of lucidity, but overall, he's not coherent anymore."

"From what we gather, it started the day he got to France. He flew out there to see a friend, but when things got bad she abandoned him. Somehow he managed to board his plane back to the U.S., and we all know what happened from there." Ginger sighed.

"Did he say anything useful? He couldn't help at all?"

Kale frowned. "No."

I downed the rest of my coffee and thumped the cup on the table. "We need that blood."

"Even if we find it, there's still a problem," Brandt said.

I let my head fall into my hands. "Isn't there always?"

Brandt chuckled, but when I picked up my head to look at him, his expression was serious. "They've been working around the clock to produce Domination. My contact on the inside says they've used nearly all the blood."

Kale glanced from me to Brandt. "If we're lucky, there'll be enough left to cure one person."

"But the Domination serum has the blood in it, right?" Dax tapped the edge of the table and Mom grabbed his hand. They were so perfectly in sync with each other. "What if we got our hands on some of that?"

"It's a possibility—and it might be a last resort—but there's not much in it. If that Wentz guy can make it work, it might be enough for someone who hasn't already entered the decay state but someone who's already showing signs? I don't know." Brandt looked away. "Plus, there's the risk. Only half the people given the drug survive. From what I've heard, it's not pretty…"

"It's better than nothing," Mom said coolly.

"What about Reaper's blood?" Alex piped up. "He's been given the serum. Couldn't we make a fix using him?"

Mom shook her head. "We don't know how Domination affected him. Before he was given the drug, Kale's blood used to keep Sixes compliant. I don't think it's worth the risk."

Kale nodded, resolved. "Getting the drug will be slightly easier than getting the blood, but I think we can do both. Dez can take the blood and the others can get Domination."

"No way," I said, and for the second time that morning every eye swiveled in my direction. I was starting to feel like a neon spotlight followed me everywhere I went. At one point in my life I would have reveled in it. Now? It was getting annoying.

Alex jumped to his feet, snapping, "Why the hell not?" while Kale slammed a hand down on the arm of the couch and said, "Yes, you will."

"Whoa." Jade appeared in the doorway. She looked from Kale to Alex before her gaze fell on me with one of her usual sneers. "Looks like everything's back to normal."

"Who is this?" Kale asked, looking her up and down. He didn't seem impressed, which gave me all sorts of warm fuzzies.

Jade's lips split with a wicked grin as she crossed the room, wedging herself between Kale's chair and mine. "It hurts that you don't remember me. We shared something very special."

He looked from her to me, then back again. "Incredibly hard to believe. I don't find redheads the least bit attractive. Maybe if you looked more like Dez I could see it." Unlike the old Kale, who would have simply spoken blunt and to the point, this version added the tiniest bit of a barb—and I loved him even more for it.

Jade opened her mouth, then closed it again, retreating to the coffee pot without another word.

Ginger slammed her cane against the table. The sound was like a shot through the room, ending the bickering in an instant. "While I suspect that falling into old patterns might help Kale feel more acclimated, this is not what I had in mind. Could we possibly focus, people? Or do I have to start swinging?"

I sucked in a deep breath. "I think Ben should get the blood."

"Of course you do," Alex hissed, flicking a hand in Kale's direction. "But what good is Rain Man's memory going to be if

Domination kills you?"

"Ben can't do anything to help Kale—try to keep up. This has nothing to do with that," I snapped. "He's the worst off. He should get it. If not him, then Brandt."

"I'm not taking anything till I know you're okay," Brandt said. There was no argument in his tone. Only simple resolve. It was fine. He didn't need to agree. I'd cram it down his throat while he slept if I had to. "Besides, I don't need it. We went over this, remember? Technically I can't die."

"No, you can't," I shot back. "But who exactly are you going to jump into? Feel like picking someone from this room?"

Brandt's eyes widened and he didn't respond.

"You're being stubborn," Alex interjected.

"*Stubborn*? What gives me the right to take it? I'm no better than any of the rest of them."

Alex looked like he wanted to argue, but he locked his jaw and turned away. He had to know I was right. I wasn't any more important than the others. The guaranteed cure should go to the one furthest along. Right now, that was Ben Simmons.

"This isn't the issue right now," Mom said. "We need to get our hands on both the blood and the drug before a decision can be made. Not to mention Franklin Wentz will need to produce a working cure."

"How is he, anyway? I still haven't seen him."

Brandt stretched. "He's locked away in a lab Ginger had set up for him. I saw him this morning. He's trying to come up with an alternative cure. Something that doesn't need Penny Mills's blood. Not having any luck, though."

Mom turned and swiveled her gaze between Kale and Brandt. "How do we get in?"

Brandt hesitated. I didn't like the look in his eyes. I was all too familiar with it. "I have an idea—but I don't think Dez will like it."

"Not a good way to start," I mumbled.

"I've been gone a while now. I don't know where they're keeping it, and my contact is only on the outside edge of the inner circle. But..."

I narrowed my eyes, willing him to stop right there. I knew exactly where he was going with this, and he was right. I didn't like it.

"Kale could go back," he continued cautiously, watching me from the corner of his eye. "I'm betting he knows where the vial is. He can get it and get out."

I expected everyone to jump on the objection train but no one said a word. I had to be the voice of sanity? *Really?* Fine.

"Bad call. Kale has spent too much time with me. No way they'll trust him. And what happens when they expect him to start up daily sessions with their Resident brain-basher? How will he keep her from going in and figuring out that he remembered? Not to mention the chance of her scrambling things up again." I clapped my hand for dramatic effect. "Oh, and we removed his tracker. How do you propose we explain that?"

"Dez makes some good points," Mom said. "If they start to play with his memories again, then we lose the last chance we've got to save the kids." She glanced at me. "That's not a risk I'm willing to take."

"Agreed," Ginger said with a *click* of her cane. I couldn't help noticing how everyone relaxed when she set it down beside her chair. A room full of people with extraordinary abilities and we were all afraid of an old woman with a cane.

"It's risky," Brandt agreed. "But in theory, he wouldn't be there long enough for it to matter. Get in. Get the blood. Get out."

I sighed. "Because anything is ever that easy? Too many things could go wrong. And like I said, how do you explain the tracker?"

Brandt frowned. "I *said* you wouldn't like it. As for the tracker, I'm not sure."

"Kale *should* go back—but not alone," someone said from the other end of the table.

Everyone's attention turned to Vince.

"I've been here a while, and I owe you all a great debt. First, for coming to warn me, then taking me in when I had no safe haven." He set down the paper. "I want to see these people fall just as much as the rest of you. They took my life from me. Everything I've worked so hard for—gone."

Ginger watched him carefully for a moment before leaning back. There was something in her eyes that made me twitchy. I couldn't put my finger on it, but she either didn't trust Vince or knew what he was going to say and didn't agree. "So what do you suggest?"

"Kale needs to go back. I think that much is a given. But he should go in with support." Vince nodded toward Mom. "Sue's right. If he goes in alone, everything we've done in regards to getting him back could be too easily undone. He needs a show of good faith…"

"Good faith?" Kale asked, suspicious.

Kale didn't understand what Vince was getting at. I did— and it was kind of brilliant in a scary, impulsive, and reckless sort of way.

"An offering," I said, rushing on before I gave it too much thought. "Me. I'll go."

24

Everyone's mouth opened in protest, but I held up my hand. Sure. Now they spoke up.

"I know, I know. This is crazy, but hear me out at least, okay? I think Vince is on to something here. Dad is a douche but he's smart. He's going to figure Kale's already been corrupted. Think about it. There's no way they didn't see us together at the airport. Hell—the whole place saw us. If he shows up back at home base, they're going to wanna be sure he hasn't switched sides. But," I said, taking a deep breath. "If he shows up toting the one thing Dad wants—me—and says it was all an act, I bet my board they won't question him. Denazen wants to silence the Underground. If he thinks I can tell him where we've been hiding, and that Kale is still loyal, he's going to shit rainbows of happy."

Mom frowned, apparently not sold on the idea. "What about the Resident using her ability to keep Kale's memories at bay?"

"Like Brandt said, hopefully we won't need that much time," Vince said. He turned to Kale with an encouraging nod. "Stall them. Make excuses. Tell them you let Dez remove the tracker to gain her trust."

Dead silence.

"I don't like it," Kale said quietly. "But she's right. They're less likely to suspect something's wrong if I don't show up empty-handed. Without, as Dez said, a show of good faith, I might not be able to get anywhere near the blood." He turned to Vince and nodded. "There's something very familiar about you. Are we friends?"

"Vince was the last person we visited over the summer to warn about Denazen," I said, smiling. "See? Things are starting to come back."

"That must be it," Kale said, but something about the way he watched Vince didn't leave me convinced.

Unfortunately, now wasn't the time to worry about it because Alex was going berserk. "This proves you've flipped to the other side of the moon," he growled at Kale, stomping his foot. "There's no way you'd let her do this if you were in your right mind."

"*Let me?*" I choked. "Are you serious? Since when—"

"I won't let anything happen to her." Kale stood and leaned across the coffee table, expression loaded.

"Why? Because you *love* her? You can't even remember how much you hate me, and brother man, that's saying something."

"I may not remember any of you, but let me guess. You're the ex, right? The one who can't let go?" He glanced back at me and I fought a shiver. There was a gleam of something feral in his eyes. Something possessive. It was a hint of the old Kale mingled with something new. Something darker. "Seems like she made her choice."

"You're a dick," Alex spat.

"Something tells me I feel the same way about you," Kale countered, straightening and folding his arms.

"And something tells me this is going to lead to a migraine," I said, standing. No one looked happy, and I couldn't blame them, but we were kind of low on options and time was running out. "Like it or not, this is our best bet."

"We need to move quickly," Kale agreed. "She's showing signs of decay."

I groaned and let my head fall back into my hands.

"I knew you didn't feel that cut at the party," Alex snapped.

I picked my head up. "We knew it was inevitable. My ability already spiked and changed. It was only a matter of time."

"How bad is it?" Brandt asked. He looked a little pale.

I tried to shrug it off. "It's not. Little things here and there—nothing major. Some issues like keeping focus and"—I turned to Alex—"*occasionally* a lack of physical pain."

Kale frowned. "It will only go downhill from here."

"But walking straight into hell?" Mom practically squealed, frantic. Well, Mom's version—which looked a lot like annoyed with a side of homicidal anger. It had taken some time, but I pretty much had her moods and expressions pinned, not that she had many. She shot Vince a furious scowl, then turned it on Kale. "I know what goes on behind those walls. *You* may not remember, but *I* do. The idea of letting my daughter willingly walk into the devil's den isn't something I can agree to."

"Do you think I want to go?"

"Yes." She folded her arms and hit me with her best *Mom stare*. She had perfected it over the last few months. She'd gotten pretty good, too. "I think you probably see it as a challenge."

Ouch. She knew me so well. But she had to see it was more than that. This was about survival. Adrenaline junkie or not, even I wasn't willing to skip through Denazen's doors without a really good life or death reason—and that's what this was now. Life or death. Mine and a whole lot of others, too.

"Last call for brilliant ideas." I looked at Mom. "If you can come up with something better, believe me, I'd be thrilled to hear it."

But she had nothing. I could see it in her eyes. Defeat and, ultimately, acceptance.

Looking back to Kale, I said, "How should we do this?"

He didn't answer me. Only stared. I'll admit it. In that moment, I started having doubts. There was something foreign in his eyes. A spark of something I didn't recognize. It was dark, but worse than that, it was angry—and I didn't know if that anger was directed at the situation or me.

• • •

"Are you scared?"

Everyone had gone their separate ways, leaving Kale and me alone in the hall. I started walking, too antsy to stay in one place. "I'd be crazy not to be, right?"

"I won't force you to do this," he said softly. "We can try to think of another way to get the vial."

"There is no other way."

"Agreed."

A bitter laugh escaped my lips. I couldn't help it. "Alex was actually right about one thing. *My* Kale would never have agreed to this."

He didn't answer right away, and when I turned to look at

him, his expression was a cross between angry and stricken. "I don't remember what we had—yet—but I know now in my heart, in my soul, that I *am* your Kale."

I reached over and ran my fingers across his cheek. He felt the same. The same electric tingles shot through my body each time we touched, and that dizzy, falling-into-oblivion feeling overcame me each time our eyes met, but there was something else. An almost scary, raw gleam that reminded me of darkness. "Are you?"

"I'm different than I was—and maybe I'll never be quite the same—but the one thing I'm sure of… The one thing I know without a doubt in my heart is that I'm yours. I feel it with every breath I take, Dez. From that moment behind Ashley Conner's house, I felt it bubbling inside each time I looked at you. And if you and the others feel like I'm being careless by bringing you to Marshal, then think again." He took my hands. "Maybe the old me wouldn't have agreed to this because he was scared. I'm not scared. I think we make an amazing team. Together, I know we can do this. You're the most able person I know."

"One hell of a pep talk," I said with a nervous giggle.

He started to say something, the hint of a smile tugging at the right corner of his lip, but someone down the hall let out a terrified scream. We bolted toward the sound, rounding the corner of the last room at the end of the hall.

"What the hell?" I snapped, busting into the room.

Lu was on the ground, scooting along the far wall as Ben loomed above.

"Y'all watch yourselves! He's lost it."

Ben whirled around with a sick grin, and I had to force myself not to look away. He was pale as paper, eyes sunken and bruised. At the corner of his mouth, a thin trickle of blood trailed down, collecting at the tip of his chin. Every few seconds a tremor would run through him, shaking his entire body.

"Bubbles have come to make it all better, aye?" Lu forgotten, he advanced a step in our direction. Rapping his knuckles against the side of his head, he said, "The swirly soup in there is all amiss. All sorts of holes like cheese." He froze, then let go with a bout of hysterical laugher before exclaiming, "Like Swiss!"

Kale stepped in front of me, black gathering at his fingertips, but I pushed him aside. "No way. He's sick, remember? We can save him. We just need to get the cure." I inclined my head toward the door. "Go. Make the call you need."

Kale's eyes went wide. "You want me to leave you here with him?"

I turned to Ben, whose expression had changed, and pulled out the chair in front of Lu's desk. "Take a seat, Ben. It's gonna be okay."

After a moment of hesitation, he nodded and sank down. "The bubbles in my brain are hurting me," he whined.

"I know." I turned to Kale. "See? We're fine. Go—and let Ginger know we're probably going to have to keep Ben quarantined for now. I'll meet you back in the common room."

He didn't look thrilled about it, but he left.

I stepped around the chair and held my hand out to Lu. Her hair was sticking up and the sleeve of her hideous pink sweatshirt had been torn, but otherwise she looked fine. "You okay?"

She let me help her up. "Right as country rain."

"What happened?"

She waved a hand back and forth in front of Ben's face. He didn't so much as flinch. She stepped away and fell back on her bed. "He came in and just stopped in the doorway lookin' kind of like this. Then he yelled something about soup and charged me."

I remembered all too clearly the encounter with Fin as the Sanctuary began to burn. The guy who'd attacked us had been barely human. "It's the drug—I've seen it before."

Her eyes were wide. "This is normal?"

"Well, I don't know about *normal*, but this is what happens." I snuck a peek at Ben. He was silent and staring at the wall. The tremors seemed to have subsided. "That's what would happen to us if we didn't get the cure—which we will. Don't worry."

Lu sighed and looked at the clock above the door. She seemed sad all of a sudden. Folding her hands in her lap, she said, "You're a good egg, Dez. I like you. I wish we could have gotten to know each other."

"We have plenty of time. When this is all—" It was in that moment I remembered the conversation we had her first night here. It was also in that moment Ben let out a feral roar and flew from his chair, straight at Lu.

It was over before I could even blink. She never tried moving from his path. Ben's hands were a blur, wrapping around Lu's neck. There was a horrific sound—the almost echoing crack of a brittle branch—and then silence.

Three seconds. Possibly four. That's all it had taken. I hadn't even had the opportunity to try and stop it.

Lu's eyes were wide yet unsurprised as she wobbled for a moment, then fell sideways across the bed. It was pointless—the whole thing was over and done—but I screamed it anyway. "No!"

It wouldn't help Lu. It *couldn't* help Lu. But it did remind Ben that there was someone else in the room.

25

Ben's lip twitched with the slightest hint of a smile before he charged.

I managed to sidestep him—barely—but ended up tripping on the corner of the rug in my haste. I went down hard, the side of my head kissing the corner of the small dresser. Stars exploded behind my eyes and the floor tilted sideways as the room began to swirl.

I tried to roll onto my side but a heavy weight on my chest prevented movement. "You're just like the others," Ben said with a snicker. "Beautiful and deadly and made up of bubbles." He leaned close, yanking a chunk of my hair aside so he could whisper in my ear. "I'm onto you, though, Bubble Girl. You can't have the soft stuff inside my head!"

"Ben, please…" The room still spun but things were getting clearer. I sucked in a deep breath and tried to push him off with no success. For such a scrawny guy, he sure as hell was heavy. "You're sick. You're not the kind of guy who goes around hurting people."

Although I was pretty sure Lu would have had a different opinion on that.

"Self-preservation," he snapped. All the amusement in his expression was gone, replaced now by something dark and unreasonable. "If I wipe you away, you won't be able to hurt me anymore."

"Wipe me—" And then I understood—he intended to wipe my mind.

And honestly? I freaked the hell out.

Bucking and kicking, my arms flailed in every direction. A chunk of hair, a patch of skin—anything that would shift his weight and allow me to wriggle free. But the way he was on me didn't allow for any advantage. I couldn't move much and it was hard to breathe. Playing the distress card turned my stomach—but I had enough common sense to know when I needed help. So I did the one thing I blasted movie starlets for doing—I called for help from the big strong man.

"Kale!" Over and over, I screamed for him, but he didn't come. Of course not. I'd sent him away. Assured him there was nothing to worry about.

Ben's hands clamped around my head, the tips of his fingers digging through hair to reach my scalp. The pressure was enough to make me scream. In fact, I did. I let out a howl that probably could have shattered glass just as another voice rang out.

"What the fu— Shit! Dez!" Alex.

I gasped for air, on the verge of praying for death to come swiftly. Every second Ben's hands stayed attached to my head, the pressure continued to build. Scenes—memories—rose like a dust storm in my mind. Each one I focused on—Dad screaming about me breaking curfew, a particularly bad book report in eighth grade English, ten minutes in heaven with Steve Gander at my first co-ed party—exploded with the tiniest of pops, stealing what little air was in my lungs and disappearing forever.

Something above me shifted, and suddenly there was air. Lots and lots of glorious air. I threw myself sideways, coughing, in time to see Alex haul Ben off the floor and fling him toward the bed.

"What the hell happened?" Alex helped me off the floor.

Obviously he hadn't paid attention when I told him Ben needed the cure more than I did. "Supremacy decline. Lu…"

When he didn't answer, I followed his gaze to the bed. Ben sat there, skin pale as paper, staring down at Lu. His lips moved, but no sound came out.

Alex took a step closer. "Is she—"

"She knew," I whispered, keeping my eyes on Ben. If I didn't look—didn't blink—then I wouldn't cry. I wasn't ready to subscribe to Ginger's school of thought—don't ask, don't tell—but it seemed to me that the Sixes with an inside line to the future had more to deal with than anything I'd ever want to consider. "She told me when we first met that she was going to die."

"And she just accepted it?" Alex turned back to the bed, angry.

And that was it. The last thing I truly remember in detail. I was there, talking to Alex, and a blur of white and blue came at us from behind. The room dipped sideways and a sharp pain bloomed on the right side of my head, just a few inches from my eye.

There was a scream—something I'd never forget for as long as I lived, and then, there was nothing…

• • •

"She's okay," someone said. He sounded muffled and far away. "I think she's okay." It was Dax.

"Back away. Give her some damn room." Ginger. Definitely Ginger. There was no mistaking that bark, along with the distinct sound of her cane tapping the floor.

"She's right," I mumbled, opening my eyes. Kale, who was on the floor behind me, helped me sit up. "Kinda hard to breathe with you guys sucking up all the air. What happened?"

No one answered.

"Anyone feel free to jump in," I tried again. "Alex?"

My heart gave a squeeze as I looked to the bed where Lu's form was draped with a blue afghan. Peeking out from the edge was a single finger adorned with a pink plastic mood ring. On the floor a few feet to the right, another body lay still beneath a sheet.

No. It was the word that repeated over and over again inside my head. Like a CD on skip. *NoNoNoNo.*

I shoved Kale away and rose up onto my knees, crawling several feet before falling back. The room started to swim. "It can't — "

Kale was right there beside me, trying to pull me away, but I wouldn't be moved.

"Alex— He— " And that was all. I couldn't push any more words past my lips.

"It's not him," he said quietly. "It's Simmons."

It was horrible, and I knew in the back of my mind I should be appalled, but the joy that swept through me was overwhelming. Alex and I had our differences, but a part of me would always love him.

"I was on my way back. I made the call. You weren't in the living room so I came here." He cupped my face, thumb passing lightly under my eye to catch a tear. "He was on top of Alex when I entered. I separated them. I hit him, but not hard. He was fine—and then he just fell down."

"Heart failure," Dax said, frowning. "His body couldn't fight it anymore—that would be my guess."

"Insanity then death," I said with a shiver. "Where's Alex?"

"By the time I arrived, Alex had stopped screaming. I pulled Ben off but I think I was too—"

"No," I snapped, turning to Mom. "Where is he? Where is Alex?"

"They're doing everything they can."

• • •

"Hey," someone said from the doorway.

I rolled my eyes. Jade. "Don't you knock?"

She snorted and closed the door behind her. "You wouldn't have answered. Would you?"

"Of course not. Maybe that should be a hint?"

She settled in the chair by my desk, picked up my favorite bottle of nail polish—Passion Purple—and started painting her nails. After a moment, she asked, "Where's Kale?"

"Hoping his lack of memory gives you another chance to play kissy face?"

"Please," she said, waving the bottle in my direction. "It was obvious before all this went down that the boy has no taste. He picked you."

I sighed. "Was there something you actually wanted, or did you just come in here to piss me off?"

She flipped her hair but avoided my gaze. "Just wanted to

see how you were holding up."

Jade and I hadn't become friends over the past few months—I doubted that would ever happen—but our relationship had warmed to cordial. Most of the time. In the beginning, right after Kale went back, she'd bring me coffee in the middle of the night, sometimes just sitting with me in silence until dawn. We never spoke about it and I'd never thanked her, but really, I think she liked it that way.

"It's getting better. He's starting to remember. Little by little, I think."

"What about you? How are you *feeling*?"

It was funny. I didn't feel the need to sugarcoat things with Jade. Maybe because I'd convinced myself she really didn't care. "The decline is starting to show. Nothing major yet, but it's there."

"I met the scientist guy. Wentz. He's…different."

I looked up. "Different?"

"He introduced himself—then immediately after assured me he loved animals."

"Um, okay."

She finished painting her right hand and moved on to the left. "Yeah. The brilliant ones are always a little weird."

It was Jade's way of telling me not to worry, that we'd find a cure. While I wasn't sure I believed it at this point, I appreciated the gesture. "Don't you have something else to do? Other people's guys to chase? Small children to scare?"

She screwed the cap onto the polish and held her hand up in admiration. Without a word, she went to the door and pulled it open. "I can see it in his eyes, you know. Whenever he looks at you."

"What?"

"He might not remember everything, but his heart does."

And she was gone.

. . .

I'd asked Kale to stop for a moment so I could get it together. A part of me demanded I make him turn back. A little voice telling me this was the very definition of insanity. I'd infiltrated Denazen once disguised as Dad's head interviewer, Mercy. I'd been lucky and managed to get myself—and Kale—out alive. This time I wasn't so sure. I was going in as myself. And aside from being one of their Supremacy science projects, I'd done more than my fair share to piss Dad off. I had no doubt he was looking for a little payback.

When Kale and I left the cabin, Alex still hadn't woken up. Without Ben's ability, there was no way to know the true extent of the damage until he did. Ginger assured me his vitals were strong and other than a few bumps and bruises, he was fine. Physically, at least.

Sure. Fine—except half his brain might very well have been sucked out.

"I'll get you out of there—*with* the vial. I swear," Kale said.

"I believe you." But would I be in one piece when he did?

"I know this is hard, especially with everything that just happened."

I was in love with Kale. That would never change. But I loved Alex, too. It was a different kind of love—it always had been, even if I hadn't realized it at the time—but he was important to me. Still, there were things that needed to be done. Life didn't stop. My future wasn't the only one hanging in the balance. Brandt and the others counted on me. I wouldn't let them down. "It's fine. We can do this." I turned to him. "We *will* do this."

"You're incredibly brave."

If I was so brave, then why was I so close to telling him to turn the car around?

"I'm going to need you to trust me. Completely. You understand I need to make this look real, correct? That means treating Roz—"

"Kiernan," I said between clenched teeth. I knew exactly what he was talking about, and of all the horrors that waited for me inside Denazen, that was the one I might have the most trouble swallowing. Kiernan and him. Together.

"Roz," he insisted, shaking his head. "There can't be any slipups. She's Roz to me. Always has been."

Even though I wanted to argue, he had a point.

"Dez, before we go in, I need to tell you something."

I turned toward the window and squeezed both eyes closed for a second. My chest felt tight. I had a pretty good idea about where this was going, and if it were possible, I would have jumped from the car and run as far—and as fast—as my legs would carry me. I knew the conversation was coming, but I didn't want to do it now. Not here. Not after everything that had just happened. "Please. Don't—"

"I need you to understand how it was. They made me believe I loved her. I didn't feel it—I never felt it—but I was lost. Floating. I needed something to anchor me."

"So you slept with her," I finished for him. He wasn't going to come out and say it, and I'd never been a bush beater.

"Once. But it's not like you think. When I woke up I was angry—furious—and I didn't know why. I couldn't remember anything. That rage was all I had. I clung to it and it started to tear me apart. She was there with me and I felt like I was drowning. We started to argue, and..."

"So the fact that you had angry sex with my sister is

supposed to make me feel better about it?"

"No—"

"Why are you even telling me? And seriously, doing it *now*? Not the smartest thing you've ever done." I'd suspected after I'd seen him kiss Kiernan at the party. Her comment to me before Kale came in—*he's a screamer*—made sense now, and even though the whole thing felt like a bomb had gone off inside my chest, could I really blame Kale? Logic told me no.

My heart said yes.

"The last thing I want is to hurt you. I'm telling you," he said slowly, and with the smallest hint of anger, "because I have to make it appear like nothing's changed. We're going to appear…close, and I don't want you to think—"

"That you like it?"

He growled. "Do you always do that? Cut me off when I'm trying to talk?"

I shrugged.

"I don't want you to think it means anything." He grabbed my chin and forced me to look at him. "That it *ever* meant anything. I didn't know myself then, and I may not be fully aware at the moment, but my memories *are* starting to return. I know what I want. And what I don't."

"So you're apologizing in case you have to do it again?"

His face grew pale. "Of course not. I—I know it doesn't make sense considering all that's happened, but I would never—"

"Never what?"

It were almost as though he was in physical pain. He rubbed his face, then balled both fists tightly and slammed his head back against the rest. "Step out," he blurted finally. "Now that I'm with you again, I would never step out on you."

"We should go," I whispered as the tears came. He didn't

understand what he'd just said but I did. "Before I chicken out."

He nodded and started the engine. The ride was fast, which was probably a good thing. The more time I had to think about this, the more monumentally stupid our plan sounded. Kale called someone—I didn't know who—and told him or her we'd arrive at the back door shortly.

"Wait. They ordered me terminated. How did you explain bringing me in alive?"

He hesitated. "When I called earlier, I told them I was sure you'd break under pressure and reveal the location of the Underground. Marshal seemed pleased…"

I tried not to let his words alarm me. *Break under pressure.* Yeah. That sent waves of happy rolling through my system.

Just before we pulled into a large parking lot, he said, "You're supposed to be unconscious. Is there any chance you can mimic a bruise? To make it look like I hit you?"

I leaned over and closed my eyes. "This conversation is bordering on surreal. Just FYI." I concentrated on the memory of the bruise he'd given Alex when they'd fought in September. Across the right side of his face. "How's that?" I asked without opening my eyes.

A warm, feathery-light touch trailed down the left side of my face, and Kale sighed. "Disturbingly perfect." The car listed to the left, then stopped. "Remember. You're unconscious."

A moment later, I heard the door open. "She's still out."

"You hit her?" an annoyingly familiar voice breathed as Kale's door closed. They were faint, but his footsteps could be heard as he walked around the car, then a second later I felt the chilly air hit my skin as my door opened.

A pair of strong arms caught me before I tumbled from the seat, then slid beneath my legs and neck and hefted up. "She wasn't going to come willingly."

"I don't understand," Kiernan said. I could almost see her expression. Eyebrows forming a deep *V*, lips curled into a disbelieving sneer. "I saw you at the airport. You *helped* them get that Supremacy kid."

We were moving, Kale barely jostling me as the cold wind bit at my skin. "Of course I helped them." His tone was condescending and angry. I couldn't help it. It gave me warm fuzzies to hear him talk to her like that. "How else were they going to think I believed what they said?"

"I told Daddy. I *told* him there was no way you'd turn on me. What we have is far too strong." I could hear the smile in her voice. Apparently Kale's tone didn't faze her.

What they have is too strong? If he didn't get me inside and away from the sound of her voice, there was a chance I'd give myself away by reaching out to choke her.

Kale's arms tightened around me as the chilly air warmed and something metal-sounding clicked behind us. We'd entered the building. There was no turning back now. "Nothing on this earth could make me forget about the girl I love, Roz. Nothing."

26

I was losing track of time. Kale had left me what seemed like hours ago—I didn't know where, because I hadn't dared open my eyes—and no one had been by since. In reality, it had probably only been about ten or fifteen minutes, but it felt much longer. Slowly, I cracked one eye, and then the other.

The room was barely bigger than a walk-in closet, with one door and no windows. I'd never been claustrophobic, but spending too much time in there might change that. There was a tiny bulb hanging from a wire in the middle of the ceiling—very *Sopranos*—and a single white folding chair in the corner with suspicious-looking dark stains on the backrest that trailed all the way down the right leg. They'd long since dried, but I had a pretty good idea what they were and could imagine all too well the ways they might have gotten there.

I climbed to my feet and scanned the ceiling, inch by inch, then did the same with the walls and floor. No sign of a camera.

Next I tried the door, which was, of course, locked. I

crossed the small space and slid down the wall directly across from it. How long would it take for Kale to get in, get the vial, and get me out? It might have been pure delusion—or maybe the Supremacy crazies setting in—but I kept my fingers crossed that they left me alone until then.

Some time passed. I thought about Lu—another senseless tragedy of this whole mess—and all the others we hadn't reached in time. Ashley. Conny. Innocent victims of something they probably never even understood. Denazen's reach was far, but the things Penny Mills said before she was killed terrified me. How many more lives would be destroyed before we could take them out—*if* we could take them out? Each day that passed, they seemed to gain more of an upper hand. I was starting to wonder if killing the beast would be impossible.

The idea that this was all hopeless was too depressing and I needed to stay focused. I recited the lyrics of several Powerman 5000 songs, then counted to one thousand—twice. I was halfway through the third time when the doorknob rattled, announcing that I had a visitor. When the door opened, I was only slightly surprised to see Kiernan, and not Dad, step through.

"Well, well, well," she said, closing the door behind her with a snap. "Look what *my* hottie dragged in."

"Oh, please. The only way you could get a guy like Kale is to wipe his brain clean. Kinda sinking low, even for you. Don'tcha think?"

"You told me he was an awesome kisser. Holy crap—you weren't kidding!" She pulled the folding chair from the corner and sank down with a superior smile that begged to be wiped away. It took every ounce of self-control I had—and then some—but I stayed in my corner on the other side of the room.

"Is there a point to this? I mean, you're not here to

just gloat, right?" I let out a little gasp and covered my mouth. "Or...are you? Dad doesn't trust you to do anything important, right? That's why he sent Kale with Aubrey to off Thom Morris. Maybe he was afraid you'd screw it up."

She shook her head, grin never wavering, but I could see the tightening set of her shoulders. I'd hit a nerve. "You can't bait me, bitch. I'm in way too good a mood. I've got my guy home safe and sound, and I get to be the one to find out where the Underground is currently holed up." She held her hand out to examine her nails. Bright purple with lavender tips. Very Kiernan. "I know you're not just going to tell me, so, yanno, I'm *really* looking forward to this."

"Oh," I said in mock fear. "Is that supposed to, I dunno, scare me or something?"

She leaned forward, face serious. "I *resent* you."

I rolled my eyes. "For *what*, exactly?" My jaw clamped shut just in time. I'd been about to call her on her misplaced anger over our respective childhoods, but then she'd know Kale spilled and his cover would be blown. Instead, I focused on the things I knew. The things she'd personally let slip. "This can't all be out of some misplaced sense of loyalty to Dad!"

"This is because someone like you doesn't deserve to breathe," she spat, voice full of venom. "You had everything and you threw it away."

"Everything? Check your facts, sister. I had crap."

"You had a home and a father who loved you. You had friends. Food. Clothing. All you ever did was try to push him away. To make him angry. I would have given anything to be in your place. I had nothing!"

The hate in her voice made me cringe, and my heart broke just a little. "I don't know what happened to you before we met, Kiernan, but I promise you my life was not the stuff of

Disney fairy tales. He didn't love me. Never did."

"You're a liar. An ungrateful, hateful liar," she said with a menacing step forward. "Where did the Underground go after the hotel burned down?"

Arguing with her over Dad was pointless. She was convinced I'd lived the perfect life and was somehow betraying him. If she was ever going to see his true colors, it had to be in her own time. "Seriously? You *really* think I'm gonna tell you?"

The smile on her face grew wider, and from her back pocket, she pulled out a small black thing. At first it looked like a garage door opener. But as she got closer I realized it was a Taser. Tossing it into the air and catching it again, she winked at me.

"Yep. I really do."

• • •

We'd been at it for a while now, and although I couldn't see it, I was pretty sure she'd given me a black eye. I hadn't gone down without a fight, though. Her bottom lip was swollen, and she favored her right arm. I'd bent the left one back on her last try. Something had popped and she'd let out a horrible wail right before jamming the Taser against my hip.

She'd retreated to her side of the room and me to mine. "I can go at this all day. Can you?"

I shrugged and forced a smile without answering. The truth was, I didn't know how much longer I could do this. I was sure there were no cameras in the room. There was a point where I'd almost completely overpowered her, nearly wrenching the Taser from her fingers. If there'd been a camera, surely someone would have come running.

Kale was out there somewhere, risking his neck to get me the vial. While I hadn't *really* expected us to be in and out in ten minutes, I was starting to worry. When Kiernan came at me again, I had a plan. I didn't know how good it was or if it'd even work with how weak I was, but it was worth a try.

"I'm gonna ask one more time. Where's the Underground?"

Instead of replying, I busied myself by skimming the dirt from under my fingernails, whistling the theme from Tree Busters—a local brush removal service. When I looked up, she'd stopped about a foot away.

"No? Then maybe I'll go get Kale." She waggled her brow and flashed a wicked grin. With each step closer, it grew bigger. "I'm sure he'd *love* to help, since, you know, you're the reason he almost died and all."

She waved the Taser like a Fourth of July sparkler, but she was cocky and too careless. Lightning fast, I sprang to my feet, grabbing her wrist and twisting it around so the tip of the device angled at her instead of me. She tried to squirm away but there wasn't enough time. My other hand covered hers and I jammed her finger down over the button.

Kiernan yelped and crumpled to the floor, surprised. She'd always been too cocky for her own good. Thank God some things never changed. I regained my balance and turned the dial one click higher, then hit her again. She twitched, eyes rolling back then closing, her breath evening out to tell me I hadn't—unfortunately—killed her.

Grounding her was the easy part of my plan. What came next would either make or break the whole thing. Falling to my knees, I grabbed her hand and took a deep breath. At first nothing happened and I panicked. Frustrated, I concentrated harder, picturing my own face as it was when I looked in the mirror this morning. It wasn't a big surprise. When we'd gone to the airport for Ben, I'd done two major mimics in a short span. Granted, I'd gotten some rest, but apparently that hadn't been enough.

Determined, I closed my eyes and tried again. I felt a cool sweat break out across the back of my neck, and after a second, a familiar snap. When I opened my eyes I was relieved to see I'd effectively swapped us. It was my body lying on the floor, unconscious, as I moved to the door in Kiernan's. A part of me felt weirdly vindicated. Not that I had a desire to spend time inside her skin, but she'd swapped us and tried to steal Kale. This felt, at least a little, like payback. Maybe I'd walk through the hall digging deep for nose-nuggets or pretend to pick at an atomic wedgie. Hell, maybe I'd strip down and run through the halls singing "Old MacDonald Had a Farm!" I might be Dez on the inside, but it technically wouldn't be *my* goods on display for all to see.

I wobbled a bit getting to my feet but got my balance under control and headed for the door. As awesome as it would have been to disparage my sister's reputation, I had something more important to do. I reached for the handle, breath held and determined to find Kale, but the door pushed in, knocking me back in surprise. Kale poked his head through and looked from me to Kiernan-as-me lying motionless on the floor, then frowned. "Can't get information out of her if she can't speak."

I stepped through the door and he followed, locking it behind him. "She had it coming," I said simply, taking his hand.

He looked down at our hands, smiled, then shoved me hard against the wall. "I missed you," he growled in my ear, warm breath sending shivers of excitement throughout my body, before he claimed my lips. It started out as something savage. The kind of kiss you see between two tortured souls who hate each other yet are undeniably attracted. But then it changed. It became less controlling and more needy. It felt like I was the air and Kale was a suffocating man desperate for breath.

When he pulled away, he rested his forehead against mine, wrapping a strand of my hair around his index finger. "Are you okay?".

It was hard to hear the concern he had for her—fake or not—but I kept my voice even. This was an act. He had a part to play, and for the sake of all our survival, he had to be flawless. "Of course. Like that little—"

"Not too tired?" he asked, voice lower. "From the switch?"

It took me a second, but when I realized what he was asking my heart sped up. "How—"

He pulled back. I could see his whole face now and not just the dazzling blue of his eyes. "I know my girl."

I know my girl.

Those four simple words were nearly enough to make me forget where we were and melt into him, but I pushed off the wall and nodded down the hallway.

"The panel room," he said. "We should make sure our guest stays asleep for a while."

I nodded, not sure what he meant, and let him tug me down the hall. We climbed a set of stairs, then wound around to another hallway and knocked on the second door twice before pushing through.

A petite brunette looked up from her magazine as we walked in. "Kale," she said with a flirty smile. "Welcome home."

"Devin. Kiernan is being uncooperative at the moment, and Roz needs a break," he said to her. She sat in front of a large panel of buttons. There were a million of them. Every shape, size, and color you could imagine. Some were blinking, some unlit—all looked ominous.

With an unimpressed roll of her eyes, she looked me up and down and said, "*Of course* she does."

Huh. Apparently people here didn't think much of my sister.

"She's in containment room D," Kale said. "Put her under."

Devin nodded and snapped her fingers. A moment later she winked at Kale. "Done. She should take a nice nap." To me, in a much cooler tone, she said, "You probably have a few hours, but don't stretch it. Cross wants that info pronto."

"Believe me, so do I." Adding a wicked grin, I said, "And it'll be so much fun getting it."

We left Devin to her job—whatever it was—and headed up another flight of stairs. "Have you found it yet?" I whispered as we pushed through the door at the top. I had no clue where we were or where we were headed, but I hoped it was right out the back door.

He shook his head. "It was moved—but I know where. A little harder to get to but not impossible."

"What are you doing up here?"

I froze, stopping short as Dad, in a meticulously pressed suit and a sprinkle of newly gray hair, stepped into our path.

"She wasn't playing fair, Daddy." I flashed him a sly smile and a wink. "I told her I was off to spend some *quality time* with my boy. I figure I'll let her stew for a bit, then go back and hit her hard."

A curt nod, and then he brushed past us. "I have a meeting with the heads of the European divisions in half an hour. I'm taking it from home. There are too many distractions here, but I'll be back in three hours. Make *sure* you have that information by then. I want to move forward."

Without waiting for an answer, true to form, Dad stalked

away, head high and shoulders squared. Kale waited until my dad was through the door at the bottom, then pulled me forward. "This is perfect. The vial was moved to his office. No one goes up there except him and a select few."

"Yeah but I'm sure it's locked. I can mimic the handle to get us in though."

"No need." He reached into his pocket, and a second later produced a small silver key.

I planted a quick kiss on his cheek. "Hot *and* resourceful."

The hall was deserted as we made our way to Dad's office. Once there, with one last look over his shoulder, Kale jammed the key into the lock and swept me inside.

"There's a hidden safe," he said, crossing the floor in three long strides. Without missing a beat, he began running his hands along the wall. "I'm not sure where, only that it's here. Aubrey said they moved the vial yesterday."

I scanned the room. "Well, how hard could it be to find?"

We set to searching. Kale took one end of the room and I took the other. We went from corner to corner, respectively, then switched in case the other missed something. Apparently, the safe was very hard to find.

"I know it's here," Kale snapped. He was in the corner by Dad's bookcase, running his hands along the bottom of each shelf. When he came up empty-handed, he stood and kicked the corner. "Damn it!"

I wasn't sure I'd ever get used to hearing Kale curse. I made my way to him, taking his hands in mine. With a squeeze, I said, "It's okay. We'll find it."

Something tapped against the back of my hand. His fingers. One. Two. Three. "Lives depend on finding it. Your life depends on finding it. How can you be so calm?"

"Calm? Trust me, I'm not as calm as I seem. I'm actually

kind of a mess."

The tapping stopped and he reached across to cup my cheek. "A mess? No. Not even close, Dez."

This was dirty pool on the universe's part. To push us together after being pulled apart for so long. All I wanted to do in that moment was kiss him. Thankfully it was one of the few moments lately that I didn't find distraction plaguing me. I was able to pull away. "Come on. We don't have much time."

27

It killed me to walk away from him, but this wasn't the place for *Kale Time*. I made a move to cross the room. There was a file cabinet in the corner we still hadn't checked. But Kale stiffened and clamped a hand across my mouth. I waited, breath held, and then heard it, too. Voices in the hall.

Kale grabbed my arm and made a move toward the door, but there was nowhere to go. The office had no closet, and the desk wasn't big enough for both of us to hide under.

But I had an idea. After shoving Kale toward Dad's leather sofa, I pushed him down, tore off my T-shirt, and straddled him, bending down just as the door flew open.

"What the hell is going on?" Dad growled.

Doing my best impression of Kiernan's innocent stare, I lifted my head from Kale's and frowned. "Sorry, Daddy," I said, snapping up the shirt and clutching it to my chest. "We were just—"

"I can see what you were doing," he barked. "How did you

get in here?"

Déjà vu. When I'd snuck into his original office in Parkview, he'd asked me the same question—only that one had been easier to answer. There was no way he'd buy that the door was open.

"Gino let us in." Kale sat up, coolly elbowing me aside. He inclined his head in my direction. "She wanted to go someplace private."

Dad's face was a mask of rage. "Of course she did. This is all one big game to her." He stepped closer, finger jabbing at the air inches from my face. "If you don't straighten up, I'm putting you right back where I found you. You've done nothing but screw up since the moment you got here! Deznee is a pain in the ass, but she's a thousand times smarter than you are— now *get out!*"

I didn't need to fake the stricken look I knew was plastered all over my face. Dad had always been distant and cold to me. Then, when I found out who he really was, he'd shown his true colors. A man with no heart. But until this moment I truly believed he must have had some semblance of human emotion—even if it was buried deep. If this was how he treated her, why the hell did Kiernan stay? Why did she resent me for growing up with him when she couldn't? The man was a bastard.

We didn't move fast enough. Dad slammed his hand against the doorframe and said, "Don't make me tell you again."

I stuffed my arms through the shirtsleeves and stumbled off the couch, Kale at my heels. We were out the door and into the hall before I took another breath. "Holy crap. That was close."

"We didn't find the vial," he growled.

"We'll have another shot." I almost sounded like I believed it, too. The truth was, every minute that ticked away, our window of opportunity got smaller and smaller.

Kale stopped walking. We'd made it to the staircase. "No. *We* won't. You're leaving. She won't be out forever, and just because she looks like you doesn't mean she won't be able to prove what you did. A few select questions from Marshal and this will explode in your face."

"But we can—"

"Too dangerous. Bringing you here served one purpose. To get me back inside as a trusted Denazen affiliate. That's done. There's no reason for you to stay."

"What about that speech in the car? What a great team we made?" I fumed. He couldn't force me to leave him behind. I wouldn't stand for it.

"I changed my mind," he snapped.

"You changed your— Holy crap! This is so not right!" While I wanted my Kale back in his entirety, the new version seemed to have slightly more faith in my ability to handle things on my own. And now he was reverting?

His eyes widened and he leaned closer. "Can you possibly blame me? When I agreed to this, I had no clue what these people were capable of. Now that I'm starting to remember, I don't want you here."

I folded my arms. "And how are you going to explain my disappearance?"

He matched my stance as well as my stubborn expression. "You're wearing Kiernan's face. You left me in the hall and walked out on your own. Not complicated."

Talk about role reversal. "Everything's *complicated*," I mumbled. He was right, though. Kiernan wouldn't be out forever. A prolonged stay wasn't something I had any interest in, but there was still one minor problem. "What about Kiernan?"

"What about her?"

I had to tell myself to close my mouth. "Um, she's still wearing *my face*? Trust me—I've been down this road before. It's creepy, not to mention she's the last person I want walking around in my skin."

Kale frowned. "I hadn't thought about that."

Further proof that he wasn't himself. My Kale was sharp. Always thinking—always aware.

"If I swap her back and leave, you promise to lift the vial and get out, right?"

"Yes."

I sighed. The idea of leaving him behind—especially with Ms. Gropey Fingers—made my skin crawl, but there weren't a whole lot of options at this point. "Fine," I relented. "Let's get back to the room. According to what Devin said, she should be out for a while longer. That'll give me enough time to switch her back and slip out before anyone notices."

"There!" I shouted from the bottom of the stairs.

Well, Kiernan-as-me shouted.

My sister had woken up early.

28

I whirled to run the other way, but four agents were just coming through the door on the landing above us. There was no way I'd get through them. Not without Kale's help—and I couldn't get that. Not without blowing his cover. And if his cover was blown, not only would we both be trapped here, but any hope of snagging the cure would be gone forever.

In short, I was screwed.

Kiernan stomped up the steps, eyes on me and expression fuming. "That's Kiernan, Kale," she spat.

Kale, to his credit, shot her a look of confusion that would have even fooled me. He looked from me to her and took a step away from both of us. "What's going on?"

"She mimicked and knocked me cold."

Hand on hips, I curled my lip like I'd seen Kiernan do a thousand times when annoyed. "Bullshit. She's lying!"

"If I'm lying, then how did I get out of the room?" Kiernan growled.

That was a good question—and then I remembered Kale opened the door as I was leaving the room. Kiernan had locked it after stepping inside. Of course she'd have the key to open it. Knowing there was no way out of it, I shrugged and nodded to Kale.

"Busted," I said simply and closed my eyes. I felt a shiver run through me and when I opened them and looked down, it was my own form I saw, not Kiernan's.

"Change me back," she snapped. "This face makes me sick."

"Make me."

Her anger melted into smugness. "I don't need to make you," she said, grabbing Kale's arm and tugging him close. "He will."

He turned to me and, even though I knew it was an act, the threatening tone of his voice gave me chills. "Fix this. *Now*."

As I touched her hand, I contemplated giving her a little something extra, but with this many agents surrounding me, I decided against it. Instead, I closed my eyes and pictured her as she'd been—the day we first met. Clothes and all.

When I stepped away, Kale stared at her. Her hands flew to her face, a panicked light in her eyes. "What? What did she do?"

"Your hair is different. Purple."

Kiernan looked horrified. Worried the color might spark Kale's memory, no doubt. But she recovered quickly. With a smug smile, she said, "Very nice, Kiernan—but sticking *your* old hair color on me won't work. Kale remembers me."

"Does he? My bad. He didn't realize the difference when he was kissing me a few minutes ago," I said, even though I knew I should have kept my mouth shut. I couldn't help it, though.

Kale grabbed my arm and spun me closer to the steps. Wiping his mouth with a disgusted expression, he looked at Kiernan. "She's telling the truth. We did kiss."

"Is that all you did with her?" She looked genuinely hurt and it took every ounce of self-control not to scream.

Kale never got a chance to answer because Dad appeared at the top of the first landing. "Is there anything you manage to do without screwing it up?"

Kiernan tensed and Kale's fingers around my arm twitched.

Descending the stairs, Dad locked eyes on Kiernan. In all the years I'd spent with him, and all the stupid crap I'd pulled to get his attention, he'd never once looked at me with as much venom. There was no love in his gaze. No compassion. There was only anger and hate so potent, it made me shudder. "Is there *anything* you're capable of succeeding at?"

Her cheeks flushing, she looked away from him. "I'm sorry. But in my defense, she — "

"Your *defense?* We don't need your excuses." He turned away and said to Kale, "Put Kiernan in holding — *restrained*, please."

Kale nodded, then guided me down the steps. Kiernan made a move to follow, but from the corner of my eye I saw Dad stop her. He pointed to the door at the top of the steps, then turned on his heel and breezed through.

I'd hoped Kale would bring me down to holding — wherever that was — by himself, but Dad sent two agents with us so there was no choice but to keep up the charade.

We didn't travel long, and when one of the agents unlocked the door and Kale pushed me inside, I had to remind myself it was all an act.

He shoved me toward the wall and wrenched my right hand up, snapping the same cuff he'd worn just months ago into place. As he moved to restrain the left one, our eyes met. He snapped it closed, then glanced over his shoulder at the two agents standing by the door and back to me.

I knew what he was thinking—and it was too dangerous. We were too close to getting our hands on the vial to ruin it now. I shook my head slightly and let it fall so my hair framed my face. "Don't," I whispered. "Please."

His hands, still on my left wrist, twitched, but after a moment he backed away. Without another word, he turned and breezed through the door, the agents on his heels. Several sharp clicks and a clatter followed as they locked me in.

I held my breath, waiting for them to leave. As soon as the door clicked closed, I'd mimic these puppies and get the hell out of Dodge—but of course, Dad would have thought of that. As the agents walked out, he walked in. "How are you finding the accommodations, Deznee?"

"Why don't we switch places and you can see for yourself?"

He laughed and closed the door, punching a four-digit code into the keypad on the wall. "There's that bravado. I have to say… I've always found it admirable how you can stand tall even in the face of disaster." He turned to me. "Or maybe you're just too ignorant to be fearful?"

"Aww, there's the Dad I know and hate," I spat. Leaning as far forward as the chains would allow, I winked knowingly. "So let's have it—just between you and me. Not exactly brimming with pride over your other spawn, are you?" This was the first time we'd been alone since Kiernan had revealed our shared parentage.

Dad sighed and pulled over the desk chair on the far side of the room. "Kiernan has been somewhat of a disappointment."

"Who's her mom?"

Dad shrugged, face impassive. "No one important. An unwilling Resident chosen for her ability to conceal objects by camouflaging them. I'd hoped Kiernan's ability, aided by the Supremacy drug, would surpass her mother's."

"She can move around unseen—and unheard. I'd say that's an improvement."

"Oh, it is," he agreed. "Unfortunately she inherited her mother's stupidity."

"Wow." I chuckled. "Must have been a *West Side Story* kind of love, huh?"

Dad stood and began pacing from side to side. "I trust you appreciate the gravity of your predicament. You were created to be a boon to Denazen, not a hindrance. I'm sure you understand that I can't let it continue."

"Is that your way of telling me my time is almost up?"

He smiled, and I was struck by how wrong the expression looked on him. "In a manner of speaking, yes."

"Well, then at least let me ask you one thing."

"I don't see what it could hurt at this point."

"Are there any more?"

He stopped pacing and faced me, interested. "Any more what?"

"Kids. Do I have any more freaky sibling science experiments running around out there?"

Dad sighed. He made his way over to the desk in the corner and began pulling open drawers. I couldn't see what he was doing because he purposefully blocked my view. When he turned back to me, his smile was even wider than before. "I'm going to answer your question, Deznee. I'm going to tell you something I've never told another living soul."

"This should be good," I mumbled as he stopped a few

inches from me. There was something in his pocket. He'd taken it from the desk.

"I loved your mother."

Laughter. Hysterical and unabashed. "You've gotta be shitting me."

His expression didn't change.

"Holy shit, you're actually serious?"

He didn't seem insulted by my disbelief. "I know, I know. But it's true. She was beautiful and wild and something about her called to me. I was in upper management at the time and viewed Sixes as nothing more than a means to an end. But she was different. For her, I made an exception."

"If locking her up in your institution of crazy was your way of showing love, then I'd hate to see how you treat the people you hate."

Smile still firmly in place, Dad lashed out his hand and clipped me hard across the cheek. "*You* should know. I hate you. Still, I kept you even though I knew the truth."

The air thinned, and despite the stinging itch spanning the entire right side of my cheek, a chill had settled in the room. "Truth? What truth?"

"I lied, of course. Had a test done and changed the results in my favor, but as you grew, it was so obvious. That's how much I loved her, Deznee. I put up with you."

"What," I snapped. His words were making me dizzy. "*What* was obvious?"

He came close—so close that we breathed the same air. A moment later something sharp pricked the skin on my forearm. When he pulled away, he wiggled a small hypodermic needle in front of my face. "The answer is yes, Deznee. You do have a sibling—and it's not Kiernan because *she's* my daughter. You are not."

29

"Dez?" a familiar voice called. Something shook me and it took some effort, but I opened my eyes.

Everything was bleary at first, but when it cleared I saw Brandt standing over me. His lips moved enthusiastically, but there was only intermittent sound. Like a bad cell signal.

"...it together. I need you...Kale...Dez?"

I climbed to my feet, rubbing both eyes with the heels of my hands. I wasn't in the holding room anymore. We were standing in the middle of a lush field chock full of daisies and bordered by a trickling brook. Somehow, I'd gotten outside.

No. I hadn't. I'd fallen asleep.

"Brandt?"

He took my hands. "Dez, look at me. Are you all right?"

"Vial," I managed to get out. My tongue felt heavy. Like it was weighted down with rocks. The inside of my mouth tasted weird, too. Like I'd been sucking on pennies. I tried to spit it out but that only made it worse. "We still haven't found it."

He rolled his eyes. "I know. I told you, I have a contact."

"Dad's office. It's in there. We almost had it but— How did you know I was sleeping?"

"Kale told me they drugged you with some pretty hardcore stuff. Forget about that now. Listen carefully, Dez. Uncle Marshal wants to make an example out of you. We need to get you out of here." He closed his eyes and for a second, I swore he faded in and out like a hologram. It reminded me of something you'd see in a sci-fi flick.

"This is Kale's fault. He should have never suggested this."

"Technically, Vince was the one who had the idea…"

"Dez…"

I shook my head and leaned closer to him. This was a dream. We were inside my head. Still, Brandt smelled like Brandt. I inhaled and let my head fall against his shoulder. "No. This was the only way. Did he get the vial?"

"Kale's having some issues. Cross has armed agents standing at the end of the hall now. He's not taking any chances."

"Where does that leave me?"

"I told Ginger. She knows what's going on and they're coming."

The scratchy fabric of his sweater itched against my skin. "Okay…"

"But I don't know if they'll get here in time, Dez. Or if they'll even make it inside. We need to get you out now."

I tried to shake my head but sharp pain prevented it. "No. Kale's close. Don't give up yet. Please. Give him one more chance."

"Getting you out is more important right now."

"Give it another day. Just one more day." Although the idea sickened and terrified me, I wasn't ready to give up.

Without that vial, it didn't matter if I got out of here alive or not. Without that vial, I was a goner. So were the other kids.

"You don't understand." Brandt pushed me away. His eyes bore holes in mine. "We don't *have* another day. Cross is staging a very public termination in a few hours. Like I said, he intends to make an example of you. I know what they gave you is strong, but you're stronger. You have to wake up and get out. Now."

Wake up? "Exactly how am I supposed to do that?"

"Try. You can do it. You have to, because that's not even the worst part," Brandt said.

"Not the worst part?" How the hell did it get worse than termination—AKA death? And a public one to boot?

"Brandt, tell me what's going on."

He looked uncomfortable. "Cross plans on having Kale do it."

• • •

When I woke from the dream everything was filmy and raw. I was alone and still in the holding room; Brandt was nothing more than a shadow passing through my mind. Whatever sedative I'd been given was wearing off, taking the comforting numbness right along with it. My arms felt like they'd been ripped from their sockets, and my wrists were more than likely perma-bruised from holding all my weight in the cuffs.

The moments right before passing out came flooding painfully back. Marshal Cross wasn't my dad. Kiernan wasn't my sister. The revelation should have made me happy. Knowing I didn't share any tiny bits of genetic material with those whackjobs should have had me Snoopy dancing until the cows marched home on Judgment Day.

Marshal Cross was a mind-twister, though. There was always a slim possibility he was lying just to mess with me. Kiernan and I shared similar facial features and the same went for Dad. But I supposed if you looked hard enough at most people, you could find similarities among them. I decided, for now, that he'd told me the truth—and that it was good news.

I needed good news.

With that out of the way, the next order of business was to find a way out of this mess. If what Brandt said was true, my clock was ticking. Ginger was sending people, but even if they could get inside, we didn't have nearly enough manpower or resources—despite Dax and his big fat bankroll—to launch an all-out raid on a place like Zendean. I hadn't seen much of the complex, but from the way Kale spoke and the things Brandt said, it had to be massive with huge amounts of security. The building itself had stretched on forever—I'd peeked as we pulled into the lot.

Cringing, I tugged on the chains to test their security to the wall. They didn't budge. Not that I could have reached, but now would have been a perfect time to test that hairpin theory Brandt had about picking locks.

I sighed and accepted the truth. Getting free from the chains was going to be impossible. At least without a key. So that simply meant I had to get someone to unlock the cuffs *for* me.

I scanned the room. On first sweep I didn't see a thing. There was the desk in the corner, the chair Dad had pulled closer, and a small table a few feet away with a pack of cigarettes and a lighter sitting on top of a stack of papers.

Papers.

Wow. My focus issues were getting worse. Why worry about picking a lock when I could simply mimic my way out of this mess? I closed my eyes and pictured paper. It was a small object, resulting in nothing more than a tingle, which was a relief. After mimicking Kiernan and myself earlier, there was no way I had another full-body swap in me. At least not for a day or so.

The familiar tingle raced up my spine, and when I opened my eyes, I tore the cuffs from the wall with ease just like I had with Ben's at the airport. That's why Dad had put me to sleep. Since my ability had surged, it was the only way to keep me under control. But how long did they think I'd be out? And how long *had* it been? There was a good chance they'd be back any minute to haul me off to their public hanging. Brandt was right. I needed to be gone by then.

I crossed the room, fully intending to mimic my way right the hell out, but something caught my eye on the way to the door. It was a painting in the corner, leaning against the wall and partially concealed by the desk. I knew I needed to go, but something about it wouldn't let me leave. Not until I saw the whole thing.

Hurrying across the floor, I swiped the painting from behind the desk and laid it across the top. The tarnished silver plaque on the bottom said *W.V.K.* The man depicted, somewhere in his forties if I had to guess, sat tall in a high-backed chair and wore a black brimmed hat and a dapper-looking suit. I couldn't date it—I'd failed history miserably—but it was definitely old. Early 1900s, if not older. The man looked so familiar and yet I couldn't place him. He had a long black beard and mop of thick hair with the slightest curl at the ends, and his expression was fierce. Like a hunter scanning the wild for prey. It reminded me a little of Kale's.

I reached for my phone and, of course, found it missing. Duh. They'd taken it. A picture was out, so I committed as much of the picture to memory as I could and started for the door.

I got two steps before someone walked in.

30

I frantically dove to the desk for something to use—or mimic—into a weapon. I grabbed for the only thing I could find—a stapler. Spreading my legs, ready to wield my office supply of death, I faced the door.

"Dez?"

The stapler fell from my hands and clanked to the desk with a rattle, then rolled onto the floor. *"Aubrey?"*

Something shoved him aside, and a blur of black and blue stormed the room and flew straight at me. Kale swept me into his arms and squeezed so tightly I had a hard time breathing. "Are you all right?"

"Fine," I gasped. "Can't—breathe—but fine."

Kale looked confused for a moment before letting go and stepping away. "Oh. Sorry." He glanced from me to the wall, then back again. "If you're free, what are you still doing in here? We need to leave."

He was right. If this kept up, I'd need a babysitter. God

only knew what would happen the first time something shiny passed in front of me.

"We have to hurry," Aubrey said, tapping the doorframe to get my attention. "I caused a distraction, but we don't have a ton of time. We need to get to the lab."

Kale nodded, and we followed Aubrey from the room.

Aubrey led us around the first corner and down the hall. Tinted bubbles lined the ceiling, making me nervous. They were smaller versions of the ones you saw in department stores. "Aren't these cameras? Can't they see exactly what we're doing?"

Aubrey smiled. A sly, mischievous grin that made him look years younger. "Not everyone here agrees with what Cross and the Council are doing. We've got the cameras covered. Don't worry."

The lab was three floors below the holding room, and when we got there, I was surprised to find it empty. We skidded through the double doors and Aubrey took off toward a tall glass cabinet on one side of the room, while Kale made a beeline for a small desk by the door marked Exit on the opposite side.

"What are we looking for? Is the vial in here?"

Aubrey threw open the doors and started pulling things out. Several glass bottles crashed to the floor, and I cringed as they shattered, causing an echoing clatter. After a moment, he exclaimed, "Got it!"

"Got what?" I flew forward to get a better look. "What are we here for?"

"These." He turned and held out a tray of glass vials filled with smoky gray liquid. Domination. It had to be. "We came for these."

"Found it," Kale called on the other side of the room. He

raced toward us, something small and golden in his left hand. "Where is she?"

"Right here!" someone else called, bursting through the door. "Right here. Everyone's tied up with that electrical issue and the fire."

It was the girl from the panel room. "Devin?"

She flashed me a smile and winked. "I'm a friend of your cousin's."

"You're Brandt's contact?" I didn't know why, but the fact that she was a *she* surprised me.

Devin wrapped her arms around me, gave a quick squeeze, and took the tray from Aubrey. Then, she took the gold thing from Kale—a door key—and disappeared through the exit without another word.

"Domination," Kale said, taking my hand. "We needed to get a batch. Just in case we don't find the blood. Devin is taking it out to one of Ginger's people."

A small blossom of panic bloomed in my chest. "You didn't find the vial yet?"

"He found the safe," Aubrey interjected, closing the cabinet doors. "But the blood wasn't there."

"Maybe the blood is gone. Used." Kale frowned and nodded at the door where Devin had taken out the case. "That was a brand-new batch. They could have used the last of the blood to make it."

"There wasn't much left and Cross had the lab working nonstop to pump out as much of the drug as they could," Aubrey said. "If the blood is gone, that batch might be the only chance at a cure we have."

I couldn't speak. If the blood really was gone, our only hope was Domination. With a 50 percent survival rate, I wasn't loving the chances.

Kale tugged me toward the door. "We have to live long enough to worry about it first, and that means getting out of this building in one piece."

"That's her!" a man shouted from the front of the room. Three additional agents burst into the room behind him, cutting off our escape.

I glared at Aubrey. "Is there anyone you didn't invite to our little escape party?"

One of the agents pulled out what looked like a cross between a walkie-talkie and a cell phone. "They're in the lab. I repeat. In the lab."

"Why are we standing here?" I whispered with a nod toward the exit door. "Shouldn't we, I dunno, make a break for it?"

Kale tensed. "Devin took the key. That door doesn't open from the outside—or inside—without it. We're trapped."

I turned my attention back to the four agents by the door. The one in front with the walkie shook it then growled, tossing it to the ground. The electrical distraction Aubrey mentioned. That must be why it wasn't working.

Three of the agents sprang forward in attack mode, while the fourth ran the other way. I had to stop him before he told anyone where we were or what we were doing. I darted after him, ignoring Kale's screams to stop. The deck was stacked against us, but if every agent—and loyal Resident—in the building came down on us, we were as good as dead.

He was fast, making it up three flights of stairs and to the third floor landing with impressive speed. I had a hard time keeping up, but managed—barely. That was it. My mind was made up. When this was all over, I was going to take up running again.

I rounded the last corner on the third floor landing just

as he disappeared through the door. The building had a weird setup. The stairs ended, but a small sign with an arrow directed me to a set of elevators. I burst through the door just as he reached the elevator at the other end of the hallway.

I kicked as hard as I could, urging my feet to carry me faster as smoke started filling the hall. Great. Now something was on fire? This just kept getting better and better. The elevator doors opened with an echoing *ding* and he slipped inside, furiously mashing the button on the wall. The doors started to close. I wasn't going to make it.

With one last push, I propelled my body, kicking my legs forward and tilting back. I hit the ground, right hip first, sliding the rest of the way. Across Zendean's pristinely polished floor—and into the elevator just as the doors whooshed shut.

Of course, now I was alone in a steel box with an armed man three times my size.

31

He laughed as I pulled myself upright. "Not exactly what I had in mind, but this works, too."

"Don't suppose I could talk you out of whatever you're thinking, huh?"

He folded his arms and widened his grin. "You can try. I get a kick out of women begging me for things."

Begging? What a frigging scumbag. "Sorry. I don't beg."

Without another word, he lunged for me as the elevator jerked upward. I managed to dodge him, but it wouldn't last. There wasn't a hell of a lot of room in here. He made another swipe, and I made another dodge. It probably would have gone on like that—back and forth until one of us finally got tired— but the elevator jolted to a stop, sending us both toppling to the floor.

"Oh," I groaned, feeling a tiny bit queasy. "That can't be good." This was it. I finally understood Kale's loathing for these things. I was never getting into another elevator for as long as

I lived.

There was a horrible noise—a cross between a metallic crunch and an odd snapping sound. It was followed by the elevator whooshing into motion again—only this time it was in the wrong direction. Down.

And at about five times the normal speed.

I loved roller coasters. The thrill of soaring high above, inside and out, upside down, and sideways. It was the kind of crap I lived for. I'd done the free-fall ride at Great Adventure one year with Brandt. He'd hated it, keeling over promptly as our feet touched solid ground—but I'd been in heaven. As the elevator plummeted, I tried to remember what the appeal of it all was.

I managed to climb to my feet again just as the car came to a bone-jarring halt. Of course, the motion of the sudden stop brought me to the floor again. I made another attempt to stand, but the agent, pale-faced and determined, stumbled upright first and shoved me back, reaching toward the ceiling to knock out the emergency door. It clattered open and he wasted no time jumping and hefting himself up. I tried to grab his legs, but he kicked out, getting lucky—or so I told myself—and caught me in the side of the head.

Everything swam and I went down again as the elevator jerked into motion once more. Down. Stop. Down. Stop. I didn't know how many floors the building had or exactly how high up we were—and I had no desire to find out.

Positioning myself beneath the hole, I stretched and kicked off the ground to reach the opening. It took me three tries, but I finally grabbed the edge and hauled myself to the top of the car. The agent was there, balanced precariously on the edge, trying to reach a metal bar that jutted several feet above his head. He was too short.

I peered over the side, hoping we'd stopped near a set of floor doors, but there was nothing for at least several feet. I could try dropping down to a ledge below, but there was a chance I wouldn't have enough time to pry open the doors and slip through before the car started falling again. I didn't relish the idea of getting crushed. Plus, there was a chance I could miss and plummet to my death.

The agent let out a growl, still trying and failing to get to the bar. I was about to tell him we should work together, but my stomach lurched as the car began to fall again.

The guy screamed, losing his balance and lurching to the side—and over the edge. He caught the rim of the car, but by the time I crept toward him, his fingers had started to slide. "Here." I extended my arm. "Let me help you!"

He didn't argue, making a move to take my hand. But a terrible squeal filled the air, and the car jerked a few feet. The sudden shift dislodged his grip from the elevator.

I peered over the side and watched the darkness below swallow him. He didn't scream, which made the whole thing more eerie. Despite the fact that he was an agent and had technically tried to kill me, I said a silent prayer for him. No one deserved to die like that.

Standing, I took a deep breath and was careful to move slowly as I inched across the top of the car to the wall. I had no intention of falling to the same fate as the agent.

The elevator had slipped a few feet and I saw a bar with a floor door beside it. There was a good chance I could reach it. If successful, I could swing to the small ledge and hopefully pry the doors open.

On tiptoes, I reached for the bar and prayed Kale and Aubrey were having better luck than I was. My fingers brushed the surface, but I was too far away to wrap them around for a good grip. The car shimmied, and I was sure it would continue its plunge, but it remained still. Deep breath. I could do this.

I tried leaning forward and stretching, but it was no use. I was a hair too short. My only chance was to jump and hope I caught it on the first try. Any sudden movements would send the car crashing down.

"Okay, Dez," I said to myself. There was a slight echo and the hint of smoke. "This is just another stunt. Something they said you couldn't do."

I thought about Kale and how my life had changed since he'd stumbled into it. I wasn't a believer in fate. We all made our own way—despite what Ginger would have me believe. And my way was to live a long, crazy life with Kale by my side. It didn't end at the bottom of an elevator shaft in a Denazen building.

Bending my knees slightly, I arched my back, arms up, and jumped.

For a drawn-out moment, there was nothing but air beneath my feet. A bubble of panic formed in my chest, but it faded as my fingers closed around the cool metal, right hand locking like a vice.

A moment of victory, followed by one of terror as my left hand slipped off. The car beneath quaked as I used the tip of my sneaker to give myself the nudge I needed to grip the bar again—this time with both hands.

With an echoing scream and a rush of stale air, the car dropped from under me, disappearing into the abyss. There was a deafening noise and a reverberating rattle as it hit the ground. Judging from the distance, I'd gotten off just in time.

"Holy shit," I gasped, and swung toward the small ledge. My feet touched solid ground again, and I pressed myself tight against the elevator doors with a silent prayer of thanks.

The doors weren't as hard to pry open as I expected. I slipped through and fell to the floor to catch my breath as alarms wailed all around. I let myself rest for a moment. A short span from the count of one to ten—that was all I could afford. Kale was still here somewhere. And so was Aubrey. He'd helped us, and I wouldn't leave him behind any more than I would have one of the others. Whether he liked it or not, he was one of us now.

I wondered what this would do to his relationship with Able…

By the time I got to ten, I was on my feet and running. The building had erupted into chaos. People were running down the hall—some with fire extinguishers and others with boxes and stacks of papers. They were all too busy to pay any attention to me.

Room after room was the same. People trying to put out little fires everywhere.

I stopped short as I passed the holding room where they'd kept me earlier. There was someone inside. Flash of flannel and a mop of unruly dark hair. "Vince?"

He looked up from the charred remains of the desk, startled. "Dez!" Stepping to me, he threw his arms around me and squeezed. "You're all right!"

I returned the hug, slightly awkward, and pulled away. Vince was a nice guy and all, but we'd never been hug-friendly. "What are you doing in here? What's going on? Are the others here, too?"

"Whoa. Slow down." He took a deep breath. "We got a tip that the vial was in here. I'm searching while Sue and Dax and the others take the guided tour with your friend Aubrey."

"Kale! Where's Kale? Have you seen him?"

"He's looking for you. I think Denazen figured out he was

playing for the other team."

"We should find the others. Regroup. This place is a madhouse, but that doesn't mean someone won't get bagged and tagged. Plus, whatever's on fire is spreading. The whole place is liable to go up like a roman candle any minute now."

Vince chuckled. "There's no fire, Dez. This is the work of a Resident. Carley, I think her name is."

Carley. The name sounded so familiar. It took me a moment, but I remembered where I'd heard it before. "That's the freak-show who made me think they'd kidnapped Mom back in September."

Vince nodded. "Apparently she's done with Denazen." He turned back to the desk. "Go find Kale. I have a couple places left to look, then I'm right behind. I want to be sure we don't miss it."

I didn't think for a minute they'd stashed the vial in here, but I didn't correct him. He was finally taking part in the action, and I knew from experience it felt good to do something productive and helpful. One last nod and I was out the door and racing down the hall.

The entire building had erupted in chaos, and I needed to find Kale. Bursting through the door at the end of the hallway, I twisted to go left but froze when I saw an agent flying full speed in my direction.

I pivoted to the right and found Kale. He was on the other end of the hall, crouched low to the ground. His hand pressed flat against the linoleum as a swirl of black gathered, going from wall to wall.

When he looked up and saw me coming, it was too late.

32

"Dez, no!" he screamed, jumping to his feet. His expression contorted—pure panic. Something rare on Kale's face. He pointed to the ceiling. "Up!"

With the inky black mass barreling toward the agent—*toward me*—I froze and looked up. Above my head was a thin pipe that ran the length of the room. Kicking off the ground with all my strength, I grabbed the pipe and drew my legs up just as the churning mass zoomed past. I counted to ten—to be safe—then dropped to the floor and turned to watch the darkness continue on its path. Either the agent didn't understand, or he was so oblivious that he didn't see, but he hadn't made any attempt to move. He was still coming fast.

And then he wasn't.

Kale's darkness hit him. The agent never even slowed. One minute he was only a few feet away, zooming toward us and solid, the next he was a million tiny particles of dust scattered in my face. I cringed, waving a hand back and forth to not breathe him in.

"Are you okay?" Kale said, coming up behind me. "I almost—"

"I'm fine. Promise. Cavalry has arrived. I just came from Vince, and he said Mom and Dax are in the building searching for captives."

"They're in the building?" Kale's eyes went wide. "How did they get inside?"

"According to Vince, some of the Residents Denazen thought were wrapped around its fat little finger aren't so compliant anymore. Seems Brandt and Devin organized one hell of a coup."

He smiled. "Trojan horse. Like what Kiernan did at the hotel."

My mouth fell open, and for a second all I could do was stand there and stare. Just for a second, though. The next, I threw my arms around him, squeezing as tight as I possibly could.

He returned the embrace then pulled away. "It's confusing. I can only see fragments. And sometimes the things I see don't make any sense. What I just said, I don't understand. I can't see the memory clearly. But I have a good idea what's real and what's fake now."

"This means it's fading, Kale. We're going to be okay."

He kissed me quickly on the forehead and took my hand. "Hurry. This is our last chance to find the vial."

"We have the case of Domination. Forget the vial—I'll take my chances. There's no way we're going to find it now. This place is huge and we have no idea where it's being kept." At this point, we were only pushing our luck. I was free, I'd found Kale, and we had the serum. Brandt used to tell me I didn't know when to walk away. I'd done some growing up since then, though, and that wasn't the case anymore.

"There's one last place to look," Kale insisted. He tugged me forward and I let him. "Come on."

We sprinted to the other side of the building—floor sub-level seven—and climbed staircase after staircase. The higher we got the more activity we saw. The smoke grew thicker. I kept telling myself that it wasn't real, like Vince said, but it smelled real. It felt real, too. The temperature in the building seemed to have jumped a good thirty degrees.

Kale pulled me into an unmarked room at the end of the hall and closed the door behind us. We entered a wide landing that overlooked a room full of scientific equipment. Microscopes, rows of beakers and tubes, and a huge glass tank full of water. It was the one thing that looked ridiculously out of place. It reminded me of something you'd see at an aquarium. A shark tank—or maybe a mermaid.

Crap.

If there were mermaid Sixes out there, I was turning in my membership card.

Kale took my hand and pulled me down to the second landing, pointing to a row of metal cabinets. "Marshal brought in a scientific team. This is where they did the research on the blood with the formula that was stolen from Wentz. They might be keeping it here."

"They might be," someone said from the doorway above us. "But wouldn't that just be too easy?"

We looked up to find Kiernan standing in the open doorway.

"Isn't this a nipple twist." She looked from me to Kale, eyes settling on our joined hands. There was red-hot fury in her eyes, as well as a spark of hurt. "Mind explaining, lover boy?"

"I told you," Kale said slowly. His fingers tightened around mine. "Nothing could make me forget the girl I love."

She blinked, staring like she'd heard him wrong. "So it was all nothing? Everything we shared? You didn't love me at all?"

While I'd never been driven to the same level of desperation Kiernan had, I understood the way she felt. Sort of, anyway. Dad had ignored me most of my life. I did anything and everything possible to get his attention. To feel some kind of connection. I'd wanted the same thing she did. A family. The difference was, I found friends. There were people out there who genuinely cared about me, and with them in my life, Dad's lack of interest didn't matter quite so much. My sister hadn't had that. I'd seen the way Dad—*Cross*—treated her. She had to have seen it, too. She might not be willing to admit it just yet, but I was betting Kiernan had finally realized the love she craved wasn't going to come from Marshal Cross, so she'd foolishly pinned her hopes on Kale.

Kale's lips twisted into an angry scowl as she started down the first set of stairs. "It was all a lie. Something you forced on me. I love Dez. I've always loved *Dez*, and only her. The things that happened between us weren't real, and they weren't about love."

"Maybe not at first, but it turned into something more," she insisted. There was the slightest crack in her voice. Desperation and betrayal. Despite what she'd done, my heart hurt for her. It didn't excuse her actions—there was always a choice—but she was hurting.

He shook his head. "No. It didn't."

Kiernan stepped onto our landing. "I'm sorry I lied to you, Kale. It was the only way to make you see the truth. Daddy only wants what's best for us—*for you*." She pointed to me, lip curling into a cruel smile. "She doesn't love you. She's only using you to take us out."

Kale once told me that he loved how I never made a big deal out of his social awkwardness. How I accepted him the way he was, even though he didn't get the jokes others did or sometimes took things too literally. He didn't understand because he'd been a prisoner at Denazen since his birth, every detail of his life at the mercy of cruel men with their own twisted agendas. But I didn't *accept* these things. I *loved* them. Kale was Kale, and there was no one else on earth like him. He wasn't your average chocolate chip cookie. No. Kale was a mocha cookie with coffee-flavored chips and a gooey caffeinated center. He was one of a kind—and I wouldn't have changed that for anything on earth.

"What's best for me is Dez, not you. You're—" He tilted his head, lost in thought for a moment. "You're crackers on crazy," he declared, proud of the analogy. When he responded in true Kale fashion, the part of me that had shriveled away when he left came bounding back to life, bigger and brighter than before.

It was crazy on a cracker, but God, I loved this guy.

"Fine. Go ahead," she said with an ugly sneer aimed at me. "Smile. Laugh. Think you won because you turned him against me. How long will your stupid happiness last without this?"

She reached into her pocket and pulled out something small. Balanced between her thumb and pointer was a glass tube filled halfway with thick red liquid. Penny's blood. The vial.

She was the one who had it.

Kale tensed, ready to pounce, but I stopped him.

Kiernan didn't miss it. She laughed and wiggled the vial, blowing him a kiss. "I know what you're thinking, Dez." The blood coated the inside of the glass, turning it an opaque red. "You're thinking no big, right? There's still a chance with that batch of Domination you stole. A fifty percent chance of survival is better than zero, right?"

I opened my mouth, then closed it. How did she know they'd taken the drug? Had Devin been caught?

As if reading my mind, she nodded and I tried not to panic as she tossed the vial into the air, then caught it. "Dad had a feeling you'd go for it so he left an extra-special batch in the lab. I'm sure you guys have snagged it by now."

"Special?" Kale asked. He inched forward as Kiernan backed away. She was on the second step now, leaning against the railing, and I was terrified that any sudden movement would cause her to drop the vial.

"*Very* special. Your batch shares some of the same ingredients as ours — only it's missing a few *key* elements."

"It's lethal," Kale said, fingers curling around the banister.

"Wickedly so," she confirmed. "Takes a while, too. Guys in the lab said someone could last up to five days after taking it — and wish for death the entire time."

I pushed aside the sick feeling in my stomach and stepped up to meet Kale, who'd paused at the base of the stairs. "Why even tell me?"

Kiernan backed up another step. With a smile I'd never forget, she wiggled the vial again over the edge of the railing and said, "Because I wanted the satisfaction of seeing your face when I did this — "

Time slowed. A scream spilled from my lips, the agonized sound bouncing off the walls and echoing through the corridor. I threw myself forward to catch the vial as it dropped over the side of the banister, but it was too far. The tips of my fingers brushed the edge but instead of drawing it closer, I flicked it farther away. Horrified, I watched as it fell, crashing not into the large tank of water but to the concrete floor below and shattering, the small amount of liquid splattering everywhere.

I couldn't move. Couldn't breathe. My future was there on that floor. On the stairs above me, Kiernan laughed, and when I climbed to my feet and turned, Kale was backing her up against the wall. The tips of his finger swirled black.

I grabbed his arm and pulled back. "Stop—this is between us. Me and her."

If Kale disagreed, he didn't show it. With a simple nod, he stepped back to our landing as I took his place in front of the girl who had tried so hard to shred my life to bits. There was no fear in her eyes. Only resentment.

I knew the feeling. Any love or sympathy I had for my *sister* was officially gone.

"You had everything," she whispered.

"So you decided to take it?" I countered. "I have a newsflash for you, Kiernan. You didn't get to grow up with your father—lucky, by the way—but neither did I. Marshal Cross *isn't* my dad."

She looked like a five-year-old who had just been informed the Tooth Fairy was a fraud. "Liar!"

"Why the hell would I lie about that? He told me himself. He's not my flesh and blood—he's yours. And trust me, you can have him."

She started to speak but I pushed forward, knocking her flush against the wall.

"You had to see who he was—what he was doing. And you still helped him. You helped him burn down the hotel. *You* killed Rosie. You took Kale from us. From *me*. And why—so you could get the approval of a man who doesn't give a crap about you?"

"My father loves me!" she screamed. But there was no conviction in her words. She didn't believe it any more than I did.

"No, Kiernan. He doesn't. Marshal Cross doesn't love anyone. He's not capable of love. You're so desperate to win his approval that you don't see what's really going on."

I took a deep breath. "I thought we were blood," I said, grabbing her hand. "I could have forgiven almost anything. You were confused. *He played you.* I understand that. Sleeping with Kale, helping Able—I might have been able to get over all that. *Eventually.* Because you did it to me. But what you did to Rosie—and *Kale*? Dropping that vial didn't just kill me, Kiernan. It killed other people. Innocent people. People I care about." I leaned closer. "Those are lines you shouldn't have crossed."

Kiernan let out a nervous laugh. "So, what? You're going to kill me?"

I hadn't crossed that line yet—and I hoped I'd never have to. As much as a large part of me wanted to, I wasn't going to start with her. Backing away, I let go of her hand and said, "I don't have to. If you stick with Cross and Denazen, you're killing yourself."

"Maybe—but at least you went first." She wasn't looking at me. Her head was tilted up.

The next few things were kind of a blur. Kiernan winked and stepped aside. At the same time, two echoing pops split the air. I didn't know what they were at first and there was no time to react. For a normal person, at least.

In a flash, Kale shot forward and elbowed Kiernan in front of me, while at the same time yanking me hard down the first two steps. She screamed and lunged forward, but Kale pulled me from her path and she fell to the landing. I blinked. Just once. One minute Kale was beside me, the next he was propelling himself up the stairs toward the agents who had burst into the lab.

I watched for a minute as they danced on the landing above us—trading blows and swinging back and forth in what looked like a choreographed Hollywood fight scene. One swung and Kale ducked, sending him over the banister. His screams faded, ending with an echoing *thump* as his body crashed to the ground below, to the left of where the vial had fallen.

Kale loved the thrill of the fight but had obviously had enough. At the tips of his fingers, the black mass began to swirl, and the remaining agent—the one who'd fired the gun—took a step back.

I was so wrapped up in watching Kale, I'd forgotten all about Kiernan. Unfortunately, she hadn't forgotten about me. She was climbing to her feet, blocking me from the stairs—and Kale. The front of her light gray T-shirt was splattered with macabre red and I thought she might have spilled some of the vial on her.

She saw me watching her and laughed. No. It was more like a cackle. She tugged at the shirt and I could hear the wet sound it made, sick and wrong. With a nod toward my shoulder, she said, "I know, I know. It's worse than yours. Probably fatal."

Mine?

I followed her gaze and nearly crumbled. The air left my lungs in a single, chilling breath. Down the front of my shirt was my own trail of macabre blood, spilling from a sick-looking hole in my shoulder. One I hadn't even noticed.

"But don't feel bad. If I'm going down, I'm taking you with me."

And with an almost inhuman roar, Kiernan charged me. It all happened so fast. Half a heartbeat. A fraction of a moment. I heard Kale call out as the ground beneath my feet disappeared and the world flipped. One minute Kiernan's hands were wrapped around my throat, the next a sharp sting assaulted my entire body. Like a full-body slap—then icy cold water all around.

The force of the impact separated us, and I fought against the urge to suck in a deep breath. Surface. I needed air. My foot came in contact with something solid—Kiernan. She made an attempt to grab my ankle, but I avoided her and kicked hard for the surface. My head crested the water, and I lunged for the rim of the tank to haul myself out, but she grabbed my leg and forced me under again. I managed a shallow breath before I went down, but it wasn't enough.

My lungs were on fire, and my heart felt like it would explode at any moment. Kiernan, with her singular focus on dragging me to the grave with her, didn't give up. Each time I pushed her away, she came at me with a renewed sense of energy.

In a panic, I started thrashing. My knee collided with the side of her head, sending her far enough away for me to make one last escape attempt—only I couldn't. Kiernan was no longer holding me back, having drifted away and down to the bottom of the tank, but I couldn't move. My foot was stuck on something. Frantic, I twisted and bent, trying to find the source, but my time ran out. Everything dimmed around the edges, and my entire body went numb.

I don't know how long it lasted. One minute I was giving in to the inevitable, the next, a soft voice was calling my name. Over and over. Begging and pleading for me to stay.

"Dez," it breathed. Warmth pressed against my lips, followed by a burst of air. A second later, a foul rush of fluid surged up my throat, choking off my newly found source of air. Strong hands rolled me onto my side, allowing me to breathe easier.

"You weren't breathing. Dez, I thought you—"

I tried to sit up, but nothing happened. "Kiernan—"

"Stay as still as you can." He pulled the hoodie over his head, the edge of his shirt catching and riding up to reveal well-toned muscle. Normally I wouldn't have an issue with the view, but I got the distinct feeling something was wrong.

He wadded the hoodie into a ball and slammed it against my shoulder. I tried to wriggle free—the pressure didn't hurt, though it felt weird—but he was too strong.

"Dammit," he cursed, and I tried not to laugh. It sounded so strange coming from his lips.

I tried again to pick up my head, but it felt as though someone were holding it down. I did manage to turn it sideways—and was sorry I had. "Oh my God." The words spilled from my lips as my heart skipped a beat. I'd forgotten all about getting shot.

"Shh!" he whispered in my ear, arms slipping beneath my legs and behind my head.

The world tilted sideways, and then up. "I don't feel anything. Did I—" I squinted into the tank below. There was a dark, unmoving figure at the bottom. "Is she—"

"It's not bad," he said, taking the steps faster than I would have dared. They were metal, and everything was soaked from me dripping everywhere. "It's not bad."

I wanted to tell him that when people repeated themselves—him in particular—that was the very definition of *bad*, but I didn't. Or couldn't. My lips, like my head, were too heavy to move.

Kale's expression was fierce. Oddly *familiar.* As everything faded to black I figured out why the painting in the holding room looked so damn familiar.

I just hoped I lived long enough to tell someone.

"Am I dead?"

Brandt-as-Henley rolled his eyes. "Seriously? Would I be the first person you saw right before entering the Pearly Gates?"

"Fiery pits of hell maybe," I mumbled, sitting up. I was curled around a large, soft pillow, scrunched in a comfy armchair. "Did we make it? Is everyone okay?"

"More or less."

More or less? I didn't love that answer.

"So I missed it all? The big escape?"

He shrugged. "You didn't miss much. Actually, consider yourself lucky. Ginger has been on a rampage over Kale's little stunt at the airport."

"Kale's—" Then I remembered. He'd used his ability in front of a huge crowd. "Oh, crap."

"Yeah. She's been playing damage control all day." Brandt winked and waggled his brows. "Cabin's a bit more crowded now, too. That goth guy came back with us. A hot chick named Carley, too."

I was right. We were totally going to have to expand. "Kale?"

"He's okay," Brandt confirmed, and I breathed a sigh of relief.

"So, let's not beat around the bush. I was shot, right?"

He frowned. "Yeah. You were."

"And I almost drowned."

"The way Kale tells it, you *did* drown. He said you stopped breathing. Poor guy looked physically ill just telling Sue about it."

"So the gunshot thing, am—am I okay? You said 'more or less' when I asked if everyone was all right." I took another look around the room. The ceiling was papered with Powerman 5000 posters and the air smelled like coffee. "I'm in some freaky coma, aren't I?"

"Nah. It's not that bad. You're dreaming. I wanted to pop in and see you. You were pretty lucky. It shattered bone. You'll be rocking a cast for a while, since, oddly, we don't have a healer, but you're gonna be okay."

I let out a relieved breath.

"Kale told us what happened to the blood, Dez, and that the Domination we have is no good."

"I failed," I said miserably, letting my head fall into my hands. "I blew my life and all the other Supremacy kids' lives."

"Not necessarily. Wentz is working on it. He's got an idea. If this works, then you *saved* them, Dez."

I wanted to ask him what he meant, but he was gone. And so was I.

• • •

If there was one sound I hated worse than whistling, it was humming. Everyone knew this. I'd once given Alex a fat lip for humming after repeatedly begging him to stop. It wasn't him—the pitch was wrong—but someone was in the room with me.

Humming.

"Oh my God, dude. That is the most grating sound in the world."

The whistler laughed. An amused chuckle, followed by something warm tugging up around my shoulders. When I opened my eyes, I gasped. "You!"

Vince leaned back in his chair and sighed. Brown eyes peeking out from under a mop of black-as-night hair. "I suppose that answers my question."

"And I suppose that answers mine," I replied, hefting myself into a sitting position. My arm was in a sling and my fingers felt numb—the beauty of painkillers if I had to guess—and both my legs were asleep. But I knew what I was looking at. I was looking at the guy from the painting.

Vince smoothed the bedspread, pulling the corner up and around the edge. "What question would that be?"

"Whether or not I was crazy."

"I take it you saw the painting," he said with a sad smile.

"W.V.K?"

"Winston Vincent Kale—or, as my current driver's license says, Vincent Winstead." He extended his hand. "Very pleased to meet you."

I took his hand, realizing how incredibly surreal the whole thing was, and shook my head. "Winston Kale. As in, a descendant of Miranda Kale's?"

"Winston Kale, as in, the one and only. Ginger has her facts confused. Both she and Kale are relatives of mine, not Miranda's. Miranda had no living descendants. She and my son died from the black plague not long after I drove them away."

"Let's forget a ton of things—mainly that if you're who you say you are, you're, like, ancient—and focus on the big issue. You're saying that you're Miranda Kale's husband? *You're* the sonofabitch who started Denazen?"

He sighed and stood. "There is so much you all don't understand. About me, about Miranda—about *Denazen*. Things are not what you think. *Denazen* is not what you think." He frowned. "At least, it wasn't."

"I can't tell if the pain meds are sending me on one hell of a trip or if you're really standing here."

"I reacted badly to Miranda's confession about being a Six—not that we called them Sixes in my day. In those times, things like that were considered dark. Evil. I treated her horribly and not a day goes by that I don't regret it."

I still couldn't wrap my brain around it. "But you'd have to be hundreds of years old. No one lives that long."

"I'm a Six, Dez. I devoted a lot of time, after losing my wife and child to ignorance, to research, and I believe that I'm the *first* Six. I traced lineage on hundreds of different lines and from what I can tell, my body was the first born with the genetic abnormality. I was born in Virginia in 1810. My mother died in childbirth—as so many did back then—but it was because of a strange infection affecting pregnant women. Between June and December of that year, twelve women contracted the infection—all dying in childbirth. Neighboring towns panicked. They crept in one winter's night and burned the town and all its inhabitants to the ground."

I let my head fall into my hands and squeezed my eyes

closed. "This isn't really happening."

Vince grabbed my hands and pulled them away. "It is, and you need to listen because I'm afraid I don't have a lot of time. All modern-day Sixes are descended from one of the children born in Tunstal between June and December of 1810. There were twelve of us. Ten survived the town fire. After Miranda and my son died, it brought the number to nine. Nine people survived to produce offspring and carry on the abnormality. Nine of us: the mothers and fathers of the Six race."

A thought turned my stomach and kicked up a heap of bile. "All related. Oh, God. Is there any chance Kale and I—"

"Are not related. Kale is from my line. You are from another. But I digress. I created Denazen as a haven for people like us. A place we could always go and be ourselves."

I couldn't help laughing. "Well then you failed, man. In case you hadn't noticed, Denazen is kind of the polar opposite."

"Again, you think you know what's going on, but you haven't even scratched the surface. Cross? The other heads of division? They're nothing more than worker drones." He stepped away from the bed. "I turned my back on Denazen some time ago, and because I chose to walk away instead of fight, it has become what it is today. You and Kale made me see my error. By risking yourselves to warn me—warn the others—you renewed my faith."

"It was you!" I exclaimed, recalling our visit to Ben Simmons's apartment. "Ben's roommate said three people came looking for him. Kale and me, Aubrey and Able—and you."

"I feared he wouldn't be found in time. He was essential to my plan…"

"You're talking in circles. Plan?"

He smiled. It was weak and full of unspoken sadness. "I have to leave. There are things to do and further information to gather. I don't expect you not to tell the others who I am, but I beg you to please give me a full day's grace." He backed toward the door, eyes never leaving mine. "Please believe that I am on your side and truly wish to right the wrongs I've committed. We *will* see Denazen fall."

"And that's it? That's all you're going to tell me? Not what information or who's really in charge—not to mention what the hell they're really doing?" I slapped a hand down against the bed. "And more specifically, why tell me? There's, like, a crapload of other, more powerful Sixes out there. Why do the big reveal to me?"

"Ginger has seen Kale's destiny. Fated to become the Reaper, he will be crucial to bringing down those who wish to enslave us all. But he's not the only one. There are others. Others like you. *You* are also crucial."

Crucial? Nothing like dumping a twenty-ton weight on a girl's shoulders. "So then what exactly are they doing?"

"What they're doing, Deznee, is readying for war. Think about the limitless power that comes with limitless resources. Control the governments, the economy—the people—and you control the world. The people behind Denazen, the real puppet masters, want nothing short of that." He opened the door, pausing. "Take care of Kale. He is, after all, my own flesh and blood." Vince winked. "And the fabled Reaper."

And before I could reply, he was gone.

I sat there for a while, stewing over what Vince had said. I went back and forth but, in the end, decided to honor his wishes and wait until tomorrow to tell the others. One day. What would one day hurt?

I must have dozed off, because when I woke again, Kale

was sitting next to the bed.

"Hey," I said, thrilled to see him.

He smiled. "How do you feel?"

I wiggled the fingers of my left hand. "Arm's still attached, so that's a plus."

"I was worried."

"That makes two of us." I sighed. "I heard I almost took a permanent sleep with the fishies."

Kale blinked.

"I almost drowned," I clarified.

"Oh. Yes. And from this moment forward, we will never speak of it again."

I threaded my fingers through his. "Ya got a deal. What about you? How do you...feel?"

"I'm okay, Dez. I don't have it all back, but it will come." He sat in the chair beside the bed and sighed. "I don't think things will ever be the same, though."

A chill raced up my spine. "What do you mean?"

"My memories are coming back, but there's a sense of detachment. I've been through so much since that first day in the woods. Things about me have changed—and a lot of that happened while I was at Zendean."

"Oh," was all I could manage. I didn't know exactly what he was getting at, but his words were like a ten-ton weight on my chest.

"I will understand if you don't want me anymore."

Wait, what?

"Kale, what are you talking about?"

"I don't like cheese anymore."

I couldn't help laughing. "Well, then deal's off. I can't possibly be with someone who doesn't like cheese."

But he didn't smile. "I understood that to be sarcasm. As

you've pointed out, I have a different vocabulary. I'm not the same Kale anymore."

I pulled him closer, rolling my eyes. "Of course you are. The more time you spend away from them—in the real world—the more acclimated you're going to get. It has nothing to do with who you are."

"Maybe," he said softly. "But one thing is different—and it's something that scares me."

"What?"

"I remember feeling this…this blackness. Like a bubble in my chest. Anger, Dez. For everything they did to me. To all of us. It's hazy, but I remember keeping it locked away. Controlled. It was something that took a conscious effort but I managed."

"And now?"

He shook his head. "And now I don't know. It feels different. *I* feel different. Like sometimes I don't want to lock it away. Sometimes, I like feeling angry."

"I think that's normal, Kale. After everything you've been through—everything *we've* been through, it's normal. I kinda feel the same way…"

He looked hopeful. "Really?"

I nodded. "Really. We're gonna be okay. I promise. We all are." Brandt told me everyone made it out of Zendean okay, but then I remembered Alex. "How is Alex?"

"He's awake. He wanted to come see you, but Ginger asked him to wait."

"Wait? Why?"

He looked away for a moment. When he turned back, there was regret in his eyes. "He wasn't undamaged by Ben's attack."

"Wasn't undamaged," I repeated, throat thick. "What does

that mean?"

"He's missing a few memories. It's nothing to worry over, though. He's truly fine."

"Okay," I said, not sure whether to believe him or not.

"And right now, you have something more important to concern yourself over."

I swallowed. He was right. The sand in my hourglass was almost up. "I... Brandt said— We don't have a cure, do we?"

He looked away, hesitating for a moment before looking me in the eye. "Brandt's strange friend is working on it. The scientist, Franklin Wentz—although don't call him that."

I blinked. "Call him what?"

Kale lowered his voice and leaned close. "Franklin. Something about babies. I don't understand, really."

I couldn't help my smile. It was so Kale. His mannerisms, his tone—even the way he moved. "So, what about this friend who we won't call Franklin? How far has he gotten?"

"He's working on a synthetic cure. He says he thinks he can even duplicate my blood if the Underground wants."

"I thought that was impossible?"

Kale shrugged. "I guess he's special."

"Wait—doesn't he need at least some of Penny's blood? We don't have any. Kiernan destroyed it all."

"That's not true. We had your shirt. The one you were wearing when Penny Mills was shot."

"My—" And then I remembered. I'd gotten blood all over it. "That's kind of brilliant."

"I know." He grinned, but it didn't last. "A lot has happened. I need to know if we're okay."

"Okay?"

"Dez, I killed people. I killed them *for* Denazen." He bowed his head, ashamed. "That is something I swore I'd never do again."

"You can't blame yourself for that. Denazen killed those people, not you."

"And what about the things I did to you? Was it Denazen, too? I… Kiernan—"

"Yes," I replied quickly.

He looked like he wanted to argue, but he simply sighed, leaning forward to rest his forehead against mine. "I love you, Dez. Please tell me you know that."

A lot had happened. Denazen, Kiernan—Kale and I would always have mountains popping up to stand in our way. But if anything, this last one proved to me that no matter what happened, we could weather anything.

"I know that, Kale. I promise you, I know."

34

Things were starting to feel normal again—whatever that meant. I moved back into my own room two days later and, that morning, found a note taped to my door from Alex asking me to meet him at noon at the picnic table outside the cabin. Everyone I'd asked refused to talk to me about his condition, saying only that he was fine and had asked to speak to me himself.

It was the first time since the day at Zendean that I'd been outside, and the chilly January air bit at my skin—but it was wonderful. I'd missed New Year's Eve—and Kale's first New Year's kiss—but I was determined to spend the next few weeks making up for it.

"How're you feeling?" Alex sat down beside me. I hadn't even heard him come up.

I wiggled my fingers and smiled. "I'm good. I got your note." I gestured to the bench. "Obviously."

"I wanted to come see you right away, but they told me to

let you rest. Said you got shot."

"Surreal, right? But I guess now I can call myself a true badass. Wasn't that what we said? It takes a bullet?"

He shifted uncomfortably.

"Oh, come on. You have to remember. That night at Memorial Park? We had this conversation about—"

He looked up from the table, head shaking slowly from side to side. "No. I don't remember." Sighing, he tapped the wood twice, then turned so he sat sideways, facing me. "Most of my memories are gone."

"But they'll come back."

"No. They won't. That Ginger chick is pretty sure they're gone for good, and I can't explain it... I think she's right. I remember my first name and that I'm a Six—a telekinetic. I know that everyone here is important to me. My family...but that's about it. Everything else is just gone."

"I... No. That can't be—"

He took my hands in his and smiled. "Don't sweat it. I'm alive. From what I understand, there was a girl with me who wasn't so lucky."

This had happened because he'd helped me. Alex and I, even with our intense history, were just bad for each other. It wasn't intentional, but somehow we just kept hurting the other. It was like there was a force field around both of us that turned our intentions to poison. Nothing we did in regards to the other ever turned out right. "Lu. Lu was killed. Ben attacked me. You came in. You saved me... I'm sorry this happened to you."

"Don't be." Sighing, he leaned his head back and blew out. "I'm not sure why, but I get this feeling that I had a lot of unresolved issues. Things I couldn't get past." He tapped the side of his head again. "I think a lot of them had to do with you. Whatever they were, they're not a problem anymore."

I swallowed, fighting against the lump in my throat. "That's true."

"I think I have to look at this as an opportunity. A gift, ya know? This is my chance to start over with a clean slate. That Dax guy said I was kind of a dick."

A small giggle escaped my lips. "You, um, had your moments."

"I don't really remember much, but I get this heavy feeling when I look at you. He said we were friends, but it was more than that, wasn't it?"

"It was," I admitted. "At one time."

He nodded, justified, and stood. I noticed there was a backpack on the floor at his feet. "Anyway, I wanted to stop and say good-bye."

"Good-bye?"

"I'm a new man—literally. I want to help with this whole Denazen thing, but I think I need to figure out who I am first. Yanno, find myself?"

Alex had a wide array of faults—faults I took great pleasure in pointing out every chance I got—but he had genuinely loved me. I loved him, too, but Kale had my heart and soul, and that would never change. Even the loss of his memory couldn't kill what we had together. This was a way for Alex to finally be free. Even though I wanted to stop him, to keep him close and safe, I knew in my heart this was best for him. It was time to really let go.

"I think that's a good plan."

He turned and started away, stopping a few feet from the path. With a wink over his shoulder, he said, "Who knows? Maybe I'll find myself a great girl. Someone like you."

I sat there until he disappeared from sight, then stood,

wincing as I turned the wrong way and wrenched my arm. I didn't mind, though. The pain was a relief. Brandt and his friend were working on the cure and insisted it'd be ready in less than a month. In the meantime, I worried about the little signs creeping up and increasing.

But no worries. I had plenty to occupy my time until then. There was a lot of work to do. I had no intention of sitting around waiting for Vince to return with answers. I planned on getting them myself. If Marshal Cross was simply a worker bee, then we needed to know who was above him in the chain of command. We needed to know where his orders came from.

First I'd verify that what Vince told me about Denazen—and himself—was true, then I'd work on getting names. We had a handful of new Sixes under our roof now, and I had a plan that would use the ability of every last one.

I was about to head inside when the black leather bracelet on my wrist caught my attention. It was the one I'd mimicked purple the night after Kale went back to Denazen. I didn't remember consciously changing it back, but I let it go for now. I had more important things to worry about.

There was a conversation I needed to have with Mom.

I needed to know who my father was.

Keep reading for a bonus scene from TREMBLE, as told in Kale's point of view...

Aubrey's Promise

Whatever was in the needle Cross gave me earlier was wearing off. The edges of the room were becoming steadily sharper, and the sick feeling in my stomach was nearly gone. How long had I been back? Four days? Five? Maybe it was longer than that. At Denazen, there was no real sense of time.

They tried to break me. No food. No water. Pain. Threats. But all these things meant nothing to me. I'd been here before. In this same exact place. The only thing that mattered now, the only thing I wanted, was for her to be safe. I could endure anything as long as she was okay.

I was about to drift off again when a small noise came from the door. A moment later, someone tall with long, dark hair, dressed all in black, slipped into the room. I eyed him for a minute, debating whether he was actually there or not.

"I'm sorry," Aubrey said, approaching slowly. "This is the first chance I've had to see you."

I considered not responding. Cross was getting desperate to break me. There was no trick beneath him. But I needed to know. "Dez?"

He stopped a few feet from me, pulling up a metal chair. "She's fine. I healed her."

I nodded, silent. There was nothing more to say. At least for me. Aubrey, on the other hand, wasn't finished.

"I don't know how much time I have," he said, taking a deep breath. "So I need to make this quick."

Still, I didn't speak.

"When we met in September, my view of the world was... different. I believed in what I thought they were doing at Denazen. I believed Cross. My brother did, too." He shifted in the chair. "Able and I, we were raised by an honorable man. Brought up to always keep our word and show no respect to those who don't deserve it. Cross intended to go back on his promise to cure Dez. After you left with him, he told me not to cure her unless she came with us willingly."

That caught my attention. My head snapped up, the chains giving a painful jingle at the movement. "You said—"

"I cured her anyway. My point is, my eyes were opened that day. That night, I told Able what happened." Aubrey stood and started pacing. I wasn't sure what he was trying to tell me, but it was obvious he was uncomfortable. "Able's always been a little bit of a follower. He would have gone along with Cross if it weren't for me. But I talked him into leaving. We were going to pack up and get the hell out of town before sunrise."

"You're still here."

Aubrey nodded. "I went to get Able that night, but he'd changed his mind—with a little help from one of Cross's Sixes. Mindy."

"I don't understand..."

"They hijacked his brain. He's still my brother…sort of… but he's different. Cross must have gotten wind that we were planning to bail. Able has an offensive ability. Cross doesn't let go of those easily. You should know."

"Why are you telling me this?"

"Because I made a promise to Dez and I want to keep it. I can't stop what's coming, Kale, and for that, I want you to know I'm sorry. In a few hours, you won't even remember this conversation—"

Unease swept over me. "You're saying Cross is going to do this to me? This brain hijacking?"

Aubrey sighed. "They've created a successful trial of the Supremacy drug. Domination, they're calling it. Cross plans on giving it to you, but he needs to know he'll be able to control you first. He plans to wipe away all memories of Dez and the Underground."

"No!" I was weak, and even though I knew it would do no good, I pulled hard against the chains restraining me. Raw and bruising pain shot down my arms but I ignored it. "They'll never be able to do that. Nothing can take Dez away from me."

The sympathy on his face made me angry. He thought I was wrong. "They will. There's nothing you can do." He started toward the door, then paused a few feet away. "Like I said, you won't even remember this conversation by the time they're done, but I wanted you to know I'll be here for you. With you. If there's any way for you to find your way back to her, I swear to you that I will help."

"Why?" I stopped fighting the restraints, knees giving out. Conserve. I needed to conserve what little energy I had left. I would need it. "Why would you help me?"

"No one deserves the things they've done to you. No one deserves to have someone he loves taken away. Cross knew

I'd never leave Able behind—so he made sure Able stayed. I'll never get my brother back. I've got no one now. Not really. Even if you never find your way back to her, I wanted you to know you'll have me. I'll stand with you."

Acknowledgments

As always, a huge thank you to my family—my parents who are always supportive, and my brother for his computer wizardry. And to my saintly patient husband who is willing to forage for his own food when I get too wrapped up in work (which is most days).

My editors, Erica, a trusted friend and sounding board, and Liz, who continues to take chances on me, I'm eternally grateful.

A special thank you to Cathy Yardley for brainstorming titles with me. T is a lot harder than you'd think! And to Mary, JJ, and Marie for taking the time to share their thoughts and suggestions on the early drafts of this book.

For the hard work of my publicity team, Dani and Anjana, thank you. You guys are awesome and rock my socks ten times over.

Don't miss PROPHECY GIRL *by*
Cecily White
Available online and in stores now!

**Amelie Bennett. . . . Ending the world, one prophecy at a
time.**

I was born to slay Crossworld demons.

Big black flappy ones, little green squirmy ones. Unfortunately,
the only thing getting slain these days is my social life. With
my high school under attack, combat classes intensifying, and
Academy instructors dropping right and left, I can barely get
my homework done, let alone score a bondmate before prom.

Then *he* shows up.

Jackson Smith-Hailey. Unspeakably hot, hopelessly
unattainable, and dangerous in all the right ways. Sure, he's my
trainer. And okay, maybe he hates me. Doesn't mean I'll ignore
the wicked Guardian chemistry between us. It's crazy! Every
time I'm with him, my powers explode. Awesome, right?

Wrong.

Now my teachers think I'm the murderous Graymason
destined to bring down our whole race of angelbloods.
Everyone in New Orleans is hunting me. The people I trusted
want me dead. Jack and I have five days to solve the murders,
prevent a vampire uprising, and thwart the pesky prophecy
foretelling his death by my hand. Shouldn't be too difficult.

Getting it done without falling in love. . . *that* might take a miracle.

Chapter One:
The Beginning

(...five days earlier)

"I'm not going to the dance, so quit asking," I announced, extending a hand to my best friend Lisa Anselmo. "Binoculars, please."

Lisa yanked a pair of black, dual-tube goggles out of her backpack and handed them over with a calculated pout. Enough to tug the heartstrings, not enough to wreck the mascara.

"Amelie, it's our senior year. We've been planning this forever."

"You've been planning this—"

"*We've* been planning this," she insisted. "Katie and I have our dresses and everything. Don't you remember? We swore never to go to these things without each other."

"That was second grade, Lisa."

"Like that makes it *okay* to ditch a pinkie swear?'"

Groaning, I stared through my goggles into the dimly lit, fish-scented night.

The evening had begun pretty normally. Well, normal for me, anyway. Out the window by midnight, encamped at New Orleans' Commercial Street wharf by twelve thirty, scoping the area for demons by twelve thirty-three. Not that there were any demons to be found. Apart from an Irish setter who tried to hump Lisa's leg, the only activity we'd seen was a drunken sorority girl stumbling along the water's edge. She looked young. Nineteen, maybe twenty. Her green sequined minidress hung off one shoulder, dyed-blond hair in rumpled disarray. Obviously trashed.

Hmm. Why would a girl like that *be wandering around* here*?*

"Seriously, Amelie, a pinkie swear is a pinkie swear. It's like BFF code. You of all people should know that." Lisa glared at me, her frosted plum lips curled down at the corners. "And don't give me any garbage about how you can't get a date."

"I didn't say I couldn't get a date," I muttered, distracted. "I said I didn't *want* a date. Now, can you zip it? We're on a stakeout here."

"What about Paul? He'd go with you."

"Waterfall Paul? After the Jell-O shot incident? No, thanks." I flipped the visor down to increase the power on my new night vision binoculars. (Okay, not *mine*, exactly. Borrowed. Certainly not stolen.)

"How about Zeke?"

"Beer-breath. And he wears skinny pants."

"There's always Matt," she suggested hopefully. "He doesn't drink."

"Matt's awesome. He's also in love with *you*," I reminded her.

Lisa flicked a handful of thick chestnut curls over her shoulder and gave a tolerant sigh. "I don't understand why this is so hard. We're *Guardians*."

"We're trainees."

"Same diff. *Every* Guardian Channeler needs a Watcher. We're *supposed* to bond with them, Ami. It's like *destiny* or something. If our friendship means anything to you, you'll do this for me."

Uh, yeah. Like I would dignify *that* with a response. At this point, Lisa's friendship was less of a choice than a fact of life. It worked out well—kind of symbiotic, actually. I beat up anyone who messed with her, and she made sure my homework got done. Fair trade, right? Honestly, if not for Lisa's constant nagging, I'd probably still be crouched in our kindergarten sandbox eating glue and playing with Neferet demons.

"Are you even listening to me?" She prodded me annoyingly in the shoulder.

I swatted her away. "Look, if it means that much to you, I can ask Keller Eastman. I'll probably get herpes from holding hands with him and die a miserable, humiliating death...but for you, Lisa, it's worth it."

"Amelie Lane Bennett." She gave me that look—the one she reserves for small children and people who wear white after Labor Day. "You need to take this seriously. Guardian bond assignments go up at the end of the year. It doesn't matter how pretty you are, or how well you fight, or even how perky your boobs have gotten since last summer."

I frowned and shifted my ladies so they tucked benignly against the concrete wharf ledge. "Can we leave my boobs out of this?"

"I don't know, can we? I mean, look at you! Stained sweats, holey T-shirt, no makeup. And...*this*." She flicked a clump of sweaty red hair poking out the rubber band at my neck. "You have so much potential, Ami. Must you waste it?"

"Lisa!" I grumbled. "Focus! This is life and death we're dealing with."

"I *know* it's life and death," she insisted. "There's *nothing* more crucial than this dance."

"Oh, for the love of—"

"I'm just saying, your mom had a great bloodline, but there's no guarantee you'll carry it. And with your parents' history..." She trailed off, too polite to finish the sentence. "You're lucky they let you stay at St. Michael's after your mom died. I mean, you could easily have wound up in residential. Or worse, the human sector. Would it kill you to play by the rules occasionally?"

"Would it kill you to mind your own beeswax?"

"Probably," she admitted.

I tried to concentrate on the sorority girl, but Lisa's accusation drilled into me. Loathsome though it was, she had a point.

When my parents, Bud and Charlotte Bennett, abandoned the Guardian Community seventeen years ago, they'd tried to pretend things were normal. Not easy, since my dad had been labeled a defector and my mom a traitor to our mission. I suspect they planned to lie to me indefinitely—you know, *ignore* the fact that our family was about as human as the Loch Ness Monster's. They'd put me in a human preschool, hid the broadswords and spellbooks, let me have human friends...right up until the day I channeled our kindergarten class turtle into the demon realm.

Thus began my career at St. Michael's Guardian Training

Academy.

My parents enrolled me mid-year with the understanding that I would be properly trained, sheltered from harm, and, most importantly, they would never hear another word about "the war on demonkind." That denial lasted two years—the exact amount of time it took Mom to get shredded by a demon at a holiday PTA event. Merry Christmas, right?

I suspect Bud still awakens each morning with the faint hope I'll transform into some tree-hugging, dirt-loving hippie daughter he can be proud of. I, by contrast, awaken each morning with a nasty urge to kill things.

Demonic things.

Big black flappy things, little green squirmy things... We don't talk about it. It's one of many topics we don't talk about.

I lowered the extra binocular lens and tipped up my night goggles.

"Lisa, this is the third night in a row we've staked out this location. And the third night you've spent driveling about Watchers and bonds and dances. I know it's important to you, but I need you to respect that *this* mission, sanctioned or not, is important to me. We're technically at war here. Professor D'Arcy's body was discovered not thirty feet from where we sit, and I, for one, am interested in finding out who killed him. Now, are you going to help me or not?"

She squinted her eyes, contemplative. I could practically see the thoughts processing in her head, the gravity of the situation weighing in. Finally, she spoke.

"What about Lyle? He still likes you. *And* he was at the top of class rankings last year. Any girl would be lucky to land him as a bondmate."

"You're not going to let this go, are you?"

"Nope."

I gave a weary sigh. Seriously, the girl was like a dog with a giant wad of beef jerky. "Lis, I'd rather die a cat lady than go out with Lyle Purcell again."

"There's an idea. You could borrow Brutus for the gala," she mused. "You might get a hairball off the goodnight kiss, but his kitty carrier would make a nice accessory."

"You're hilarious. Now shut up."

I flipped the goggles back down and kept scanning the horizon. A good thing, too. Sorority Sally had collapsed, giggling, against a wrought iron bench, head lolled back and throat bared like the cover of a Gothic romance novel. I guess the greasy homeless dude napping two benches down must've had a thing for Gothic romances. As soon as he heard the giggle, he pried open a bloodshot eye, emptied his rum bottle, and hauled himself vertical. Streaks of dirt clung to his coat and his shoulder-length hair dripped with sweat as he staggered toward the girl.

"Hey, Lis, we've got a situation."

"Vamp, were, or demon?"

"Vamp, I think."

She pulled a wooden arrow out of the quiver and watched as I threaded it into my bow.

"Remember," she cautioned, "you have to wait until human blood is spilled. Any unprovoked attack on a Crossworlder violates the Peace Tenets. Do you need thermal imaging for vamp confirmation?"

"Do we have thermal imaging?"

She rummaged in the backpack. "No."

"Add it to the shopping list."

Thermals or no, I was ninety-eight percent sure this was a vamp attack. Maybe ninety-seven. My hand drew back the bow as the dude crouched over Sorority Sally, a predatory look in his eye. His fingers tapped her cheek, tenderly at first, then harder. I could see his lips forming the words, *Hey, baby. Want to party?*

Yeesh. After a hundred thousand years of verbal evolution, could a guy not produce a better pick up line than that? I barely had time to stifle a groan before the girl's eyes fluttered open. Faster than thought, her hands gripped his collar, her mouth in a vicious twist.

That's when I released the arrow. The shaft wasn't as tight or familiar as the weapons at school, but it flew straight enough.

"Bull's-eye," I said as it entered her shoulder.

I'm not even sure if the poor schmuck noticed, he was so wasted. *She* definitely noticed. Her eyes narrowed to angry slits as she turned in our direction, fangs bared. Served her right. Maybe next time she'd remember to flick some water on her face before she went hunting. Only vamps and zombies wouldn't sweat in this humidity.

"Duh, why didn't you just kill her?" Lisa asked, annoyed. "Two more seconds and it would have been justifiable vampicide."

"Lis, for all we know, she volunteers weekends at the soup kitchen. Besides, it wasn't a vampire who killed D'Arcy."

"Yeah, well," she sniffed, "it wasn't a demon, either."

I was about to ask what she meant when I noticed a stirring in the distance.

The blond girl had shooed her would-be snack on his way and was in the process of working the arrow out of her shoulder when something dropped from a tree about fifty feet away. It scuttled toward her, razor sharp talons scraping the pavement, a bubbling snarl at its lips.

"Oh, crud. New target. UV arrow."

It took me less than two seconds to reload and take aim, but by the time I did, the demon had already launched itself at the girl. Its skin was black and mottled, with coarse, oily hair along its shoulders—one part beetle, one part gorilla, three parts Sicilian mafioso.

"Uh, Lis? I need an ID."

Lisa slipped on a second pair of night goggles and started paging through the ginormous Encyclopedia O' Demons she'd brought along. Headmistress Smalley *seriously* needed to get that thing in an e-book format.

"Got it! Rangor demon, third level. Head shot only, everything else is armored. Left eye for the kill," she summarized aloud. "I hope you know what you're doing."

"Me, too."

The Rangor slashed at Sorority Sally with manic glee. For a second, it looked like they might topple down the embankment into the Mississippi where I couldn't get a clear shot, but the girl recovered enough to get her arms up. She rolled to the ground, tossing the beast over her head. Not as fast as some of the vamp videos we'd seen in training class, but way faster than *I* could have moved in that dress. Impressive.

"Hey, Guido," I called.

Startled, the demon jumped to its feet *(um, claws?)* and ran toward us, gathering momentum. Arms raised, it let out a howl of fury. Its whole face seemed to fold open, rows upon rows of teeth bared in serrated ridges.

That's when I sent off the second arrow.

The shaft pierced the beast's left eye, spilling bright UV liquid down its face in a trickle of purple acid. A cry ripped through its throat. Inhuman. Screechy. Like the emergency brakes of a railway car. Lisa clamped her hands on her ears.

"Wow, this is super subtle," she yelled over the ruckus.

"Maybe next time you could take out an ad in the *Times Picayune*?"

In hard lurches, the demon writhed and twisted on the ground. Rangors weren't known for their passive deaths, but really, it seemed to be taking longer than necessary. In the distance, horns honked and garbage trucks clanged, sure signs of human approach.

"We're so gonna get busted."

I sighed. Lisa was right. If a Guardian caught us, that would be one thing. But involving humans was a whole other enchilada.

"All right, give me a knife," I ordered.

She handed me a hooked blade about the size of a banana and stood back.

It took less than twenty seconds to separate the crucial parts, at least enough to stop the twitching. By the time I finished, my arms were scratched, my hair was clumped with mucus, and the vampire had fled into the night.

"You're welcome," Lisa yelled after her. She humphed and turned back to me. "Omigod, did you see that? Ungrateful toads, every last one of them."

"Tell me about it," I said, wiping the demon goo off my arms. "You want to get the body or the weapons?"

"I'll get the body. You'll probably end up summoning a demon horde if you try to dismiss it. Remember Veronica's sweet sixteen?" She smirked. "Priceless. I thought she'd never get her hair back to its normal color."

I frowned. "It's not my fault I have allergies."

"Oh, is that what we're calling it?" Lisa gestured to the boardwalk where the drunk human lay, passed out in a pool of vomit, not twenty yards from my pile o' demon. "Amelie, how many times do I have to say this? Birthday parties are one thing, but it's *illegal* for unbonded Channelers to mess around with Crossworld beings. Not without a Watcher present, and *certainly* not around humankind. Our handbook specifically says, *The fist of eternal damnation shall fall heavily upon he who knowingly reveals the existence of the Guardians.* Didn't you read it?"

I had read it, actually. That handbook was where I got my best ideas.

"Well, technically, we didn't channel anything. And *that*," I said, pointing at the Rangor pieces, "is not a 'fist of damnation.' That's just an obese demon. There's no law against killing obese demons."

"There is, actually," Lisa noted, "for trainees. Which we aren't going to be anymore, unless we get this mess cleaned up and get to class."

I grudgingly gathered the weapons and spread some fallen leaves over the sticky, tar-like substance that had oozed out of the Rangor demon. Gulls flew in slow, lazy circles overhead, pastel light glinting off their wings.

Lisa called open the Crossworld channel. "*Inergio.*"

As soon as the word was spoken, yellow flickers appeared and a narrow gash of light tore through the air. Chill winds swirled around the rift, spits of black fire lapping at the demon body.

Lisa sank to her knees, out of breath. "I'm done. You're up."

"*Exitus!*"

Instantly, the flow of power shifted to me, a hard fist in the middle of my chest. Fingers of Crossworld poison trailed over my skin, reaching into me with claw-like insistence. Without a Watcher to drain it, my defenses were weak. Lisa had done most of the work, as usual, but I still couldn't shake the unsettling sensation of drowning in darkness.

When there was nothing left but a few gloppy demon chunks, I collapsed next to her. "That sucked."

"My thoughts exactly."

"Maybe we should take tonight off."

She rolled to her side just enough to shoot me a nasty look. "Maybe you should get a boyfriend."